WORK FOR IT

THE NAIAD NOVELS SERIES

LEILA BURNES

Copyright © 2023 by Leila Burnes.

All rights reserved.

Published by Said What Press, LLC.

No part of this book may be reproduced in any form or by any electronic or mechanical means, including information storage and retrieval systems, without written permission from the author, except for the use of brief quotations in a book review.

This book is a work of fiction. Names, characters, places, and incidents either are products of the author's imagination or are used fictitiously. Any resemblance to actual persons, living or dead, events, or locales is entirely coincidental.

Cover Images © Milatoo, Paulaparaula, alenaganzhela
Editor: VB Edits • vbeditsromance.com

ISBN (paperback): 978-1-961032-01-9
ISBN (special edition): 978-1-961032-02-6

For content warnings, please visit www.leilaburnes.com

For Flamingo House. Who's going to stop us?

PLAYLIST

CUENTA PENDIENTE • Paty Cantú, Alejandro Sanz

REGGAETÓN LENTO • CNCO

CLANDESTINO • Shakira, Maluma

ME PORTO BONITO • Bad Bunny, Chencho Corleone

GO FUCK YOURSELF • Two Feet

SHE LOVES CONTROL • Camila Cabello

YA LEIL • Remenkimi

DOWNTOWN • Anitta, J Balvin

TOUTA • Haifa Wehbe

MAÑANA ES TOO LATE • Jesse & Joy, J Balvin

YO X TI, TU X MI • Rosalía, Ozuna

DOS GARDENIAS • Buena Vista Social Club

NOVEMBER

CHAPTER 1

"The next time I see him in person, I'm going to physically fight him."

On the laptop screen in front of me, Marianne throws her head back and cackles at my comment. Despite her laughter, she knows I'm not joking. She's well aware of just how much I hate Daniel Santiago and every problem he's caused me. She should be. I've only threatened to kill him about a thousand times over the last two years.

Our delightful coworker is the reason I've been screwed out of money, why I'm continuously kept in the dark about projects, and why I consider taking blood pressure medication every morning. Because when I see his face in that little box on Zoom during our daily team meeting and I'm forced to listen to his condescending voice, I'm convinced I'll have a rage-induced stroke.

He's also part of the reason I have my job in the first place, but that's not as important.

"He fucked me over *again*," I huff, still fuming from the Zoom meeting with the acquisitions team that just finished.

"What did he do this time?" Marianne asks.

I take a breath, gearing up for another Daniel-inspired rant. "He told me the continuation of Kimmy Petes' *Burned by the Billionaire* that I've been working on for months would be released on the app last week. So, of course, I got her all hyped up about the release of the new chapters we wrote for her. And I told her she could start posting all the marketing material and dive into all the fun author stuff on social media to promote it. Sounds good, right?"

"Right…"

"Well, it's *not* good." I scowl. "Because the release date comes and goes, and then Kimmy emails me demanding to know why the new chapters aren't posted, telling me she's promised her readers something that wasn't delivered. And she's *pissed*."

"Oh shit."

"Uh, *yeah*. And guess who's taking the brunt of that anger since she's the production lead for the new chapters and has become Kimmy's punching bag at Naiad Novels?" I point to myself. "This stupid bitch."

Recounting the story only makes me angrier. As a fellow author and one who has had her own books continued by Naiad Novels, I get it more than most. I'd be livid if my publisher didn't release the super-hyped, much-anticipated continuation of my best-selling book when they promised. And as an employee of Naiad Novels—the hottest serialized fiction platform on the market, currently revolutionizing the publishing game—I know a fuck-up like this is colossally unprofessional.

It doesn't matter that Daniel and his team are in charge of posting chapters on the platform. I'm running point on her project, so *I'm* the one Kimmy is furious with.

Normally, I'd chalk something like this up to miscommunication inside the company and move on, but this isn't the first time Daniel has made my professional life hell. I swear he's determined to ruin all the projects I'm assigned to. And I hate him for it.

This feels like a personal attack. I put my blood, sweat, and tears into ghostwriting these new chapters of *Burned by the Billionaire* on Kimmy's behalf, working tirelessly on a project she would be happy to put her name to. Kimmy may have written the original story—the first thirty chapters—but after that, the work is all mine. I'm talking *hundreds* of chapters. At Naiad Novels, our slogan is *What if your favorite story never had to end?* And these things really do not fucking end.

Until they stop bringing in money, that is.

We buy, or *acquire*, as Daniel would remind me to say, romance novels from top-selling self-published authors and continue them. We post a new chapter each day on our app, creating never-ending tales. Like soap operas or telenovelas in written form, with a lot more steam.

So yeah, I spend most of my day writing smut. And it takes a hell of a lot of skill.

"Don't be so hard on yourself, Selene," Marianne gently scolds. "It's not like this is your fault."

She's right. Daniel changed the release date without telling me. And, in the meeting we wrapped up ten minutes ago, he implied it was my fault for not checking our internal calendar for changes. I could have accepted the blame if that had been true, but I'd checked the calendar almost obsessively, only to see the release date change an hour before the first ten chapters of the continuation were scheduled to go live on the app. By then, it was too late. I could do nothing but brace myself to pacify a livid author.

While I had to rein it in when I spoke to Kimmy, I was just as angry. Because even though her name is the only one that will appear on the story, *I* came up with the plot and the character arcs for the continuation. *And* I edited the hell out of her original manuscript to make it more appealing to serialized readers. It's the most work I've put into any project besides my own, and I'm proud of it, even if I can't publicly claim credit, thanks to my employment contract and too many NDAs to count.

So letting its release day come and go, angering thousands of readers who had been anticipating the promised new content from their favorite author, is a slap in my face as well as Kimmy's.

Thus, I'm more than ready to fistfight Daniel Santiago.

"Has Kimmy calmed down at all?" Marianne asks, a concerned frown marring her face.

I shoot the laptop camera a dry look. "Not in the slightest. In her latest email, of which there have been *at least* twenty since this fiasco started, she asked me how I could work for such an unscrupulous company, and how I, as an author, ever trusted them to continue my work."

"Well… You *didn't* trust us to continue it to your standards," Marianne points out. "That was why Daniel suggested bringing you on as a full-time employee. So you could do it yourself. And make us a ton of money in the process."

I scowl at the reminder of how I found myself at Naiad Novels, not wanting to give him credit for the one good thing he did.

"Money he cheated me out of as an author," I grumble. "I could have made so much more in royalties if he hadn't screwed me over in the acquisition deal for the books Naiad bought."

"True, he lowballed you," she concedes. She's well aware that the percentage of royalties I earn is far lower than that of our other top-performing authors. "But that's how the industry works."

That may be true, but I can and will be bitter. "Yeah, and I'll still punch him in the face for it."

Marianne cackles again. When she's caught her breath, she stares into the camera, wide-eyed. "Ooh, you'll be in the office next week, won't you?" Her face lights up over the video feed. "Will the showdown happen then? If so, could you film it? I won't be in New York until the week after, and I do *not* want to miss this."

Thanks to the pandemic, I haven't been to our New York City office in nearly eighteen months. My position at Naiad has always been remote, and in the Before Times, I traveled from my home in

Baltimore to the city about once a month to attend important meetings. After shutting down the physical office for a while, the higher-ups finally reopened it two months ago, and the company has gone with a more hybrid approach, giving employees the choice to come in or work from home.

It's taken some time, but I've finally scrounged up enough bravery to get on a train and work face to face with people next week—Daniel included. I can only hope he chooses to stay home those days.

I snort out a laugh. "Buy your tickets now for the fight of the century."

"I'd watch this on pay-per-view in a heartbeat. Price doesn't matter."

"Maybe I'll wait to go after him until you're there. Save myself the effort. And the filming fees."

"Gives you more time to train too. I want you in the best fighting shape to take him on. Daniel better watch himself."

She's right. Because when I see that maddening man in person, I swear, it's on sight.

CHAPTER 2

"Please don't commit murder. I don't have time to come up to New York and bail you out of jail."

My darling roommate gave me the same warning when I went up to the city last week, and here she is, repeating it again.

"Hey, I didn't kill anyone when I was there before." I shoot Carly a look as I climb to my feet and stand my suitcase on its scratched wheels. "I got my new key fob for the office, put in my hours writing sexy stuff, and got out. No blood spilled."

"Because Daniel wasn't in the office those days," she says, her dark eyes wary. "Didn't you say *everyone* would be there tomorrow? Is that going to lead to a manslaughter charge?"

I ignore her question. It's wishful thinking, but I'm still crossing my fingers that he'll choose to stay away again. "I never said I was going to *kill* him. Just give him a solid punch to the gut. Maybe a kick to the dick. That's all."

She shakes her head, her tight curls bouncing as she does, and blows out a breath. "I don't trust you in the slightest."

"Good, you shouldn't," I chirp, leaning in to kiss her deep brown cheek. With my purse in hand, I snag the handle of my suitcase. "I'll be back Tuesday night. Another quick turnaround trip."

"Want me to order your usual for taco Tuesday?" she asks, following me to the front door of our apartment. "I can stick it in the fridge so you have something to eat when you get home."

Carly is my favorite mother hen. She always makes sure I'm properly fed and remain out of prison. We met during our freshman year of college and have lived together ever since, though I doubt it will be long before she and her boyfriend are engaged and move in together. Until then, I'm lucky to have her around to keep me alive and (mostly) out of trouble.

"That would be great." I squeeze her arm with my free hand. "Thank you."

She nods and zips my coat up to my chin, brushing my long, dark hair over my shoulders to keep it from getting tangled. "By the way, the front desk called." Her eyes flick up to mine. She's five-foot-one, and while I'm six inches taller, I still feel like a small child when she babies me like this. "You got another package. More lingerie?"

Pressing my lips together, I duck my head and grin. I can't help that I like pretty things. Especially the kind that make *me* feel pretty. And if that means a good portion of every paycheck goes toward lace and silk, then so be it. "My favorite indie shop was having a sale on bralettes, and I couldn't resist."

I may not have a boyfriend or a fuck buddy to model the handmade pieces for, but just wearing them for myself brings me joy. I'm a sucker for sexy underwear, even if I'm the only one who sees it.

"Would you grab it for me?" I ask. "I'll open it when I get home."

"Sure. Text me when you're on the train?"

We both travel for work—New York City for me, and Philadelphia for her—and long ago, we established a system of checking in during every stage of the journey. Mostly at her insistence. Sometimes I think Carly worries about me more than my Arab mother, which is truly telling.

"Have a good time," she says as she opens the door. "And choose peace, not violence."

"You clearly don't know me then."

She heaves a weary sigh. "I know you too well. Remember, kicking someone in the dick isn't your only option."

"Not just *someone*. The devil himself."

"Selene," she warns, like a mom telling her rowdy child not to terrorize the other kids. "Play nice."

I flash her a grin, heeding exactly none of her caution. "I make no promises."

CHAPTER 3

"Look who's here."

I glance up from my laptop, leaving the sentence I was writing unfinished. Next to me, Marianne has been helping with ideas for the story I'm working on, but we've mostly spent the morning shrieking and jumping up to greet coworkers we haven't seen in over a year and catching up on office gossip.

I crane my neck to peer through the glass wall of the conference room, expecting to see someone else I can wave wildly at.

Instead, it's the last person I wanted to encounter today. Daniel.

Our office building's security system was updated while we were working remotely, and when I came in last week to pick up my new key fob, I managed not to run into him at all. But since our bosses have planned an after-work outing tonight at the bar across the street, it seems Daniel has decided to bless us with his presence.

I try not to glare as he drops his messenger bag next to one of the long tables in the main office area and hugs a grinning Stephanie, one of his acquisitions teammates. He straightens up a moment later with his back to the conference room and shrugs out of his leather jacket, revealing a crisp white T-shirt underneath.

Similar to a lot of tech and creative start-ups, we don't have an office dress code, which means I'm wearing leggings, sneakers, and an oversized sweater—my standard uniform. Daniel is dressed casually in jeans, but instead of looking sloppy like the majority of the office, he's the epitome of put together. The least he could do is take one for the team and look as shitty as the rest of us.

But *of course* he stands out. He's one of two men in our combined twenty-person acquisitions and productions department, and the only straight one, which means he's already a rarity around here. And in addition, though it pains me to admit, Daniel is…attractive.

He's handsome and he knows it, which plays into his charm—another thing I can't stand. He's a salesman through and through, with the silver tongue to prove it. That particular talent has helped him seal major deals and poach self-published authors who were already making millions of dollars on other platforms. Not to mention, he's convinced his connections at several major traditional publishers to give us the rights to post their backlist books on our app. Undoubtedly, he's played a big role in the success of our company.

Still hate him, though.

"Oh, my favorite person," I say dryly, glancing back at my laptop as it flashes a low battery warning at me.

Sighing, I lean down to search for the charger in my bag beside my chair, still keeping tabs on Daniel from the corner of my eye. When I've rooted through what feels like every pocket of my oversized purse and still can't find it, I look away from him and focus my attention on sifting through the mess I've brought with me.

I've just wrapped my fingers around the white cord when Marianne whispers, "Oh shit, he's coming our way."

I nearly hit my head on the table as I sit up, mentally cursing myself for reacting like this. Maybe it's because I've been not-so-secretly threatening to fight this man for the better part of two years, but I'm immediately on guard.

While Marianne smiles at him when he reaches the door, I

fight back a scowl, successfully keeping my expression neutral—and pointedly ignoring the way my heart speeds up a little.

Sitting straighter in my chair, I follow the line of his bicep as he drags a hand through his thick, black curls, leaving them a little unruly and sideswept. *Perfectly disheveled* is how the heroines in the romance serials we write day in and day out would describe it. But *perfect* is not a word I would ever use to describe anything about him.

He smiles back, easy and relaxed, as he opens the conference room door. I don't think I've ever seen him upset or even tense. It's like everything rolls off him, and it leaves me itching to be the one who gets under his skin.

I want him to hate me as much as I hate him.

From the doorway, he chats with Marianne about how long she's in town for and how her trip down from Boston was. Then he turns his attention to me.

"Hi, Selene." My name rolls off his tongue smoother than I've heard anyone ever say. His voice is low and deep, but it's his accent that does it. He was born and raised in Mexico City, and those roots remain in his words. It's one more characteristic that makes my hackles rise: his sexy-as-sin voice. "Good to see you."

"You too," I reply, though it's a lie. But I can be polite for now; our fistfight can wait until later at the bar. I don't want to get blood on the office floors.

Although, now that we're in the same room for the first time in forever, I'm a little less confident I can take him on. His height surprised me when I first met him years ago, so taken aback that I could barely say hello. But in those days, he was leaner, and I was certain I could take him out with a solid shoulder to his midsection and a punch to the balls.

But he's filled out over quarantine, like he's been working out more. That doesn't bode well for my threats to fight him.

Or my attraction to him, apparently.

"I need to steal five minutes of your time later," I tell him before I can think about what I'm doing. I *have* wanted to discuss something with him for ages now, and it needs to be done in person. My hope is that by meeting one-on-one, though I despise the notion of it, I'll get a straight answer out of him for once. "I want to chat about the distribution deal for my books."

I've sent him at least half a dozen Slack messages about this. And each time, it's taken him days to respond with vague, brush-off answers. It's yet another strike against him, another reason I should be on my feet right now and socking him in the gut.

"Steal all of my time, if you want," he says, extending his free arm like he's beckoning me to him. "Come find me when you're ready."

I flash him a tight smile. Charming bastard. "Will do. Thanks."

"My pleasure."

I bet it is, asshole.

The door shuts quietly behind him a moment later. When Marianne and I are alone again, I scowl and sink into my seat.

"You handled that better than I thought you would," she commends, patting me on the shoulder. "For a second, I was worried you were going to launch yourself across the table at him."

"I thought about it," I tell her. "But I'll go with the element of surprise instead. Can't let him see the attack coming."

She laughs. "Probably for the best. He's bigger than I remember. You might need the shock factor on your side to take him down."

At least I'm not the only one who noticed Daniel's new muscles. Not that I was checking him out. Not that I'm *still* checking him out through the glass conference room wall.

With a shake of my head, I turn back to my computer screen and tap at my keyboard. "Come on. Let's get back to the adventures of the doctors who can't keep it in their pants. I need suggestions for the next place they can fuck."

Her loud exhale sums up my feelings too. I can't believe this is my job.

After Marianne and I outline the next thirty chapters of *Under His Care*, I meet with the big boss for our monthly catch-up. I update her on my current projects, and she explains the new ones I'll be tasked with. Not much has changed, except I'm getting another book dumped on my plate soon, one of Daniel's acquisitions.

She was kind enough to warn me that I'll have to do some pretty significant editing to the original manuscript to make it work better for Naiad and its market. In other words, I'll have to expand the dialogue, add new plotlines, and make sure the sex scenes are adequately steamy without violating our terms of service.

I've done the same for other manuscripts in the past, and while it's not exactly difficult, it's long and tedious work. All I can hope is that I'll be given ample time to do it before the story goes up on the app. But, of course, those deadlines are up to Daniel and his team.

When the meeting is over and I head back to the main office space, the man himself is striding my way. I try my best not to narrow my eyes at him as we pass in the hall, but it's a natural reaction at this point. Thankfully, he doesn't pay me any mind as he slips into the office I've just left.

In the small lounge area in the center of the space, I flop into one of the oversized chairs and pull my laptop back out so I can get started on the editing tasks waiting for me.

Making sure our updates go out on time means having chapters outlined, written, and edited weeks in advance, then passing the final documents along to the team in charge of uploading them to the app. That's how the sausage gets made at Naiad.

I'll admit, the first time I had to write and edit sex scenes in a room full of my coworkers, I was mortified. Writing them in private is one thing, but in public? In an *office*? It seemed obscene. But these days, I work on them while sitting on cramped trains, in packed cafés, and even at my mother's dinner table. When it comes to the written sexy word, I have no shame anymore. If someone has the audacity to read over my shoulder, then complain about being offended, that's their problem, not mine.

Across the room, Nikki and Ella are discussing a story whose title I've forgotten, but I'm pretty sure it includes the word *daddy*. From what I can gather, it's about a woman whose father's best friend is teaching her how to give blowjobs. *This* is an every-day type of conversation at Naiad and the reason the room was filled with laughter during our mandated sexual harassment training. This is the business we're in—the business of romance and sex on the page. And I wouldn't trade it for the world, no matter how untraditional the job is.

I'm editing a scene that involves very public sex when the door to the big boss's office swings open and Daniel strolls out...and heads straight toward me.

Fantastic.

He drops into the armchair across from mine, leaving nothing but a glass coffee table between us. Now that he's so close, my desire to physically fight him shrivels up and dies. There's no way I could take him in hand-to-hand combat.

Well, fine. Looks like my hate for him will have to remain internal until I can bulk up too.

"Selene," he greets with that ever-so-calm smile that doesn't touch his dark eyes. "I've been waiting to catch you. Now good?"

I smile back at him, though mine is definitely forced. "Now's perfect."

He nods and leans forward in his chair, forearms on his solid thighs as he stares me down like I'm the only person in the room. "What exactly did you want to know about the distribution deal?"

Right. Business. I clear my throat and set my laptop on the coffee table, wishing I'd closed my document first because the words *hard, thick cock* are highlighted in red at the top of the page.

"First, what's the projected start date?" I ask him, forcing myself to ignore the sentence flashing at me like a beacon on my screen. "I know the end goal is to have samples of our Naiad-produced works in all the big digital bookstores, but what's the timeline?"

In typical Daniel fashion, he explains how the timeline keeps changing based on certain factors and *blah, blah, blah*, but ultimately, he hopes it will be completed by January. He could have told me that last bit without all the other roundabout reasons, but what did I expect? It's how he conducts negotiations.

"And what about physical copies?" I ask next, which is what I'm really interested in.

When Naiad bought my books, I signed an exclusivity contract with them, which meant my original books and their continuations could only be posted on the Naiad app. It also means there are no physical copies available to readers.

During our original negotiations, Daniel promised that it wouldn't be long before Naiad produced paperbacks of my original novels. My mistake was not forcing him to put a definitive date in writing. I trusted him and his honeyed words, believing he was an honorable man who would make it happen ASAP. But here we are, nearly three years later, and he's yet to make good on that promise.

"My readers have been asking for them for years," I continue. "Think of the revenue we're missing out on by not offering physical copies of not only *my* books, but of *all* the books Naiad holds the exclusivity rights to. We could even drive more people to the app by advertising at the end of the books. It's an opportunity we shouldn't miss out on."

"We're not looking into that at the moment," he says in a patronizingly calm manner, as if I'm a small child asking why I can't have my favorite toy. "We'll reconsider in Q2 next year and decide based on how the expanded digital distribution performs. It might not ever happen."

"Come on, Daniel." I keep my tone polite, but my temper is rising. "You promised physical books during our negotiation. And there's a demand. People want this."

"So tell them to buy the e-books," he counters with a dismissive shrug. "Then we'll see."

Knowing I won't get a better answer out of him, I clench my jaw and grit out, "Fine." Then, pulling myself up a little straighter in my seat, I move on. "But if the sales *do* match up and you finally realize this has been a good idea all along, how will you go about making it happen?"

Just as I expect, Daniel launches into a convoluted explanation that doesn't even remotely answer my question, all to distract from the original topic. It's such a smarmy business tactic, one that I might understand him using if we weren't literal coworkers, but we're supposed to be on the same team.

I almost interrupt, but instead, I prop my elbow on the armrest of my chair and press two fingers to my temple as I stare him down, giving soft murmurs of *uh-huh* and *sure, right* in all the appropriate places, even though all I want to do is tell him to shut the fuck up.

Eventually, I get the *we haven't quite figured it out yet* I expected. Exhausted from having to listen to him, all I can do is sigh. This is his go-to strategy. Throw out a shit ton of jargon, circle back a few times, and ramble on until his audience's eyes glaze over, all to keep them from pushing harder for answers. The only saving grace is that he's easy to look at while he spews this mess.

And that right there is why he gets away with the things he pulls. He's tall and handsome, with a smooth voice and the ability to bullshit with the best. It shouldn't be alluring, and I know better than to fall for that kind of thing. But goddamn if there isn't a weak little part of me that's suckered by it.

That weakness fuels the fire of my hate even more, making me once again tempted to sock him in the jaw.

"Thanks," I mutter when he finally wraps up his spiel. "That's all I needed to know. I've got edits to get back to." *So you can go fuck yourself* remains unsaid, but I add a heavy dose of it to my voice.

He doesn't make a move to get up or turn his attention from me, so I grab my laptop and stand instead. The longer I'm around him, the more my fist itches to meet his face.

I make my way back to the conference room where Marianne has not-so-subtly been watching my interaction with Daniel through the glass partition.

"Your *face*," she whispers as soon as the door is shut. "You had actual fire in your eyes at one point."

I groan and drop into the chair across from her, keeping my back to the office. I don't want to look at Daniel and his stupid face anymore. "I was seconds away from committing homicide, Marianne."

"Judging from that look alone, I'm amazed you didn't." She shakes her head, grinning. "He better stay out of your way at the bar tonight. I don't take you for a relaxed drunk."

I let out a loud laugh. "I promise not to drink too much. I don't want to embarrass myself in front of our bosses."

"Not yet, at least. That's what the holiday party is for." Marianne winks at me. "Now finish your edits. I know there's some voyeurism with your name on it."

CHAPTER 4

I'm more than ready for a drink by the time we make it to the bar across the street.

After ordering a gin and tonic, I get sucked into a commiseration session with Marianne, Zoe, Nikki, and Ella over the wild things we've had to write this week. From unexpected volcanic eruptions to FBI raids of brothels, we've tackled practically everything known to man at Naiad.

Our Monday morning team meetings are dedicated to going over what we've plotted out the week before to make sure our ideas and scenarios don't overlap. We don't need a repeat of the Great Amnesia Scandal, where nearly every story that week had a character losing their memory.

Eventually, Beth from the customer service team joins us, slinging an arm around my shoulders and giving me a squeeze. "I heard you almost fought Daniel today," she says in greeting.

Marianne shoots me a sheepish grin. She's the only person I mentioned today's incident to, so it's obvious who the source of this gossip is.

I snicker. "News travels fast, huh?"

"In a company with less than a hundred people, that's a given."

"As long as he didn't hear the rumor and hasn't reported me to

HR, then that's fine." Sipping my drink, I eye the women around me. "No one has told him, right?"

"No fucking way," Nikki confirms. "I avoid talking to him whenever I can. And more than anything, I want to witness the moment you deck him and the look of shock on his face when you do."

Ella clinks glasses with her. "I second that."

Beth drops her arm and slides onto the empty barstool beside me. "The CS girls are placing bets on when you'll fight him—either verbally or physically."

"It'll probably end up being verbally," I tell her woefully. "I lost all my upper body strength during lockdown."

"I lost *all* my strength. I can't remember the last time I lifted a weight or went for a run." She snorts. "Don't even look at my Peloton stats. I got jealous when I saw you hit a fifty-two-week streak."

With a grin, I lift my drink in toast. "I'm proud of that one. My roommate and I have a competition going for who can get the longest streak, and I hate losing. Otherwise, I wouldn't have done shit."

And then there's Daniel, who looks like he built his own gym during the months we were stuck at home. I wish I had that kind of dedication, but that's the only trait of his I'd take.

As more of our coworkers arrive, Marianne, Zoe, Ella, and Nikki move down the bar to talk to them, leaving Beth and me to continue our conversation.

"How often do you plan to be in the office?" she asks. "It's been so nice having you here. I love shouting about things with you over Slack, but it's better in person."

The friendships I've developed at Naiad are the second-best part of my job—after writing, of course. I'm surrounded by creative people who appreciate the romance genre and all the things that come with it.

"Just once a month," I reply with a smile. "But next time I'll stay for—"

A loud outburst of boisterous male laughter interrupts me. The commotion is coming from the all-male app development team at a table in the corner, currently losing their minds over something it appears that Daniel has said.

"Ugh, those assholes," Beth grumbles, turning back to face me with a roll of her eyes. "I want to die every time I'm forced to bring another reported bug to their attention. They talk to me like I'm a clueless little girl. Like, newsflash, dickbags, you're not the only ones who know how to code."

I grimace. "Guess I'm lucky I don't ever have to talk to them."

There's another round of loud laughter, once again sparked by Daniel.

"Yeah, but you have to deal with Daniel, and he's the worst of them all," Beth counters. "I'd take the app development boys over him any day."

Huffing a breath, I slump in my seat. As nice as it is to know I'm not alone in my assessment, I'm still stuck working with the insufferable bastard day in and day out.

"He's just so smarmy," I sneer, my attention flicking to him. I watch as he sips a beer while talking to the guys. The rest of the production and acquisitions team is female, so I guess he has to get his man-time in somehow. "He's your stereotypical business bro. Dealing with him on the creative side is such a nightmare."

"Seriously," Beth agrees, canting forward and dropping her voice conspiratorially. "Did you know that, like, half of our authors hate him? His game of hardball during negotiations is way too intense. CS gets plenty of complaints about him."

I'm not surprised by that in the slightest. What *is* surprising, though, is that the other half feels differently. "And everyone else?" I ask, lifting my drink to my lips.

"I think they want to fuck him."

I nearly choke on my gin and slap a hand over my mouth to keep from spitting it all over her.

"He's not my type," she clarifies quickly. "I'm with you on Team *He's an Asshole*. But you gotta admit, he's tall, dark, and handsome. Not to mention that sexy voice. So I get why he's so successful at wooing potential clients and negotiating contracts. If I were a writer, I'd sign my work over to him, no question. And based on the record number of authors he pulled in last month, I'm clearly not the only one."

I'd never admit it to her—or anyone, for that matter—but I fell prey to that magnetism at first too. "I would call what he did to me less *wooing* and more *you'll never get an offer better than this, so sign our contract*. He essentially played on all of my insecurities as a writer to get me to sign."

Beth winces. "Ouch. I didn't know your experience was that bad."

"Worse," I say, feeling that familiar bitterness well up. "I renegotiated the entire contract, and I still got screwed in the end."

"That's shitty," she murmurs, squeezing my arm in solidarity. "But look on the bright side: that contract landed you a full-time job at Naiad. None of our other authors have been given that opportunity. Maybe you got screwed for a reason."

I snort and down the rest of my drink. "Don't you dare tell me I should thank him. It will be a cold day in hell before that happens."

Beth grins as she sets her empty glass on the bar and waves for the bartender. "I'd *never* suggest such an awful thing."

Once we're sipping fresh drinks, Beth launches into a tale about the ridiculous emails she gets from app users, and has us laughing so hard we can barely breathe. I'm dabbing at my eyes with a cocktail napkin when my phone buzzes in my pocket. I pull it out, greeted with a notification signaling I have an Instagram DM waiting. I swipe it open without thinking twice and scan the message.

Feeling buoyed by the content of it, I fill Beth in on the conversation

I had with Daniel about the e-book distribution deal and my desire for physical copies of my books. Then I show her the message I just received from a reader who's pleading for physical copies and swearing she doesn't care about the cost as long as she can have them on her shelf.

"Daniel doesn't believe me when I say people actually want physical copies of my novels, but this is the third DM I've gotten this week alone from readers asking for them."

Beth nods at my phone. "So show him the proof. Show him you're not the only one who wants this."

Huh. That's not a terrible idea in theory, but it would require talking to Daniel, and I've already had enough of that today.

"Ooh, he's on the move," Beth says in a stage whisper. "You should do it when he passes by us."

Fuck it, I may have already had my daily dose of Daniel, but a little more might be worth it to get my point across.

"Okay, fine." I spin on my stool and prop my elbows on the bar behind me, watching for him.

Across the room, he maneuvers through the crowd, flashing easy smiles to the people who look his way. I snake an arm out as he approaches, waving to get his attention. "Hey, Daniel!"

He glances in my direction, not quite surprised that I'm actively seeking him out, but he raises a brow when he catches sight of me.

I ignore it and shove my phone toward him. "Look at this. More people begging for physical copies of my books."

Before I know what's happening, he's wrapping his fingers around mine to steady my phone so he can read the message. The touch sends heat coursing down my arm, but I do my best to ignore it. It's got to be the alcohol hitting me at the most inopportune moment.

"Show this to me again when I haven't had a few beers," he says, still not letting go of my hand, even though he's no longer looking at my phone. No, he's fixated on me now.

A little stunned, I don't pull away. "I'll screenshot this and send it to you in the morning. So you remember."

"You're determined to do this, aren't you." It's not a question. And his hand stays curled around mine.

I look him straight in his dark eyes, unable to discern iris from pupil in the low light. "Just trying to give the people what they want."

"So thoughtful," he murmurs. Then, finally, he pulls his hand away, his fingertips trailing down my wrist as he does.

He walks on a moment later, and I resist the urge to turn and watch him go.

"How does he always manage to sound so damn condescending?" Beth asks, a note of disgust in her voice. "*So thoughtful*. Give me a freaking *break*."

But I'm still hung up on the way he wrapped his hand around mine. The way his touch lingered. "Did you see that?" I blurt as I turn back to her.

She squints, her brows drawing together. "See what? If you mean how much of a dick he is, then yeah."

Scanning her face, I nibble my bottom lip. If she didn't see it, then…then maybe I imagined it. Maybe I'm reading into things that aren't there. Maybe it was a simple touch and nothing more.

After a beat, I shake my head. "Nothing. I think I hallucinated there for a second."

"After two gin and tonics?" Beth grins and knocks my knee with hers. "You lightweight."

"Let me order one more, *then* you can cut me off," I declare, lifting a hand and grinning at the bartender.

We laugh together, but I know I'm going to be thinking about Daniel's hand wrapped around mine for the rest of the night.

"Paging Dr. Haddad to the operating room. Paging Dr. Haddad."

The page comes across the hospital intercom as I sort through the patient files on my messy desk. I sigh, setting them aside. Then I roll back from my desk and brush off the front of my scrubs. I need to get going. There are lives at stake.

But…wait. I cock my head in confusion and scan the office. I'm not a doctor. I don't save lives. I'm—

An abrupt knock sounds on the closed door before it flies open and a man barges in, a determined expression on his face. He slams the door behind him hard enough to make my desk drawers rattle.

I know that face.

"Dr. Santiago," I say, disdain dripping from the words as I lean back in my chair. "Shouldn't you be out there crushing the hopes and dreams of your patients? Breaking the news that they'll never play professional soccer again because you botched the surgery?"

"It's called football," he shoots back in that beautiful accented voice. "And don't you have a patient waiting to be left paralyzed after an unsuccessful tumor removal, Dr. Haddad?"

Shoving up from my seat, I snatch my lab coat from the back of my chair and glare at him. "Get out of my way. I'm being paged."

He doesn't move. "You're not going anywhere."

I'm hit with an overload of déjà vu as I stare him down. Oh, fucking hell. I know this dialogue. I *wrote* this dialogue—and now it's playing out in my dreams, starring the last person I'd ever willingly choose to fantasize about.

"Get out of my way," I demand, my chest heaving from fury. And maybe something else.

"You're not going anywhere," he repeats, stalking toward me, his dark chocolate eyes going molten. "Not until you let me touch you again."

I inhale sharply at his boldness. He's always been blunt, but this is so forward it makes my knees wobble.

"This is unprofessional, Dr. Santiago," I warn him, though I don't move.

He takes another step, crowding me against my desk until I'm forced to sit on the edge. "Daniel," he reminds me, his breath stirring my hair as he leans in. "Call me Daniel."

I say nothing, only keep my head turned as he brings his hands to my thighs and drags them up to my hips. When his fingers slip into the elastic waistband of my scrubs, a soft gasp leaves my lips.

"We can't," I whisper, finally turning to look at him. All I see is pure, unadulterated lust burning in his eyes. "Not here."

But he doesn't stop. No, instead, he slips a hand into my soaked panties, discovering the evidence of just how much I want him, and when the heel of his palm brushes my clit, I practically collapse in his arms.

"Say my name," he orders.

I shake my head, refusing to give in.

He grasps my chin with his free hand. "Such a naughty girl. I'll have to punish you for that."

He presses harder against my clit, dragging a moan out of me, but he covers my mouth with his to mute the sound, sweeping his tongue against mine, stealing all my resolve.

"Say my name," he whispers when he pulls back. "Say it."

"*Daniel*—"

Gasping, I wake with my fingers between my legs and his name threatening to leave my lips.

For a moment, I'm lost in the sensation of it all—his touch searing every inch of me, his voice in my ear, the hard edge of the desk pressed against my ass—before I remember where I am: alone in my hotel room, still a little drunk on gin.

Yanking my hand up over the covers, I squeeze my eyes shut and try to push away the unwanted lingering desire. Jesus Christ, what is *wrong* with me? I hate this man, unbidden attraction or not. I'm not supposed to let anything get in the way of that. But my subconscious seems hellbent on changing things.

I press my head back into the pillow and turn my face to one side. I'm greeted by the dim screen of my laptop on the mattress beside me. Once again, I fell asleep editing. And what do you know, the last page was a sex scene from *Under His Care*, our sexy doctor serial. Apparently, the content was a little too fresh in my mind when I dozed off.

At least, that's what I tell myself. I've written and edited millions of smutty words in the years I've worked at Naiad, and I've never had a dream like that. Especially one where Daniel Santiago was the star.

But brains are strange creatures, so I'll chalk it up to that. The dream didn't mean anything, even if I do find myself frustratingly attracted to the man.

This was nothing more than a fantasy. If, someway, somehow, Daniel and I ended up having sex—about as likely as a snowball's chance in hell—it wouldn't be anywhere near as hot. That mouth of his is only good for talking people into shitty contracts.

And the rest of him…

No. I refuse to let myself think any more about it. It was a dream for a reason. It will never happen.

I'd like to think that I have too much dignity to fuck a guy I hate. But even if I didn't, I've never gotten any indication that he's into me. We don't talk about anything outside of work matters, and that's okay, because we're coworkers and nothing more. Except I consider most of the other production leads to be close friends, so maybe it is strange.

God, I don't *know*. What I do know is that I need to be careful around him from now on. I can't let myself get caught up in the attraction I can't seem to shake.

Because if one touch is enough to reduce me to this, then I'm in big fucking trouble.

DECEMBER

CHAPTER 5

If there's one thing Naiad does well—other than romance serials—it's a holiday party.

The last one we had, before the whole world shut down for a while, was spectacular. I'm expecting nothing less this year, and from the looks of things, I won't be disappointed.

The only not-so-great aspect is that it's being held on a Thursday night. I don't know what management was thinking when they chose the date, but I doubt many people will show up at work in the morning. If they thought scheduling it for a weeknight would keep their employees from getting too drunk, they don't know us well at all. And if I was a betting woman, I'd say the crowd will be sloshed by ten. Myself included.

"Okay, game plan," Zoe says as she clings to my arm, teetering on her too-high heels as we step into the luxury hotel Naiad rented the rooftop of for the party. "We'll do a few shots and hit the photo booth while our makeup still looks good. Then we eat as much as we possibly can because I've heard this caterer's food is *amazing*."

"I'm down." I wore a wrap dress tonight for a reason—so I can eat as much as I damn well please and not be restricted by a tight waistline. Also, it makes my curves look dangerously good, and I don't even have to wear an underwire bra with it. I have on one of my favorite bralette and thong sets tonight, not because I expect anyone will see it, but because it makes me feel great. "I hope they hired a better DJ this year, though."

Behind us, Ella laughs. "Remember when Marsha threw a dinner roll at him when he played 'Last Christmas' for the fifth time?"

"God, I miss her!" Nikki cries. "I still can't believe that bitch left us to take a job in traditional publishing. What do they have that we don't?"

"Prestige and a 401(k)," I shoot back, to which everyone else groans in reply.

"Fuck working for a start-up," Zoe grumbles, dragging a hand through her fiery red hair before thinking better of it and patting it back into place. "Speaking of. This DJ takes requests via some new app. Maybe we should go work for *that* start-up."

I hit the button for the elevator and turn back to the group. "They're probably worse. I know we talk shit about Naiad, but—"

Despite the inquisitive looks my friends give me, I don't finish the sentence. No, I'm too distracted by the man who just walked through the door.

He's a few yards away and headed toward us, but even from here, it's clear that Daniel Santiago cleans up extremely well. For once, his hair is combed neatly, though I'm sure in about a half hour, he'll have run his fingers through it so much that it'll fall over his forehead again. His classic gray wool coat isn't buttoned, despite the below-freezing temperature outside, giving me a view of his crisp white shirt and perfectly tailored navy slacks. The ensemble is understated, but it fits him like a dream.

And speaking of dreams, I'm suddenly struck with flashes of the one I've been trying like hell to put out of my mind for the last several weeks. But every time I see his face on Zoom, it comes rushing back in technicolor. The only bright spot is that I haven't had any individual meetings with him since then. There's no way I could have looked him straight in the (digital) eye and had a professional conversation when I can't stop thinking about his hands all over me. Unfortunately, I'm thinking about it right now, all too vividly.

My heart races as he spots me. His eyes drift down my body, then flick back up, almost sharper now. Just like the night at the bar, I'm reading into it before I can stop, wondering if a look like that means—

Get it the fuck together, girl. It doesn't mean jack shit, because you hate him.

I swallow past the lump in my throat and open my mouth to warn my friends of his impending arrival, but I can't get the words out, leaving them to stare at me like they're afraid I'm having a medical emergency.

"Good evening, ladies," Daniel greets from behind the girls, causing them all to startle. In Zoe's case, she lets out a small shriek of surprise before scowling.

"Don't sneak up on us like that!" she scolds, slapping his bicep with the back of her hand.

"Selene saw me coming." He shrugs and turns his attention to me. And there it is. That same sharpness. But when he scans the others, it disappears.

Ella practically has hearts in her big brown eyes as she gives him a once-over. "Wow, you look great." She suddenly freezes. "Oh shit, am I allowed to say that? That sexual harassment training has me scared now."

Daniel laughs and slips his hands into his pockets, the expensive watch on his wrist flashing. He makes a hell of a lot more money than the rest of us do, which is just one of a laundry list of reasons to hate him. "You're fine," he says. "The conversation we had about what kind of BDSM content we allow was worse."

She snickers, and her cheeks go even more pink under the blush she's wearing. "Never thought I'd have to discuss whips and chains so in-depth with you, but here we are."

Zoe pokes me in the shoulder, grinning. "Remember the time you had to explain to me why that anal scene in *I'm Having Your Baby* was unrealistic?"

I laugh, but my face goes hot with embarrassment, especially when I accidentally glance over at Daniel. I've never been so grateful for my deep tan skin. "All I'm saying is that it would have taken *a lot* more lube than that."

"I don't think all the lube in the world would have—"

"Maybe we should wait until we're on the rooftop to continue this discussion," Daniel cuts in smoothly.

It's only then that I realize there are horrified hotel guests standing on either side of our group.

"Whoops!" Zoe says brightly, once again clutching at my arm as the elevator arrives. "Sorry, folks! We write romance for a living."

The horror only grows at her explanation. One woman's eyes go so big I'm afraid they'll pop out, and I swear another clutches her pearls.

I stifle a laugh as I practically drag her through the doors. The rest of our group follows as Daniel herds them in. Once the five of us are ensconced and the doors slide shut, I can't help but dissolve into giggles, and the other girls join me within seconds.

"Did you see that old lady's face?" Nikki gasps as she presses a hand to her stomach and doubles over. "I thought she was going to have a heart attack when Zoe said *anal*."

Ella wipes at her eyes. Her mascara must be waterproof, because it's still flawless. "She's lucky we didn't play Synonyms for Penis."

"Pecker," Nikki fires off.

"Schlong!" Zoe shouts.

"One-eyed trouser snake," I toss in.

We invented this game last year after receiving a rude email from a reader who didn't like how often we used the word *cock* to describe penises in sex scenes. Ever since, we've played the Synonyms for Penis game in our group chat on Slack.

The premise is simple: we come up with as many awful ways to describe a dick as we can. This is only the second time we've had the chance to play it in person, and it's a hell of a lot more fun this way.

Zoe turns her expectant gaze to Daniel. "Come on, give us a synonym."

I resist the urge to roll my eyes, knowing he'll decline in that haughty, artificially polite way of his, but to my shock, he throws one of his own out.

"Turgid man meat," he says without pausing to think.

Zoe and Nikki cackle in delight at his response, and Ella squeals, "Disgusting! I love it."

Soon, the elevator arrives at the roof and the doors slide open. Daniel steps back and presses a hand to the metal frame to keep the doors from closing on us. The other girls stumble through them, and I follow, ready to step out as well, but he shifts to block my exit.

"Is that seriously a game you girls play?" he asks, a note of disgusted disbelief in his voice.

My amusement fades and my blood heats to a boil almost instantly at his judgment. "It is." I cross my arms, back on guard. "Gotta keep this job fun somehow."

He shakes his head and huffs. "You have a very interesting definition of fun."

This time I don't hold back an eye roll as I shoulder past him. It's just like him to rain on the parade.

"Lighten up, Daniel," I say as breezily as I can manage. "It's a party."

I don't spare him a backward glance. I don't have time for prudes.

I was wrong before when I guessed everyone would be drunk by ten p.m. Turns out nine is more like it.

I've done my shots with the rest of the production leads, and I've eaten more deep-fried foods than should be humanly possible. Silly photos with my friends that I'll cherish forever have been taken, and I even downloaded the DJ app in order to request a few songs for us to dance and shout along to.

In the two hours since the party began, it's shifted from a polite holiday gathering into a rager. And much to my surprise, our bosses and the evil HR lady are leading the charge. I'm not afraid to let loose, but I'm also not interested in the regrets that come along with being *that* out of control.

Still, I have a pleasant buzz going as I dance to a Spanish song I only understand a few words of but love nonetheless. The classic holiday repertoire has been played out, and now the DJ is spinning a little of everything.

Despite the December cold, the rooftop space is equipped with enough heaters to keep its occupants from feeling the chill. Even in my thin dress and no tights, I've worked up a sweat on the dance floor, and after at least a dozen songs straight, I'm in need of a drink and a moment to catch my breath.

Shouting to the girls that I'll be right back, I slide my way over to the bar and order another gin and tonic with extra lime. I've taken it easy tonight so I don't make a fool of myself like some of my coworkers. More power to them, but it sure as shit won't be me.

Once my drink comes, I sit and people-watch. Zoe will probably come over and pull me back soon, but for now, she's preoccupied, doing some version of what I think is the Macarena. I can't be sure. So for now, I rest my feet and soak in the goings-on around me.

Unfortunately, it's not Zoe who sidles up to me a little while later.

"Having a good time?" Daniel asks as he leans against the bar, his attention on the crowd of our dancing coworkers, even though he's talking to me.

I was until you came over here is what I want to say, but instead, I go for unaffected. "I am, actually. Are you?"

"Surprisingly, yes," he admits, finally glancing my way. "This DJ isn't bad, but you and I are probably among the very few people here who have any sort of…rhythm."

His words are coded, but he's right. Our company is, at the very least, 95 percent white-American, and by and large, our coworkers are not the best dancers. In the entire New York team, he's the only Latino, and I'm the only one with Middle Eastern roots. We have two Black coworkers in other departments, but, sadly, that's the extent of diversity at Naiad.

"John certainly doesn't have any." I chuckle at our advertising manager, who's breaking out moves that might have been popular in the eighties *if* they were on beat. There's a small circle of clapping people—also off-beat—surrounding him, which is embarrassing for everyone involved.

"I can hardly bear to watch," Daniel mutters, but neither of us can take our eyes off John.

"It's…not great."

"It's a fucking horror show, is what you mean."

I laugh before I can stop myself. I don't want to like or find humor in anything Daniel says. He's a condescending piece of shit who doesn't deserve the recognition, and he knows it.

He shifts into my line of sight, smiling in a way that does things to me I refuse to acknowledge. "Did you actually laugh at something I said?"

"It happens sometimes." I shrug without taking my eyes off the train wreck on the dance floor. "Don't get used to it."

"I'll cherish the sound."

I suck on my straw with so much force my cheeks hollow out, all to keep from saying something I know I'll regret, and scan the mob of people. Not even the shift from the fast beat to a slow song can deter them from dancing. Several of them even grab partners and sway, laughing the whole time.

"At least they're having fun," Daniel says with a grimace. Then, suddenly, he squares his shoulders and locks me in his gaze. "But should we show them how to actually dance to this?"

I set my now empty glass down on the bar and scoff at his suggestion, even though I *could* show them all up. "Yeah, right."

"All you have to do is follow my lead."

Flashing him a wide, fake smile, I chirp, "I would never do that."

It's probably the snarkiest thing I've ever said to him. In any other setting, I wouldn't deign to stoop to this level, but it would be nice to let my guard down for once. Who cares if he knows I hate him? Everyone else does.

"Ah, I see." He nods with a frown, like something disappointing has occurred to him. "You're scared you'll embarrass yourself as badly as they are."

My head snaps up, briefly glaring at him before I can school my expression. "I just think this song is too slow."

It's a bolero, something romantic that requires a partner—and definitely the kind no one else here is pulling off.

Oh, Gavin, no… And Kelly, babe, maybe rethink this.

"Mm," Daniel murmurs, drawing my attention back to him. "Coward."

Offended, I fist my hands at my sides and stare up at him. "*Excuse me?*"

He dips his head until his cheek is practically next to mine and his mouth is millimeters from my ear. "You're a coward. It's okay. You can admit it."

Oh no. Absolutely not. This man isn't about to call me a coward and get away with it. He should know better than to challenge me. It's a well-known fact that I never back down.

"Fine," I grit out, pulling back enough to truly glare at him. "I'll dance. But you better not step on my feet."

My eyes are still narrowed when he offers his hand, perfectly unaffected by my annoyance. It only makes me even *more* annoyed with him. The self-assured asshole. I want to slap the smugness off his face.

I place my palm in his, an act that feels more defiant than it should, and let him lead me out to where several couples are attempting to dance a style they're clearly unfamiliar with. The steps I learned during my years of dance classes, something I gave up in college, come back the moment we stand face to face. And I'm glad for it now, because Daniel...Daniel knows what he's doing.

He cups my hand in one of his and lifts it to shoulder level while the other rests in the curve of my waist. Subtly, he squeezes there, a signal to ready myself. Then he steps forward, guiding me back at the same time in the *slow, quick, quick* steps. We fall into the rhythm easily, like our movements are as natural as breathing. As if we've done this together a thousand times.

"You're a better dancer than I thought you'd be," he says, almost echoing my thoughts as I watch the way his hips move.

"I'm a woman of many talents." I shake my hair over my shoulders as he dips me back slightly, not daring to meet his eyes, even though I can feel them searching my face.

When he rights me and we fall back into step, our bodies are closer. His chest brushes mine as he curls his arm fully around my waist. The warmth of his body and the heady scent of his cologne distract me for a moment, and I almost miss a step, but then muscle memory kicks in and saves me. There's no way he missed my mistake, but his only response is to slide his hand an inch or two lower on my back. Even though it's still in a perfectly respectable place on my body, something in me sparks to life at the move.

Setting my jaw, I tamp down the way my body wants to respond before the flicker of heat can ignite. The song isn't close to ending, so I can't step away without looking like the coward he accused me of being. Instead, I'll have to wait it out.

My best bet is to keep the conversation going. If our history is anything to go by, he'll have me fuming within seconds, and I absolutely need the distraction. I can't let myself think about what else he could do with his hips—things that would involve me and him and a dark corner.

"I bet you requested this song," I declare. "I can't imagine anyone else asking for a Cuban classic."

He spins me out and pulls me back again, pressing me flush to him. Despite the proximity, it's a relief, because in this position, I don't have to look at him.

"You caught me," he says as the top of my head brushes his jaw. "I couldn't resist. But you're a fan, aren't you?"

I was wrong. I don't need to keep the conversation going. The banter is only dragging me closer to the edge because of how fucking *hot* every word that leaves his mouth is. It's the manner in which he speaks, the intonations, the steady rise and fall, and how he manages to make every syllable sound worth hanging on to. I get why he's so successful at what he does, because he could negotiate a fish out of its gills.

No wonder I got fucked over.

"And that song you loved earlier?" he murmurs, his lips far too close to my ear. "The reggaetón one you and the girls lost your minds to? That was also my doing."

I desperately try to hold back the sensation, but a thrill rips through me at his words. He's been paying attention to me tonight.

But also, ew. What the fuck? Why do I even care? And why was he watching me?

Worse, though… Why do I like the idea of it?

I blame the dream. That stupid fantasy somehow changed my perception of him, and now I can't escape it. *Great.*

As soon as the song ends, I drop his hand and take two steps back. I have to get away before he leaves me even more confused. The only emotion coursing through me right now should be hate, or at the very least, vexation. Yet here I am, actually having enjoyed that dance.

What's *wrong* with me? Am I drunker than I realized? Did aliens implant something in my brain while I was sleeping?

I'm turning to make my escape when I spot the circle that's formed around us. On all sides, bright faces and hands are lifted in applause.

"Selene, you *have* to teach me how to get my hips to move like that," a girl from the design team whose name I don't remember gushes. "I don't know where you learned it, but you two are so talented, oh my *God*. I have, like, two left feet, and you guys are out here doing *that* with no practice. It's not fair."

As she and a few others laugh and chatter, I thank her and excuse myself with an awkward wave and smile, hoping no one has read into what just happened between Daniel and me. It's not my fault that style of dance is sensual. But it *is* my fault that I let him goad me into it.

I maneuver my way through the crowd, feeling suddenly overheated. At the bar, I order another gin and tonic and smile gratefully at the bartender when he sets it down in front of me. I down half of it in one go, eager to forget about the crime I've just committed. But there was no way I could ignore the dare. Daniel always brings out the worst in me and triggers my competitive side.

He's figured out how to push my buttons.

WORK FOR IT

And I'm afraid he'll never let up.

CHAPTER 6

"So, how *did* you learn to move your hips like that, Selene?" an amused voice asks from behind me a few minutes later.

I scowl into my drink. Why can't he just leave me alone? I need a chance to regroup and collect the pieces of my hatred for him. Otherwise I'm afraid I'll do something stupid. Like accidentally nurture a passing fancy into something more. But, of course, he's come to antagonize me.

"Can you just *not*?" I snap.

Daniel slides onto the stool next to me and rests his forearms on the bar top. His sleeves are rolled up, and the corded muscles move as he laces his fingers together. He searches my face in return, his gaze leaving my skin heated, but I refuse to meet his eye.

"Are you upset?" he asks, sounding genuinely curious.

As if you don't know. "I'm not upset, I'm—" I cut myself off. I don't need to explain myself to him. "I'm fine."

"No, you're not." He shifts closer, and I'm once again surrounded by his scent. It's more than just cologne. It's *him*—warm and masculine and intriguing. "You're acting like I ruined your evening. All I did was ask you to dance. If you weren't comfortable, you could have said no. I wouldn't have been offended."

I finally turn to look at him, blinking in disbelief. "You called me a coward," I bite back. "What did you expect me to do?"

"I didn't expect it to get to you that much," he says, shrugging, but he's still searching me for something. "I should have known, though. You never back down from a challenge."

"Damn right, I don't," I mumble as I lift my glass again.

"But that's not the only reason you agreed."

I freeze. The ice from my drink hits my teeth and shocks me back out of it. I refuse to believe he's figured me out and discovered my undercurrent of attraction to him. There's no way I could tolerate that level of mortification; I would have to hand in my resignation right this second and never return to New York.

"It's clear that you hate me," he continues, and I breathe a small sigh of relief. "It drives you to be competitive."

Daniel has never alluded to knowing my true feelings for him. And to hear it in such plain words… Maybe I *have* been obvious about it. Especially tonight.

"I don't hate you," I lie.

He chuckles and drags a hand through his hair. Gone is the out-of-character neatness. In its place is the sexy disheveled look that haunts me. "For a writer, you're a very bad liar."

"What's that supposed to mean?" I accuse.

"You tell lies for a living, and yet you can't do it well when having a face-to-face conversation." He shrugs as if he hasn't insulted me. "I know you don't like me, Selene. You don't need to keep badly attempting to hide it anymore."

God, this man. He never lets up, never lets things go. But I suppose, in that respect, we have something in common. Like him, I can't help but press on the same bruise and ask if it still hurts.

"Okay, fine." I set my now empty drink down with an exaggerated gentleness, even if I want to slam it. "I'll admit it: I'm not your biggest fan."

"Why?"

Turning to the crowd that's reconvened on the dance floor, I pointedly ignore him. He asked me to simply admit it, but that's as far as I go. I won't give him the satisfaction of anything more.

"Come on," he urges, low and persuasive. It's his contract negotiating voice with a hint of something slyer, darker—hotter. "Tell me why you hate me so much."

I nearly scoff, trying to tamp down on the simmering heat in my belly. "We don't have enough time for that."

"I have all night."

"Well, I don't," I shoot back with a glance at the expensive watch on his wrist. "I'm leaving soon. My feet are killing me, and I can't wait to get out of this dress."

His dark eyes flick up and down over me before settling on my face again. I do my best not to overanalyze it, but what the hell was that?

"Where are you staying?" he asks.

The question distracts me from the visual assessment he just gave me. "At a hotel near Times Square, unfortunately." I wrinkle my nose. "I didn't want to be far from the office, but that's the tradeoff."

"I'm headed to Penn Station. I'll walk with you."

"Why?" I ask, a thread of disdain mixed with dread weaving its way through me. "So you can hear all the reasons why I can't stand you?"

"What can I say? I'm dying to know."

To be honest, I don't completely mind his offer to walk with me. I've never felt unsafe in this part of Manhattan, but as a woman anywhere, I know to be extra careful once the sun goes down. Even though this city never sleeps, it's almost eleven, and the streets will be a little emptier than they were when I arrived. I'm better safe than sorry, even if being safe requires me to spend more time in Daniel Santiago's presence. I guess that means, in some way, I trust him more than most men out there.

"Okay, but I need one more drink before we go." I've got a buzz going, but if I'll be forced to endure more time with him, especially after that dance and conversation, I want the liquid courage.

Before I can order, he's already doing it—signaling the bartender and requesting another gin and tonic with extra lime for me and a rum rocks for himself, top-shelf. I want to make a comment about how he knows my exact drink order, but I don't dare strike up another conversation. Instead, I remain silent as we watch the bartender work his magic.

Once our drinks have been deposited in front of us, Daniel lifts his rocks glass and tips it in my direction. "To your hatred of me."

I roll my eyes but tap my highball glass against his. I'll certainly toast to that.

We sip in silence, letting the minutes tick by as we watch the rest of the party rage on around us. It's still going strong, but I've had my fill. I'm no longer interested in the loud music and screeching laughter. A quiet night in my hotel room, watching Netflix while shopping for more lingerie no one else but me will see, is far more appealing.

Once our glasses are empty, Daniel nods to me and stands, offering me a hand. I ignore it and stand on my own. I sway a little in my heels, but I'm not interested in his help. I'm just tipsy enough to feel flushed and relaxed, though I know as soon as we're out in the truly frigid air that buzz will disappear.

We wander over to get our jackets from the coat check as the party carries on, not bothering to say goodbye to our coworkers. As we wait, I pull up the group chat and send a quick text to Zoe, Ella, and Nikki to let them know I'm heading out. They're all still dancing with abandon, so none of them will likely see it until later. I lock my phone again, then step up to the clerk. But Daniel snags my coat first and motions for me to turn around.

I do so without protest, because the cold of the night air is quickly sinking into my bones now that we're away from the heaters. Once my arms are in the stiff, wool sleeves, Daniel runs his hands over the fabric that covers my shoulders, smoothing it out as he moves down. His touch falls away when he reaches my waist. The loss of contact makes me shiver and wonder what it would be like to feel it lower.

And then I want to slap myself. Yes, Daniel is hot. And yes, his voice sets off something inside me. And, okay, *yeah*, maybe I've fantasized about what he looks like out of his clothes. But none of that makes up for what he's done to me. Sexy or not, he's the cause of so many of my professional troubles. I have to stop this.

We're quiet as we wind our way to the elevator, and once inside, we settle on opposite sides of the metal box. Soon, we're pushing through the front doors and into the night, the street sounds and bright artificial lights hitting me all at once. The frenzy is amplified by the gin, forcing me to pause for a moment to get my bearings.

Daniel puts a hand on my shoulder to steer me in the direction of Fifth Avenue. I consider shaking it off, but he drops it once we settle into the flow of foot traffic on the sidewalk.

I don't know what to make of all these little touches. He kept his hands in all the appropriate places when we were dancing and kept just enough distance between us to be proper, and yet the connection ran deep. Even now, accidentally bumping arms as we walk, shifting closer to avoid running into others, it's like our bodies know each other.

Oh my God, stop being weird. There's literally nothing going on between you. That's fake romance novel shit.

I keep my lips pressed firmly together to prevent myself from saying something I'll regret, refusing to give him more than glances out of the corner of my eye. His shoulders are relaxed, hands tucked into his coat pockets. It's like we're friends out for a nighttime stroll, not coworkers who barely know each other and happen to be walking in the same general direction. It's terribly awkward, and yet I can't bring myself to do anything about it. I just want to get to my hotel and end the night that started out so wonderfully but wound up weird as hell.

We're nearly halfway to my destination when Daniel finally breaks the silence. "I've given you long enough," he says, his attention burning into me, though I still refuse to turn his way. "If you don't start talking, I'll have to assume you're too afraid to tell me why you hate me."

I bristle, wishing his little provocations didn't get to me so much. This time, I can't hold back the surge of anger it brings up. "You should stop goading me."

"Why?" he pushes. It's like he's spoiling for a fight. "What are you going to do?"

I grit my teeth, silently talking myself down from the ledge. It takes all my focus to hold back the venom ready to spew.

"Tell me, Selene," he coaxes with that honey voice. "Tell me why you hate me."

"No."

"Does that mean you don't hate me, then?"

"I don't think about you either way," I say breezily, though that's the last thing I feel. No, I'm trapped, cornered, like a small animal forced to choose between backing into the hunter's snare or moving straight into the wolf's snapping mouth.

"Liar." I can see him grin from the corner of my eye, bright in the darkness. "I know I haunt your dreams."

I almost trip over my own feet, horrified that he somehow knows about *the dream*. Finally, I turn to him, my heart in my throat. But his eyes are alight with humor. He's *teasing* me.

"So funny," I say, deadpan. "You should consider a comedy career."

"Someone's deflecting." He shakes his head, letting out a sigh.

"You'll tell everyone else why you hate me, but you won't say it to my face? I expected more from you."

He's provoking and prodding, making shitty assumptions, all to get a rise out of me. And this time, I'm not strong enough to resist it. I'm a fire sign; it's not in my nature to back down. The challenge makes me hot—in anger, but also, shockingly, in a way that sparks a fire in my core.

And he knows it, the bastard.

There's no holding back the inferno raging to be let out. "All right, you *really* want to know why I hate you so much? Fine." I stomp ahead of him and whirl around so I can jab a finger into his chest while I walk backward. "You, *Daniel*, personally screwed me out of so much money when Naiad bought my books. You made it seem like my contract was such a fair deal, but come to find out, you offered other authors—less successful than me, mind you—twice the royalty share."

I scoff, the words bitter on my tongue. "*Then* you put me in an impossible position creatively. You failed to mention that I would have *zero* creative control over the continuation of my books, forcing me to fight tooth and nail for it. I had to prove that I knew best for *my own stories*. And if Naiad hadn't hired me, I have no doubt I'd still be fighting. If they—if *you*—had listened to me from the beginning, I wouldn't have had to go through all that turmoil. You made my life *miserable*."

Daniel's expression doesn't change as I rant, and when I stop to suck in a deep breath, he's silent for a few beats, his expression unchanged.

When he finally opens his mouth, he has the audacity to say, "It's just business, Selene."

I throw my hands up, wishing he'd walk in front of a speeding taxi.

"Of course it's *just business*," I sneer. "But every time I advocated for myself, you were a condescending dick who gave me nothing but roundabout answers!" I let out a strangled scream that gets lost in the sound of honking car horns passing by us. "It made me want to choke you!"

"Sounds like you still want to," he tosses back with far too much indifference.

I shoot him a glare, stumbling backward in my heels. Without hesitation, he grasps my elbow to steady me and maneuvers me until we're walking side by side again. I don't thank him for it, but I don't think he'd want me to anyway.

"There's a running joke in the office that I'll fight you one day," I tell him, no longer caring if he reports me to HR. Let him fucking try. "People are literally taking bets for when I'll deck you and get fired for it."

"Based on this conversation, I'm surprised you haven't yet," he says, sounding vaguely impressed. "But come on. You want to hit me?" He shifts so I can see him better, spreading his arms to make himself a target. "Hit me. I can take it."

I snort. "I bet you can, but I'm not trying to get slapped with an assault charge in exchange."

Daniel laughs as he drops his arms again, his breath creating a white cloud in the frigid air between us. "What if I promise I won't press charges?"

"I don't trust your promises. Or contracts."

"You really *are* mad about that." He smirks and shakes his head. "You should be grateful I even found your work. Your books were popular, yes, but they never made it anywhere near the top of the charts. Still, I hand-picked you out of thousands of self-published authors."

I open my mouth to protest, but he holds up a hand and continues before I can cut in.

"*I* was the one who saw your potential. *I* reached out with the opportunity to continue your books exclusively with Naiad," he asserts.

"Then *I* pushed for you to be hired full time, especially once you started putting up a fight about having control over how they were continued."

I bristle at the reminder. He's not wrong. I *do* have him to thank for my position, but there is no doubt in my mind that I would have found success without him or Naiad. Hell, I may have found more success without them. I'm a talented writer, and I give romance fans what they want to read. I know that now. Unfortunately, when I let him talk me into signing exclusively with Naiad, I was struggling with confidence in my ability. And when Daniel spoke as if he would be doing me a favor by offering as much as he did, I let my insecurities convince me he was right.

But still, to hear this man claim that he's essentially handed me all my success sets my teeth on edge.

"You are so fucking full of yourself," I snap. "But if you want a thank you, then *thank you, Mr. Santiago.* I'd be *nothing* without you."

"I never said that." Somehow, despite the fury rolling off me, his voice is still maddeningly light. "You'd still be a phenom, but I made you *Naiad's* phenom."

"Sounds like you're firmly riding Naiad's dick."

He laughs again, deeper this time, like he truly finds humor in my response. "Maybe I am," he admits. "But they pay me to take it."

"Whatever you're making, it's not enough," I shoot back. "They should give you a raise from the royalties you cheated me out of."

Daniel is grinning, entirely too pleased with himself, as we weave around slower pedestrians. "God, you're bitter," he says. "But I get it."

I shoot him a sidelong look, nearly tripping in my heels. Again, he reaches out to steady me with a hand on my elbow, and I have to ignore the heat that shoots through me. "You do?" I ask, squinting in suspicion.

"I do." He slides his hands back into the pockets of his coat, depriving me of his warm touch again. "You want more money. Who wouldn't? But you're being a little dramatic about it."

"Dramatic!" I scoff. "Right, of *course* you'd write off a woman's concerns as histrionics."

He chuckles, bumping against me as we dodge a heap of trash bags spilling out into the middle of the sidewalk. "I'm not writing them off," he says, still ever so calm. "I'd never do that to you. But the ink on the contract has been dry for years. There's nothing to be done at this point. Feel free to continue complaining, though. I enjoy the passion."

I suck in a breath, and as much as I don't want to be, I'm a little turned on by our back and forth—especially knowing that he likes it too. "Is my anger entertaining to you?"

"Incredibly."

Again, something wild shoots through me, all the way down to my toes. He only said one word, and yet—and *yet*—it's got my insides fluttering. It's a good thing we've turned onto slightly quieter 36th Street, because I don't need everyone on Fifth Avenue witnessing my reactions to him.

"Well then, take comfort in the fact that there's so much more I could yell at you about," I huff, "but this is my hotel." I wave a hand at the revolving door of the building we're approaching.

I almost wish I'd walked slower or maybe taken a less direct route so we could keep arguing, because I'm beginning to realize that I don't want the night to end. I won't dare tell Daniel, but our verbal sparring match and his unwavering confidence has somehow made me even more attracted to him.

It's so goddamn *stupid*, and yet here I am. I might as well be wearing a sign around my neck that says *dumb bitch right here!*

"It's been nice shouting at you," I tell him, and I truly mean it. Then, before I can think better of it, I tack on, "I wish it didn't have to end."

"It doesn't have to, you know."

I frown and study him. "I'm not going to stand outside in the cold with you all night."

That brings a hint of a smile to his lips. It makes my stomach twist in anticipation.

"So invite me up," he says. His eyes lock on mine, and I swear they ignite. "Keep yelling at me."

CHAPTER 7

I'm frozen as my heart starts to race, wondering if I've heard him correctly. There's no way I have.

Invite me up.

We've been fight-flirting for half the night, but this is nothing short of a direct proposition—unless I'm reading him all wrong. Fuck, I could be, because the signals he's throwing out are so far from what I'm used to with him.

I have to play this cool. I can't bear the idea of embarrassing myself further if I've got this all wrong. And there's a strong chance I do.

Up until tonight, Daniel has been nothing but a consummate professional in my presence, even if I don't like his tactics. Maybe I'm hallucinating. Maybe I hit my head and I'm imagining this entire interaction. It's not like he hasn't starred in my dreams before.

But if I'm not hallucinating or reading into this wrong, if he really does want to come up…do I want that too?

The answer strikes me like a punch to the gut. Yes. I want to see if my burning anger can transition into something even hotter. I don't need to deny myself that chance.

But there are rules. Rules that keep coworkers from doing less than savory things together. Rules that I would usually respect, but don't have the capacity to care about at the moment.

Could this be our little secret? Do I trust him to keep it?

Hell no, I don't. And yet, that doesn't sway me.

"Don't tempt me," I tell him. It's a warning and a question—a *you want to try that again?*

In answer, Daniel steps closer and grasps my waist with one hand as he dips his head to murmur in my ear. "Don't be a coward, Selene."

Holy fuck. Holy shit. I was right.

My head spins, torn between wanting to gloat and not being able to ignore his challenge. The pompous ass knows I won't back down. And to call me a coward *again*? Oh no. He can't be allowed to get away with it. But more than that, I can't turn my back on an opportunity like this.

I want him in my bed.

And I'm going to get what I want.

Before I can second-guess myself, I grab his hand resting on my waist and pull him into the revolving door with me, his chest meeting my back. I drop his hand and push on the heavy door, wishing suddenly that the turnstile would malfunction. That we'd be trapped in here where I can relish the heat rolling off his body and the press of him against me. But the dizzying sensation is gone with a whoosh of air when our prison opens up into the lobby.

This time, he's the one who takes my hand as we move past the front desk and the crowds of late-night guests. Only moments ago, he was calling me dramatic, and now he's holding my hand, trying to get me upstairs to my room, where there's no way all we'll do is yell at each other. Yet, I'm compelled to go with it, consequences—of which I'm sure there will be plenty—be damned.

At the elevator bank, I jab the up button with my free hand and stand back. Daniel still has my other hand in his, now pressed to the hard planes of his stomach, and I shiver at the intimacy of it all. At the shock of it all.

"Keep yelling," he insists, low and teasing. "I know there's more you want to say."

I try to yank my hand away from him, but he only tightens his hold. At his reaction, I'm rocked with a realization that I've been desperate to ignore.

I want to fuck Daniel Santiago. So very badly.

"It can wait until we're in the elevator." All the heat that's been fueling me tonight rushes south. I want to keep it in my chest, to keep that fire of hate alive. And though the flames remain, they're joined by heavy desire.

We don't speak as we wait, Daniel stroking the side of my hand with his thumb. To those around us, we probably look like a couple returning from an evening out, tired and affectionate in the midnight hours. If only they knew the truth—that we're practically strangers. Yet I lean into him like I've done this a thousand times. In an act of tenderness, probably the last for the night, he brushes his lips across my temple. I like it. More than I should. But that's not what tonight is about.

We wait for the elevator to clear out, then Daniel gently pulls me into the space. He loosens his grip a little, giving me the opportunity to let go if I choose to. I don't.

Despite how busy the lobby is, we're alone for our impending ride to the eighteenth floor, and there's a beat of thick silence as the doors close that leaves me wondering what comes next.

I don't have to wonder for long.

As the elevator begins its ascent, Daniel moves, pressing his back to the wall and pulling me into him. Our hands are caught between our chests, our bodies not quite touching, but we're close enough that with one small shift, they could be.

"Tell me your next grievance," he says. A command.

I take a moment to gather my thoughts, patently ignoring the steady pulse that's started between my legs now that I know he's as into this as I am. "You made me look incompetent in front of a big-name author. In front of *Tory Mancillotti*. I'll never forgive you for that."

He chuckles, and there it is again, my anger back in full force. "I remember. You had a full fangirl meltdown."

"All because you didn't tell me she would be in that meeting," I retort, jerking my hands away from him. "I wasn't prepared and I looked like a fool."

"You did," he agrees.

He lets me go, but not far, because before I can take a step back, he snakes an arm around my waist and pulls me flush against him. In protest, I slap my hands to his shoulders to push him back, but then he moves his hips forward and—

Oh, fuck. There's no longer a single doubt in my mind that he wants me. Part of me is surprised, though the other part can't help but think *he better fucking want me*.

His dark slacks and whatever he's wearing underneath them do little to contain his steadily hardening cock. And Jesus, it's big. Undoubtedly. It presses against my stomach, and all I want to do is stand on my tiptoes and feel it lower. Better yet, I want it inside me.

Daniel grasps my chin and tilts my head up so I'm forced to look at him. It's only then that I realize I was ogling him.

"Distracted so easily," he murmurs, trailing his fingers down my throat. "Real hate isn't so easily dismissed."

Once again, the fire burns brighter. "I do hate you."

His mouth finds my ear, sweet rum on his breath. "I don't believe you."

I turn my head, forcing his lips to fall away. "Believe what you want." But then, spiteful, I press closer, trapping his cock between us, and rub against him.

When he groans, a sick bolt of pleasure surges through me. He can torture and tease me all he wants, but he won't be the only one playing the game.

"Now I believe you," he says, tightening his hold on me so I can't move like that again. "I think I like how much you hate me. Show me more."

Desire curls in my belly at the thought of doing exactly that. I'm tempted to do it here in the elevator, but right on cue, it comes to a stop and the doors slide open.

He releases me so I can step into the dimly lit hallway, but the second I cross onto the plush carpet, I'm knocked back with the reality of what we're doing.

He's my *coworker*. And even though romance and sexy stories are what we do, this crosses about a thousand different lines.

"Don't we have a policy against fraternization?" I ask, pressing my back to the wall next to the elevator.

Daniel moves in front of me and meets my eye. There isn't a shred of hesitance in the way he surveys me. "Do you care about that?"

"No," I admit. The second I took his hand, I was ready to break the rules. "Do you?"

He palms my waist again, then slips lower and drags my hips toward him. "I wouldn't have let you feel how hard my dick is if I did."

Before I can stop it, a laugh slips out, but I quickly stifle it by dipping my head. It's too late though; Daniel's already heard it.

"Twice in one night," he muses. "If I can make you laugh, I wonder what else I can make you do."

My humor fades as lust takes over once again. I pull my shoulders back and lift one brow. "I dare you to find out."

"*Ten cuidado*, Selene."

In defiance, and without breaking eye contact, I let my fingers drift down his chest, then his abs, until they're resting on the waistband of his slacks. "This isn't going to lead to a sexual harassment suit, is it?"

"Not from me." His hands roam over my hips, down to my ass, and squeeze. It almost feels like he's been waiting to do that for a while. "You going to come after me for this?"

"No," I say, succinct. There's no room for misinterpretation with something so serious. "I want—" I cut short, afraid to say it out loud. Afraid to show my hand. Because as much as this man infuriates me, I want nothing more than to beg him to fuck me.

Before I can finish, a man and woman round the corner and head in our direction. Daniel steps back but keeps a hand on my hip as he nudges me into moving again. When we pass the couple in the narrow hallway, he pulls me in front of him—mostly to keep us from running into each other, but no doubt to hide the impressive bulge in his pants as well.

An eternity passes before we reach my room, and I fumble in my coat pocket for my key. Daniel looms behind me, waiting, his presence heavy in the quiet. With the card in hand, I bring it to the sensor, but before the indicator light turns green, his hand slides around from my hip to my stomach. My breath catches at the feel of his broad palm splayed out over me, at how his fingertips span the breadth from above my navel to my mound, just centimeters away from more sensitive places.

My first thought is *How would those fingers feel inside of me?*

My second thought? *How many could I take?*

The third is *How quickly can we make it happen?*

CHAPTER 8

Despite the way Daniel's touch consumes me, I manage to get the door open. His hand falls away as I step into the dark hotel room, and it's embarrassing how much I immediately miss it.

I don't turn on the lights as we shed our coats and hang them on the hooks by the door; there's enough illumination coming in through the windows to make him out perfectly. But that's when the doubt creeps in again.

Should we really be doing this?

We've already established that this is consensual, that it's a mutual attraction, even if there are lingering negative feelings. And as long as it doesn't lead to trouble at work, then why the fuck can't we do this?

Still, my own reassurances do little to calm my whirring mind.

Daniel must sense my hesitance, because he backs me against the wall and settles his hands on my waist. "I can feel you thinking," he says, dipping his head to look me in the eye. "If you tell me to leave right now, I will."

I swallow hard before answering. "No." For emphasis, I turn the privacy lock on the door. "I want you to stay."

I swear his eyes darken as he leans in closer, finding my earlobe with his teeth and tugging.

"Tell me more about how I fucked you over," he murmurs.

This is familiar territory, and it gets me out of my head as heat shoots through me. I lift my hands to his chest and undo the first button of his shirt. "I could have been making thousands more a year in royalties if you hadn't pushed me into that deal," I tell him, though my fury is more subdued that usual.

"You didn't have to accept it."

"You didn't have to make it seem like you were doing me a favor by offering me scraps," I shoot back, working on the next button even though all I want to do is rip his shirt open and send them all flying.

With the fingers I fantasized about in the hallway, Daniel toys with the ties that hold my dress together at the waist. One hard tug, and it'll come undone, but his movements are agonizingly slow.

"My job is to look out for the company," he says. "Not you."

"Your job is bullshit."

He gives a sharp pull on the string in response, and my dress parts down the center, exposing me to him. My reflex is to cover myself, but I stand firm and stare up at him.

"Naiad could have easily afforded to pay me more," I go on as his gaze falls to my breasts. I'm wearing a flimsy bralette with twisting black serpents embroidered across it, the design barely covering my nipples. "You knew how much I was really worth and you cheated me."

"And you let it happen."

I'm on fire again, and not just because his hands have found my skin, his touch ghosting over my ribs. I'm genuinely furious. How dare he blame me for his actions? "You're a fucking asshole."

He laughs, short and mocking. With half a step back, he knocks my hands away from his chest. "You're no better. The world doesn't revolve around you, *mi amor*, as much as you like to think it does."

The sarcastic way he speaks the endearment and his simmering anger turn me on even more. His ability to match my energy brings out something feral in me. I want him badly, but when I reach for him,

I'm denied again.

The offense hits hard, though it's quickly nullified when he shoves the dress from my shoulders. The fabric pools on the floor around my heels, and then his body is pressed to mine. This time, somehow, his cock is even more prominent.

"I'm not sorry for anything I've done," he says sharply, his fingertips sinking into my hips. "And that's not what you want, is it? Contrition? No, you want me to hate you as much as you hate me."

My heart races. This sudden show after hours—no, *years*—of perfect composure is like a shock to the system. But fuck, I like it. More than I should.

And he's right. I don't want his apologies. Words don't change shit; actions do. He's figured me out, but I can't let him know that. "I don't—"

"*Cállate*, Selene. Let me hate you."

After ages of teasing, of shared breath, of near contact, his mouth finally finds mine, the kiss hard and demanding. I almost combust on the spot. His tongue sweeps across my bottom lip, and I open without hesitation, giving myself over to him. He wastes no time showing me that my dreams can come true—and that the real deal is better.

My knees go weak, and desire pools low in my belly as his hands run down my back, over my ass, and to the front of my sheer thong. When his finger traces the embroidered snake and ends right where I want him to be, I can't hold back a moan. But he doesn't linger. No, his touch disappears a moment later, leaving me yearning for more. His tongue is enough to distract me from my disappointment, brushing mine once, twice, before he pulls back again, forcing me to lean in, to follow his warmth like a moth to a flame.

I slide my hands up his shoulders and tangle my fingers in his hair as he kisses from the corner of my mouth to my jaw, nipping at the sensitive skin there. Each time, the quick pain is soothed when he flicks his tongue over it. A strike and apology. No, not an apology—neither of us wants that.

His hands find their way up my back and stop at the hook of my bralette. With ease, he pops the clasp and drags the fabric down my shoulders and past my elbows. Then it's fluttering to the floor.

"To think you've been hiding these under ugly sweaters," he murmurs as he takes me in, his lids low and heavy. "A travesty."

Before I can swat at him for insulting my fashion choices, his mouth is on my left nipple. I let out a hiss when he scrapes his teeth across it, but again, he soothes it with a light flick of his tongue. He alternates between breasts, leaving me to press my head against the wall and steady myself as he repeats it. Then he starts to move lower.

A flash of panic courses through me when he drops to his knees and curls his fingers around my thong. I'm practically naked already, but once that tiny piece of fabric is gone, there's no turning back. He'll always have the knowledge of what I'm like underneath it all.

I could stop this right now. I could tell him that this is a bad idea, that he should go home, that we should never speak about this again and return to the status quo of hate. It would be the easy thing to do. The smart thing. But I don't want to stop—I want him to touch me, to make me cry out his name over and over again. Second guessing will only leave me cold and alone, when all I want is for him to burn me from the inside out.

Daniel doesn't look up, but I know he can feel me warring with myself. His hands move to the small of my back and he trails kisses from my sternum to my belly to the top of the sheer panties. It's only then that he glances up, silently asking for permission.

I take a breath and nod. He can have this. He can have me for tonight.

A moment later, he's dragging the material down my legs, leaving me bare to him. He helps me step out of the thong, gripping my hip with one hand while he guides one foot and then the other out of the fabric. Once I'm covered in nothing more than the dim lights of the city, he sits back and stares at me in a way that feels like worship.

The look sends shivers up and down my spine.

When he's done admiring, he palms the backs of my thighs, coaxing my legs apart. I comply and open for him, even though my knees threaten to buckle from the rush of want that hits me. But he holds me firm and leans forward to brush the tip of his nose up the inside of my thigh to my hipbone, where he places a reverent kiss. From there, he makes his way over and down without taking his lips from me. The touch is so soft I nearly melt, but judging from before, he knows how to be rough.

"This doesn't feel like you hate me," I pant as his breath skims over where I want him most.

He turns to kiss my inner thigh again, and his stubble brushes my sensitive skin. "Give it time."

Then, contradicting his statement, his mouth is on my core. I throw my hands out, bracing myself on the wall as pleasure courses through me. When he flicks at my clit, already aching from the teasing buildup, a moan escapes me. With the way he's moving, he could send me over the edge in a matter of seconds. But at my response, he peers up and slows his pace, determined to drag this out.

He changes direction and technique before I can fully adjust to any one thing, pulling me up and dragging me back down. It's torture, this up and down and back and forth, and it feels so damn good.

Eventually, I run a trembling hand through his hair. It's black and thick and soft, and it takes everything not to sink my fingers down to his scalp and yank. As if he knows what I'm thinking, his eyes snap up and find mine, a threat in them. It sends another jolt through me, as if I wasn't already practically levitating.

I gasp when he hooks my left leg over his shoulder, opening me up to him even more. And when he slides a finger into me, his mouth never leaving my clit, I swear I'll lose my fucking mind. He laves at me and crooks that finger, forcing my pussy to tighten around him. God, how is he so good at this? How does he know how to break me and build me up at the same time? How can this man, who barely knows me at all, know so intuitively what I want?

I bite my lip to hold back my moans, but I can't help it; one breaks past my quiet whimpers when I'm nearly to my peak. I want to tell him I'm going to come, but I'm rendered speechless. Instead, I tighten my grip in his hair, readying myself to crest over the wave.

And Daniel must sense it, because that's when he pulls away.

"Oh, you *bastard*," I gasp as he leans back and grins sharply up at me, my wetness glistening on his full lower lip. "I was wrong. You *do* hate me."

"Let me show you how much."

The next thing I know, he's scooping me up bridal style like I weigh practically nothing. I'm not the smallest girl, and I'm definitely on the taller side, so his ability to move me so effortlessly is yet another turn on. The man is getting more and more perfect by the second.

He places me gently on the crisp white duvet, then, with his knees between mine, pressing me open, he crawls over me. I'm vulnerable to him. The cool air hitting my soaked folds makes me crave the heat of him again, in any form he's willing to give me. But right now, there's an imbalance.

"You're wearing too many clothes," I tell him. He's still fully dressed. The only thing out of place are the few buttons of his shirt I managed to undo. "Take them off."

He tsks and shakes his head. "So pushy. Haven't you realized I'm the one in control here?"

Another shiver rolls down my spine. "Who said you were?"

He leans down again, kissing me hard. My taste lingers on his tongue. "You did," he murmurs against my lips a moment later. "And I'm not giving it back."

"Fine, keep it," I exhale, bringing my knees up a little higher. He's between my legs, but he's careful not to let our bodies touch in all the places I'm desperate for, purposefully denying me. "But let me feel you."

"Say the magic word and I will. I want to hear you beg."

Jesus, this man. This fucking man. So intent on pressing all my buttons except the one I want him to put his mouth back on. But I'll give him this if it means getting what I want. "Please, Daniel."

He kisses me again in reply, this time gently, sweetly, slowly. It lingers and makes me want him even more, especially when he nips at my lower lip. Any harder, and it would have drawn blood. "Good girl."

It's so condescending and yet so hot that I feel like I'm burning from the inside out. "Take off your fucking clothes."

He laughs, but then he draws himself up to his knees and unbuttons his shirt. "Always trying to save face," he comments as his fingers work each button through its hole. "It's going to get you into trouble one day."

I'm hoping that it gets me into trouble *right now*. The kind that ends with the guests on this floor complaining about how loud the people in room 1811 are. It seems, though, that Daniel is determined to take his sweet goddamn time.

I want to tell him to hurry up, but knowing him, making any other demands will only prolong the process. Finally, he shrugs out of his shirt, leaving his broad shoulders and chest on display. A faint line of hair trails down his defined abdomen and disappears past the waistband of his pants, teasing me, begging me to trace it and see where it leads.

For now, though, I drag my attention back to his right shoulder, where a pattern of ink decorates his pec, then wraps around his bicep.

The tattoo makes him—annoyingly—even sexier.

"I didn't know you had a tattoo," I blurt.

Daniel raises a brow, though his gaze is still hooded. "Why would you?"

The words are a reminder of what I've been thinking all night. "True," I concede. "I don't know you."

"You'll get to."

Before I can question what he means, he's undoing the button of his slacks and sliding the zipper down. And then I'm at a loss for words.

CHAPTER 9

If I thought he was big just by what I felt through his pants, there's no comparison to seeing the outline of his cock in his black boxer briefs. I'm almost afraid of what I'll be met with when he finally pulls those down too.

Smirking, he watches my breasts move with the effort of my breathing, clearly knowing he's the reason for it. I want to sit up and slap the smug look off his face.

My thoughts must be written all over my face, because Daniel cages me in, hands planted on the mattress on either side of my head. "Ah, ah," he chides. "Don't ruin it for yourself."

I hate being told what to do, even if the instructions are in my best interest. But I rein in my natural reaction. Instead of giving in to the urge to let my palm meet his sharp cheekbone, I push myself up and press my lips to his, tasting his surprise. He may say he's in charge, but if he leaves me an inch of wiggle room, I'll take it.

He doesn't respond, leaving me to trace the seam of his lips with my tongue, trying to convince him to let me in. To my disappointment, he turns his head and pulls away. My stomach drops as he sits back on his knees again, wondering what I've done wrong. I made one move, and now he's shutting me down? What the hell?

My confusion only grows when he removes himself from the bed, leaving me cold and rejected. Mortified, I bring my hands up to cover myself, unable to believe that it's going to end like…like *this*.

"Daniel, I—" I begin, my voice weak.

But he shakes his head to cut me off and silently bends down. When he straightens up again, I finally get to see him—all of him.

I was right. He's huge.

His cock rests heavy in his hand, thick and veined, and I'm suddenly very, *very* worried that he might be too much for me. I prop myself up on my elbows, ready to tell him that maybe we should slow down, but he's hovering over me again before I can speak. I gasp as his weight pushes me back to the mattress, his knees positioned so that my thighs rest on them, spread wide. If he moved forward just a few inches, he'd be pressing into me, but Daniel is careful to keep his distance.

His abs flex as he leans back and caresses my calves, though soon, my gaze drifts lower and lower. His cock is all I can focus on as he works the buckle of one of my Gucci block-heel sandals, then brings my leg up and plants a kiss on the inside of my knee. He repeats the process with the other shoe, letting it clatter to the floor, but the noise barely catches my attention.

"Is something distracting you?" he asks, holding back a laugh as he curls his hands around my thighs.

I'm in no mood to laugh. Every inch of me aches for him, especially now that I know I'm not being rejected, but I have a confession to make before we go any further.

"I…" The word trails away, and I'm suddenly self-conscious. I slide my hands up to hide my breasts, as if he hasn't already had his mouth all over them.

Daniel, however, stops my movement. He snatches my wrists and pulls, uncovering my skin again. He brings my hands to his lips and kisses the fluttering pulse point of each wrist, though his eyes stay locked on mine.

"What's wrong?" he asks. His voice is still low, but the amusement is gone.

"Nothing," I say quickly. "I just…"

"What is it, Selene." It's not a question. "Tell me."

I blow out a breath and turn my head so I don't have to look at him, even though I'm still locked firmly in his grasp. "It's just…it's been a while, okay?" I admit, fighting back embarrassment. So what if it's been a few years since I last had sex? I can't imagine he'd judge me for it, but I need him to understand in case I need to take it slow.

He's silent for a few beats, and I can feel the intensity of his stare. Then he repositions my arms by my sides and leans in, his lips brushing mine in not quite a kiss.

"I'll go easy on you," he murmurs against the corner of my mouth. "At first."

I lift my hand, desperate to run my fingers over his shoulder, to trace the tattoo and feel his skin, but he turns before I can. He tilts to one side of the bed and digs through his pants pocket. He rights himself a moment later, a foil packet between his fingers.

Oh God, this is really happening.

My heart races, thumping so hard I worry it may beat right out of my ribcage. If he comes any closer, he'll undoubtedly feel it for himself, but he's still far enough away as he tears open the condom wrapper and pulls it out.

Swallowing thickly, all I can do is watch. He gives himself a long stroke with one hand, then slowly rolls the condom on. I could watch him touch himself all night, but right now, I want him to touch *me*.

What feels like ages later, he grips my hips and drags me down the bed, eliminating the space between us as he covers my body with his. We're fully skin to skin. It's fucking glorious.

I wrap a leg around his and drag up, savoring the friction of it, but I stop when his fingers dip between my thighs. He traces my slit from top to bottom and then back up, all the while rubbing circles around my clit with his thumb.

My hips buck, chasing that shock of pleasure, before I can stop them.

Daniel dips his head and chuckles against my neck. "You're ready for me." He trails kisses down to my collarbone, and without glancing up, asks, "Do you still want this, Selene?"

My answer is breathy but comes with no hesitation. "Yes."

"Yes, what?"

Bastard. "Yes, *please*."

He smiles before looking down, and my gaze follows. With one hand gripping his cock, he aligns himself with my opening, leaving me to close my eyes in anticipation. It's not long before he presses against me, hot and growing slick from my want for him.

He's slow to sink in, both of us groaning as my walls stretch to take him. It's endless, and I swear I'll break before he's fully inside.

Forcing my eyes open, I tuck my chin and watch his movement.

Jesus fuck, he's not even halfway in.

On a long exhale, I slide my hands up his arms and over his shoulders, willing myself to relax into it, to encourage him to keep going. I'm so wet I'm dripping, but there's only so much my body can do to help me out. I arch my back, searching for a better angle, one I hope will make this easier because I don't want it to stop. He assists, looping an arm around my waist and adjusting my hips.

"Is this okay?" he whispers against my ear, his forehead pressed to my temple. "Or am I too much for you?"

So cocky, even when he's filling me.

But I can't speak yet, so all I do is shake my head, even if I want to tell him off.

"You want more?" he asks, a little breathless. "Yes or no, Selene."

Part of me appreciates that he's asking, that he's giving me an out, but the other part just wants him to get on with it, to let me have all of him.

"Yes," I manage to exhale.

"Then relax."

I almost snap at him that I *am* relaxed, that he's just bigger than anyone I've had, but that will go to his head. He doesn't need the ego boost.

Still, I comply as best as I can, easing my muscles one at a time. That's all it takes, it seems. Because with one more push, I've taken in every inch of him.

I've never felt this degree of fullness before. The sensation is new and foreign and somehow *right*. Our chests heave in rival beats, but he doesn't move otherwise, which is a pure kind of torture.

Dropping my head back with a moan, I savor the sensations, the tease.

Again, he asks, "Is this okay?"

"Fuck," I gasp, working to form coherent syllables as I nod. "Daniel, *yes*. Just—*move*."

He rocks his hips into me. "Like that?" he taunts.

The move sends sparks of pleasure and pain shooting through me. I'm almost tempted to push him off and take control, but with him, the effort would be futile. I'm at his mercy now. "Again," I demand, the most I can do.

He complies, my fingers gripping his shoulders harder as I breathe through it, still adjusting. But it already feels so fucking good.

"Keep going," I urge him.

The bruising kiss I get in response is enough to distract me from any discomfort as he pulls all the way back and slides in again. He groans against my mouth as I shift to take him deeper, and the sound makes me nearly come on the spot.

But I want more—more of him, more of this growing heat.

And he gives it to me.

He slides one hand into my hair and grips hard as he thrusts, his teeth scraping down the sensitive skin of my neck. He's not gentle, not by a long shot, but he takes me slowly. He's controlled, far more than I am, proving that he really is the one in charge. Giving him that power is thrilling, only because he uses it well.

I nearly lose it when the hand that was wrapped up in my hair ghosts down my body and settles on the softness of my lower belly, his thumb stroking my clit in agonizing circles. My orgasm is already building, and with every snap of his hips, he pushes me closer to the edge.

Running my hands over his broad back, grounding myself to this moment, I close my eyes and focus on the storm of pleasure that's threatening to take over. I'm close to begging for him to let me have that release. I need it. I want to shatter under his touch. And I'm about to—

Until he stops.

My eyes fly open wide for a moment, but in an instant, I narrow them on the man above me. He's grinning, hands still on me, but our other connection is gone.

"You asshole," I gasp, furious over my second denied orgasm. "Stop *edging me*."

He rakes his gaze down my body, leaving a scorching trail, then drags his attention back to my face. "Not until you ask nicely."

"Fuck you," I spit, shoving against his chest, as if that will get him to move again.

Daniel bats my hands away. "Mm, not nice at all," he murmurs, dipping lower to cover my body with his again. But he still doesn't give me what I want. "Now you're going to have to beg for it."

I buck my hips to grind against him, but all he does is pin me down. His cock nudges against my thigh, torturing me with what I can't have.

One move, and he'd be inside me again, but he's purposefully denying me.

"I hate you," I exhale as I grip his biceps, letting my nails sink into his skin. I hope he bleeds. "I hate you *so fucking much*."

His lips find mine again, and this time, I'm the one who takes his bottom lip between my teeth. I bite so hard that he lifts his chin to break free.

"You're dangerous," he says quietly.

The fire in his eyes has me trembling beneath him. It's enough to make me beg, just like he wants.

"Please," I groan, the ache of his absence nearly killing me. "Please, just fuck me."

A shudder rolls down his spine at my words, but his voice is even as he says, "Now, was that so difficult?"

I want to rage and hiss, because nothing about giving in to him is easy. But before I can, he pushes into me. He's rougher this time, faster, like his careful control is slipping. I want to see him break, to give him that release, but not until he gives me mine.

"Harder," I whisper in his ear, wanting more. Wanting all that he can give me.

He doesn't stop as he lifts his head to look me in the eye. The intensity of his gaze is enough to make me lose my breath. "You sure?" he asks.

I meet his next thrust, inhaling sharply with the impact. "I know what I like, Daniel."

"Dangerous," he murmurs again. "So fucking dangerous."

But then he gives me exactly what I want. Hard. Brutal. Unforgiving.

I can't hold back the cry that leaves me when he angles his hips and slams against the spot where I need him most. I'm already building back up, writhing beneath him, out of my mind. When he brushes his thumb over my clit again, I'm done for.

My whole body is alight as I come harder than I ever have before. With my head thrown back and words of unintelligible pleasure leaving my lips, I clench around him, my walls pulsing as I ride the high. He thrusts faster now, breathing raggedly against my neck. When he groans and his body tenses on top of mine, I swear I come again.

I don't know how long we lie there catching our breaths, still connected, but the beating of his heart against mine makes me never want to move.

Eventually, he rolls to the side, pulling me over with him. I'm weak, and my legs are still trembling, but I have just enough wits about me to respond to his lazy kisses. I whine a little when he pulls away, though he soothes me by promising he'll be right back once he gets cleaned up. But I'd be content to stay here in the mess we've made.

I close my eyes and shift onto my stomach, the ache between my thighs setting in. I'm in a haze, aware of every inch of my body, but my mind wants to fade out. I barely notice when he steps back out of the bathroom and brushes my sweat-damp hair out of my face.

He kisses my temple and murmurs, "Go to sleep, Selene."

For him, I obey.

CHAPTER 10

He's gone when I wake up the next morning.

I didn't expect him to stay. Hell, I didn't want him to stay. But I don't recall him leaving. All I remember is coming so hard I nearly blacked out, all under his touch. A touch I never expected to feel, despite my dreams to the contrary.

For an instant, I wonder if the whole thing was a dream. There's no way I let Daniel Santiago fuck me, right? And there's no way he would live up to my fantasies. Exceed them, even.

But my body can't hide the truth. Every inch of me hurts in a good way—a way I haven't felt in years. I haven't dated or been in a relationship or even had a casual hookup since college, and I graduated four years ago. This was long, *long* overdue, even if it was with the last person I expected.

The proof of our night is littered across my hotel room floor: my shoes, my dress, my lingerie, the empty condom wrapper. I might be mortified about it all if he hadn't worked me over so well and given me what was undeniably the hottest night of my life. He took me hard, despite saying he'd go easy on me—at first. I'm going to feel this for at least a week.

Knowing I'd likely be hungover after the holiday party, I preemptively took today off. My train back to Baltimore doesn't leave until this afternoon, but I don't know how I'll walk the six blocks to Penn Station or how I'll sit comfortably on a train for three hours. My inner thighs are sore, and just perching on the edge of the bed makes me wince. I'm no doubt bruised to high heaven down there, but fuck, it was worth it.

Relishing in the memory doesn't stop my stomach from twisting into knots though, because I have no idea how to handle things with him now. What's the protocol for speaking with a coworker one fucked on a slightly drunk and angry whim? Is there a published source of rules I can reference before our next daily Zoom meeting?

For the time being, I'm resolved to ignoring it until I'm forced to bring it up again, while simultaneously praying I never have to.

I eventually drag myself out of bed and into the bathroom. I ignore my reflection in the mirror as I flip on the light, uninterested in what I look like right now. No, I'd rather imagine myself in the way I hope Daniel saw me last night—sexy enough to take to bed and edge until I begged for release.

I want to be the Selene of yesterday for a little longer. Because as soon as I leave this hotel room, it's all over. And I don't want this feeling to disappear just yet.

I'm drying off when my phone buzzes on the bedside table.

Wrapping a towel around my body and grabbing another for my hair, I step out of the bathroom and check the screen.

"Hey," I answer, putting the call on speaker so I can get dressed.

"Good, you're alive," Nikki greets. Her scratchy voice is evidence that her night didn't end nearly as early as mine. "Hang on, let me get the girls in on this."

A minute later, Zoe and Ella have joined us, also sounding a little worse for wear.

"I am so viciously hungover, it's not even funny," Nikki announces.

"Which one of you wants to come put me out of my misery?"

"Sorry, babe, but I'm not coming all the way out to Brooklyn," Zoe says. "Ella, honey? How ya doing?"

Ella's only response is a whimper and the sound of her chugging water.

"Valid," Nikki says. "Okay, let's get down to it: Selene, you abandoned us last night. How could you?"

I'm fighting with my bra clasp when the words register. Panicking, I freeze. There is absolutely no chance I'll ever tell them what happened between Daniel and me. I'll never live down the shame of it, because how does one go from declaring their hatred for a person to fucking them in a matter of hours?

I guess the typical answer would be *they don't*, but apparently, I missed that memo.

"Sorry," I tell her. "I wasn't feeling too hot after all the drinks and fried foods, so I got an Uber back to my hotel. I texted you."

Ella lets out a breath like she's finally coming up for air. "We still missed you."

"We went out after," Zoe adds. "When the party finally shut down, a bunch of us went to a bar nearby."

"Thus, the vicious hangover," Nikki groans. "Be glad you didn't go. You'd be suffering like the rest of us right now."

I relax a little as they recount their night out, relieved that they didn't notice that I left with Daniel. As long as I don't accidentally spill something incriminating, no one ever has to know. I can't imagine Daniel will say anything either, especially if he values his job.

This was a one-time thing, and now we can go back to the status quo of hate. Just as it should be.

By the next morning, I'm feeling remarkably better. But there's no way I can get on my Peloton.

"Why are you just staring at it?" Carly asks from her stationary bike next to mine. She pats the empty seat. "Come on, hop on the horse."

On Saturdays, we force ourselves to work out together in the makeshift gym we've set up in the corner of our living room. Just like with the Naiad girls, I didn't tell her what happened Thursday night—and I'm not sure I ever will, considering she also knows how much I hate Daniel. So I can't tell her that my pussy is so fucking sore that the mere idea of getting on this tiny, hard bike seat makes me want to cringe.

"I don't know if I can," I admit. It's the truth, but I follow it up with a lie. "I wore heels to the party, and it really messed up my hip."

I do have a history of hip injuries, so this is an excuse she should buy. The first, during my freshman year of college, ended my potential dance career early, and she was witness to the second one during senior year, when a game of flag football turned physical after I taunted a drunk frat boy about his lack of talent. She's well aware that I have my good days and bad ones, though in the past few months, I haven't had issues.

"You wore the Louboutin stilettos, didn't you?" she accuses with a grin. "Girl, I *know* those shoes are sexy as hell, but they're going to kill you one day."

She's right about that. And it's exactly why I didn't wear them to the party. My legs would have looked even better thrown over Daniel's shoulders with them on, but the way he kissed up my calves as he undid the straps of the block heels was still sexy as hell.

"I know, I know," I reply, backing away from the bike and its menacing seat. Even on days when I'm not nursing sore parts, it does a number on the downstairs. "I'm just gonna do a yoga class and hope I can make this feel better."

"Wow, willingly letting me get ahead in the cycling challenge," she teases. "You really must be in pain."

Part of me wants to tell her what happened, but a stronger part wants to keep this my little secret. It's one I plan to relive later when I'm in bed with no one but the memory of Daniel, just like I did last night.

That might be even more embarrassing to admit—that I touched myself while fantasizing about him and will absolutely do it again. I need to get him out of my system, because one night together really shouldn't have reduced me to this. Come Monday morning, I have to be over it. I will be.

I can't let Daniel Santiago get the best of me.

CHAPTER 11

I usually dread logging in to Zoom on Monday mornings, simply because it means it's the beginning of yet another work week, but today, that trepidation is compounded.

It isn't that I hate my job. I love the creative aspects of it, and working remotely is a dream. Sure, I'd love if my plate wasn't always so full, considering my working hours are usually from about five minutes after I wake up in the morning to ten minutes before I go to bed. But most days, I'm thankful for the steady, well-paying job I usually enjoy.

Doesn't mean I want to fucking be here today, though.

I shift in my desk chair, feeling only a bit of tenderness today. Strangely, I think I'll miss the feeling when it finally subsides. Because when it's gone, there won't be a single physical reminder left of my night with Daniel.

What we did was a mistake, and that's a fact I've reminded myself of at least a hundred times already. It was a whim, a fantasy, and a temptation I shouldn't have fallen for. But could anyone blame me? Daniel is hot as hell and aggressively confident. I hate him for it, but unfortunately, that's exactly what I'm attracted to.

The thing is, that type of man is rarely attracted to *me*. I'm brash and hot-headed. I act before I think and never reject a challenge. Those qualities are not exactly becoming of a lady, or so I've been told, but most days, I like who I am. I have no qualms about standing up for myself and speaking out, and I like knowing what I want and going after it with every atom of my being.

So the knowledge that there's a man out there who can look past all of that and still want me—or even want me *because* of it—blows my mind a little. And it makes me all the more hung up on him in return.

But this has to stop. Hell, it shouldn't have started.

With one last deep breath, I click the link to our daily team meeting—a sometimes pointless waste of time that allows our bosses to make sure we're all alive and on task—and ensure my microphone is set to mute.

Most of my fellow production and acquisitions team members are already there, but Daniel's little video box hasn't appeared, leaving me feeling somewhere between disappointed and relieved. While we wait for the meeting to begin, my coworkers chat about the holiday party and their ensuing weekends. Based on what I saw before leaving with Daniel on Thursday, there's no doubt in my mind the majority of these people were hungover the next morning and stayed home, so the postmortem is happening now.

Daniel joins just as our manager, Jim, recalls his experience at the party to raucous laughter from those who aren't muted. But all I can do is stare at the little black box that says *Daniel Santiago* until his video starts.

I wish I could say I found his disheveled hair and wrinkled T-shirt—like he just rolled out of bed—disgusting, but that would be a lie, and it's too early in the day to start lying to myself.

"Okay, we *have* to talk about what we all witnessed," Jim says, and my attention snaps back to him. "Daniel, why didn't you tell anyone you could dance so well?"

Daniel offers up a relaxed smile and a short laugh. "My family would disown me if I couldn't dance," he says, his accent a little thicker this morning. Now I *know* he's just woken up.

"And *Selene*," Jim squawks.

I scramble to unmute myself to avoid any awkward silence.

"I didn't know you could move like that either," he continues.

Smiling, I sit a little straighter, ready to crack a stupid joke about how I'm full of surprises, but Daniel beats me to reply.

"She told us she was a dancer."

Did I? I don't remember mentioning it at work. Did I include it as my fun fact when I was first introduced to the company years ago? And if so, was that seriously memorable enough to stick in Daniel's mind? Because judging from the reactions of my other coworkers, including some of my closest friends, they don't remember that at all.

"That kind of song requires a partner, and I knew she was my best bet," Daniel finishes with a corporate smile. "No offense to the rest of you."

He garners laughter and more envious comments, but all I can do is fake a smile and obsess over the thoughts swirling in my mind.

How much does Daniel know about me?

And has he been thinking of me as much as I've been thinking of him?

―――

Can you jump on a Zoom call with Daniel and Sally Marinson + her agent in a few minutes? She wants an update from the creative side as well.

Yeah, no problem, I reply to the Slack message from Jim, even though my heart has surged into my throat.

Great. Daniel will send the link in a sec.

So far, this has been the kind of quiet Monday I prefer. I've been working on edits, uninterrupted, for most of the morning. Tomorrow, I'll be stuck in an all-day meeting in order to figure out the trajectory of one of our serials, stuck talking to people for eight hours as we throw spaghetti against the wall and hope something will stick. Today, however, I didn't expect to talk to anyone after our morning meeting. My stomach lurches at the thought of being nearly one-on-one with Daniel.

We still haven't talked since our night together, minus that strange comment of his earlier, but that didn't involve us actually speaking to each other. Just *about* each other. And I didn't say a word, just smiled and hoped my camera angle wasn't terrible. I'm hoping the same thing right now as Daniel sends me a Slack message with nothing but a Zoom link.

I count to ten before I click it.

When I enter the virtual meeting, he's the only other person there. I'm tempted to leave it and then claim that my internet went down, but instead, I lift my chin and say, "Hey."

He inclines his head slightly in response. It looks like he's gotten dressed since our meeting three hours ago. Which is good, because we're about to talk to one of our best-selling authors and I can't have this fucker embarrassing us more than he already does.

"How's it going?" I ask when it becomes clear that he's not going to speak.

"Can't complain," he says easily. "You?"

My heart races. "I'm fine."

With a nod, he glances down. Probably jotting something down on the notepad I know he keeps next to his laptop. "Not too sore?"

I freeze. So we *are* going to talk about it. I just didn't expect it to be in the first few seconds of a business call while we wait for Sally and her agent to join us. They could pop in at any second and overhear our conversation, and that makes this incredibly dangerous.

I drag my fingers through my hair and regard him coolly. "Why are you asking?"

"Because I can see I left my mark on your neck."

I slap a hand to my skin and snatch up the mirror I keep on my desk. Sure enough, I have a hickey just under my jaw. "Shit." How the hell did I not notice this before?

"I was rough with you," he says casually, still not looking at the screen. "Did I leave any others?"

He absolutely did leave more. My hips are mapped with bruises in the shapes of his fingers, and I still wince a little if I sit down too quickly, but I'm not about to tell him any of it. "You weren't all that."

"You weren't saying that when my cock was buried inside you."

I don't mean to gasp like I'm acting in a black-and-white film, but I can't help the sharp intake of air just as another little box appears on the screen. It's only then that he looks up. His dark eyes are unreadable, but the corner of his mouth lifts almost imperceptibly.

That smug bastard.

"Hi, Sally," he greets, smooth and even, when the new face pops up on our call, as if he wasn't just torturing me with filthy words. "So good to see you. How are you?"

"I'm doing well, thank you," she chirps, but then her gaze shifts on the screen and a concerned frown takes over her expression. "Selene, dear, you're looking a little flustered. Is everything all right?"

Daniel dips his head and mutes his mic, likely snickering at my misfortune, although to anyone else, it probably looks like he's searching for something on the floor.

I clear my throat, hot from head to toe. "Ah, yeah," I croak. "Just one of those days, but I'm fine. Great to see you again, Sally."

Daniel soon takes over the conversation and the warmth in my cheeks subsides, but at least I have an answer to my earlier question.

He absolutely thinks about me.

And now that I know I've taken up residence in his psyche, I doubt he'll be leaving mine soon either.

"You *danced* with *Daniel*?"

I grimace at Marianne's question, glancing from face to face on the screen. She's probably been itching to ask me about it all day, but she's somehow managed to wait until happy hour. Every Monday, a few of us make drinks in our own homes and sit in front of our computers to sip them together and unwind.

"She did," Ella confirms. The pink concoction in her martini glass almost sloshes over the rim as she shifts in her matching pink desk chair. "But it was *very* clear she didn't want to."

I nod, relieved that's how it came off to everyone, but my heart is still pounding at the reminder of the dance that kicked off everything.

"He goaded me into it," I tell them. "The only way to get him to leave me alone was to just do it."

"You could still see the hate in her eyes," Nikki adds with a grin, lifting her whiskey in toast. "That's the only reason we didn't give her shit for it."

"Well, damn," Marianne huffs. "Now I wish I'd come to the party instead of visiting my kids at college."

Zoe snorts. "Get your priorities straight next time. But Selene didn't start a brawl with him, so in the grand scheme of things, you didn't miss much. She didn't even step on his feet."

"Not for lack of trying," I say, a bold lie. "But the bosses were watching, and I didn't want to get reported to HR. Anyway, Ella, how was your date on Saturday?"

Thankfully, Ella dives right into yet another of her first-date-gone-awry horror stories. She's a sweetheart, but she's unlucky in the relationship department. She'll meet her prince charming one day, though. She's impossible not to love, and the person who finally sees that will be lucky to have her as a partner. Until then, we'll all be entertained by her first date tales.

My racing heart finally slows now that the attention has shifted off me and Daniel.

I just have to make sure it never goes back.

CHAPTER 12

It's finally Christmas Eve eve, and I'm counting down the minutes until six, when I'll be free from work for the next week and a half.

It's been two full weeks since the holiday party, and I've had to stare at Daniel's face on my computer screen every weekday morning. Other than our little *discussion* before the call with Sally, we haven't spoken about our night together again. And I hope we never will.

As the days go by, it feels more and more like our hookup was some sort of fever dream. Like maybe I imagined that night and his dirty words the following Monday. At this point, now that all the bruises have faded and I can sit on my bike seat again, I really don't think it happened.

I can't decide whether I'd prefer that, though. Either way, there's nothing to talk about. Clearly it was a one-and-done situation, a heat-of-the-moment thing.

Yeah. That's all. And that's all it'll ever be.

I'm trying to keep myself from watching Daniel on the screen in our morning meeting, but I'm only half listening to Jim prattle on about organizing a team lunch in the office once we're back from the December holidays.

"Selene, Marianne, you're both more than welcome to come into the city and join," he says, his tone wheedling. "What do you say?"

I stare directly at Daniel's little box when I answer. "I'd love to come."

JANUARY

CHAPTER 13

New York in the winter is a miserable place.

Honestly, any northeastern metropolis during this time of year is gross. They're all full of dirty snow, puddles big enough to dive into, and bitter winds that whip around the buildings. It's bad enough in Baltimore, but there's something about New York that's just…worse.

And I've missed it so damn much.

I'm undoubtedly an introvert, but I've missed getting out of my house and being swept up in the crowds of the city. Do I feel completely comfortable? Absolutely not. But the thrill of it is kind of addicting.

I'm shivering by the time I push through the doors of the Naiad office building and wipe my feet on the oversized mat. As I venture through the small lobby toward the elevator, I exchange pleasantries with Rolando at the front desk. Once inside the stainless-steel car, I tap my key fob against the sensor and hit the button for the seventeenth floor, then prop myself up against the back wall and check my phone.

As the doors slide toward one another, a hand darts between them, then a man slips through. It's not until the scent of his cologne wafts toward me that my head snaps up.

"Good morning, Selene," Daniel says, low and warm.

My mouth immediately goes dry, and words fail me. This isn't the first time I've had this reaction in his presence. The second time I saw him in person, all I could do was grunt in reply to his greeting, mostly because I was holding back the words *go fuck yourself*. But it was also because I'd forgotten how tall he was. So when he stood from his chair to greet me, I had to crane my neck to make eye contact. I had a brief *is he actually attractive, or is he just tall?* moment and unfortunately concluded that the man was handsome in addition to being a giant.

Some fuckers have all the luck.

This time, I pull myself together. I swallow past the lump in my throat and mumble, "Good morning."

The doors finally shut, and then we're alone. I don't know where the conversation is supposed to go from here, but I'm leaving it up to him to decide. The last time we were in an elevator together, we ended up tangled in bed shortly after. Truthfully, I don't trust myself not to blurt out something aggressively forward like *so, what are you doing after work?*

"What are you doing after work?"

I go rigid, trying to comprehend how the words I was thinking just came out of his mouth. Is he…is he a mind reader? I look him up and down, searching for signs that he's a witch in disguise, but Daniel keeps his eyes trained on the doors.

"I don't—" I begin, but cringe at how weak my voice sounds. I clear my throat and try again. "I don't have any plans."

"Are you staying at the same hotel as last time?"

I frown, suspicious of his line of questioning. "I am, yeah."

He gives a murmur of acknowledgment. He still isn't looking at me when he says, "I'd like to see you again."

"You're seeing me right now," I reply, my stomach lurching up into my throat. Yes, I'm playing dumb. But if he wants something from me, he's going to have to say it flat out.

"Funny." The word rumbles through the small space like distant thunder. "Have a good day, Selene."

For the first time since I started here, I curse how fast the elevators are in this building, because before I can retort, we've reached our floor and the doors are opening. He exits without looking back, greeting our office manager with a nod before heading to the main office space.

I'm slower to move, still reeling from our interaction. Did I blow it? But what was there to mess up? All I did was point out the glaringly obvious, once again daring him to clarify his intentions. But this time, he didn't rise to my challenge. Instead, he left me to wonder if he was implying what I think he was.

There's no way he wants to fuck me again. No way.

I mumble a hello to our office manager as well, then head down the short hall to the rest of the office. Daniel is already settled at one of the ten long communal tables set up in the massive open space. There are a few other people around, and I greet them as well before dropping into one of the rolling chairs on the opposite side of the room. Here, I can face the tall wall of windows and keep my back to him. If I sit on the other side and face him all day, I'll never get any work done.

Even still, my mind will be racing from our thirty-second conversation for entirely too long. And I hate him a little more for it.

At four o'clock, when I've hit a slump after the heavy pizza lunch Jim organized, a Slack notification pings in my earbuds. Assuming it's one of the production girls, I don't think as I swipe over to the application. But instead of seeing a notification next to Ella's or Nikki's name, there's a little red *2* next to Daniel Santiago's name, indicating that I have unread messages from him.

My heart thuds so aggressively I worry that Zoe can hear it from where she's set up beside me. With trembling fingers, I click on his name and wait for the messages to load.

The first is a link to a cocktail lounge's website, located a few blocks south of my hotel. The second message is a time: *7 p.m.*

There's nothing else. No formal invitation. No *do you want to meet for a drink?* Just a location and a time. God, the audacity.

I'm tempted to stand him up since he's obviously incapable of asking me properly, but…why not, right? It's just a drink. What harm could it do?

A lot, the little voice in the back of my head warns.

I choose to ignore her.

CHAPTER 14

I don't know why I stop by my hotel to freshen up after work. Honestly, I shouldn't have. I should show up to the bar in the leggings and chunky sweater I wore to the office and leave my hair in the messy bun it always ends up in when I can't stand the distraction of it hanging around my face.

Instead, though, I find myself peeling off my clothes the second the door to my room slams shut. I always pack a nice outfit in case the girls want to go out to dinner after work, so I paw through my suitcase to find it. Carly says I'm an over-packer, but I'm grateful for that trait now.

I pull out a black bodysuit and a pair of jeans. Then, without allowing myself to think about the implications, I grab a matching bra and panty set too—black mesh with tigers embroidered on them in silk thread. The set will give me a boost of confidence (and cleavage), reminding me that I'm sexy no matter how this little meeting with Daniel goes tonight. There's no guarantee that he's going to see it, but if he does…

No, I can't get ahead of myself. He said he wanted to see me again, but then he promptly ignored my existence in the office, up until those messages. He didn't even look my way at lunch, despite standing beside me and reaching into the same pizza box I was. What am I supposed to make of that?

I guess I'm about to get my answers.

When I'm cleaned up and dressed, I yank my boots back on and head into the freezing night, wrapping my scarf tight around my neck. Maybe I should have stayed in and eaten room service in bed, but here I am, venturing out into the cold for a man. A man I can't figure out for the life of me.

Thankfully, the cocktail lounge is toasty and not too crowded. It's a cute little art deco place, with small tables scattered throughout and booths lining the perimeter of the room. There's a vast mirrored wall behind the bar, equipped with shelves that house every spirit known to man, and I waste no time heading over to order a drink. I don't bother to look around to see if Daniel is here yet. Even if he is, I definitely need alcohol before I face him.

I prop myself against the bar and smile at the man behind it. When he sidles over to me, I order a gin and tonic and pay, declining to open a tab. I don't know how long I'll be here, but if things go wrong, I want to have the ability to make a speedy exit.

Once I've shrugged out of my coat and have my drink in hand, I turn to peruse the rest of the place, but Daniel steps into my line of sight almost immediately.

As usual, I find myself looking up and up and up until I meet his eyes.

"I got a booth," he says. His voice is just audible over the din of clinking glasses, soft jazz, and laughter from other patrons. "Follow me."

I nod, heart racing, and let him lead the way toward the back of the room. Sliding onto one of the velvet upholstered benches, I peer up and wait for him to do the same across the marble table. Unlike me, he didn't change after work. He's still wearing a classic leather jacket, black T-shirt, and jeans. And, as always, his hair is messy from dragging his fingers through it all day. I want to reach out to him and do the same.

A flash of a memory hits me, almost knocking me back. A vision of sinking my fingers into his loose curls while he was on his knees in front of me and his mouth was on my core. And now I'm hot all over. I can only hope he can't tell.

I sip at my drink. It's a little strong, though it better be, considering I paid fourteen dollars for it. I watch as Daniel lifts his glass to his lips, and damn if I'm not mesmerized by the way his throat works when he swallows the amber liquid. If I leaned in close, I could run my tongue along his—

Fucking hell, I need to stop. He probably brought me here to make sure we're on the same page and can properly move forward without having to worry about HR coming after either of us. I absolutely cannot think about him bending me over this table and doing less than appropriate things for a public setting.

Get ahold of yourself, girl.

I take one more sip for courage before clearing my throat. By now, I've learned that he's not likely to initiate the conversation. "So," I begin. "Why did you want me to meet you here?"

He sets his drink on the table but keeps his hand wrapped around it. He has big hands—with long fingers and a prominent vein running up from the side of his wrist through his arm. Again, I'm struck with a memory, this one of his palm pressed to my belly, his fingers curling inside me.

"I figured we should talk," he says.

I can't stop my grimace. "I was hoping to avoid that."

There's a flash of amusement across his face, accompanied by one arched brow. "Really?" he asks. "You hate me so much you're going to completely avoid me now?"

"*You're* the one who avoided *me* all day," I point out, annoyed by how he's trying to spin it. "Besides, I just…didn't think we had anything to talk about."

"No?" His words are soft, but something about his gaze is heavy. "Because I think we have a lot to talk about."

I run my finger down the side of my sweating glass, trying to keep my cool. I should shut this all down, lay out that what happened between us last month was a one-time thing, and then be on my merry way. But part of me, the little part that loves to make dangerous decisions, wants to hear what he thinks we have to discuss.

That part wins out. "Like?" I prompt.

His dark eyes meet mine, pinning me in place. "Like how I left you alone in bed and how much I wish I hadn't."

My heart tumbles in my chest, and it's a good thing I don't have gin in my mouth because I'm sure I would have choked on it. "I didn't expect you to stay the night," I tell him, surprised by how even my voice is considering my whole body is vibrating with a mix of curiosity and desire.

This is the exact opposite of how I expected the conversation to go. Instead of shutting down the possibility of a repeat, he's shoved the door wide open. And he's not being subtle about it.

"Would you have wanted me to?" he asks, his full attention fixed on me in a way that makes me want to squirm.

But I resist and stay silent because I don't have an answer for him. *Would* I have wanted him to stay? I've worked so hard to convince myself it was a one-and-done situation. A one-night stand. An exquisite mistake that would only be repeated in my dreams. But if he had stayed the night, if we'd gotten an opportunity to talk after we'd sobered up and without the shroud of desperate lust, what would have happened?

I guess we'll never know, since I passed out in a post-orgasm haze, and he disappeared into the night. But I can't imagine it having gone any differently. This—being here with him tonight, talking about what transpired—is the outlier in the situation.

"Where's this all coming from?" I ask, exasperated and maybe a little breathless from the shock of what I think he's just admitted. "Before the party, we hardly spoke. If we did, it was only about business. And as you already know, you aren't exactly my favorite person."

"You aren't mine either," he replies. "But you're interesting."

The fuck is that supposed to mean? I nearly ask, but it would mean losing the cool that I'm hanging on to by a thread. "And a good lay, right?" I say dryly.

"A great lay. Don't sell yourself short."

He says it with such confidence, like there's a smirk hiding behind the words even though there isn't one on his face. He's mocking me, playing along but throwing my catty comment back in my face. It's a backhanded compliment. It's not meant to make me feel good about myself—and it doesn't. My body is still vibrating, but it's from anger instead of thrill now.

"There are a lot of interesting people in the world. Plenty of them even work in our office," I challenge, giving him a chance to redeem himself, even if he doesn't deserve it. We're both playing a game here; I just can't figure out if we're playing by the same rules. "Still doesn't explain why you went after me."

At that, Daniel tosses his head back and laughs. "You're so oblivious." He says it like he can't believe he has to explain any of this to me. "Bordering on stupid, even. You know that, don't you?"

I gape at him, fully thrown. This isn't a game anymore. Not one I'm willing to play, at least. "Excuse me?"

"You're *oblivious*," he repeats, stretching out the word. "It's why you let yourself get screwed over in those contract negotiations."

My simmering anger takes a nosedive toward rage. "I didn't *let* anything happen," I bite back, wishing I'd never come here or entertained his advances. I should have stood him up like I originally considered. "You pressured me and made promises you couldn't keep."

He rolls his eyes, but a smug smile plays around his mouth. "You think you're so smart, but half the time, you don't even pay attention to what's going on around you. You should work on that."

"And you should work on being less of an asshole," I seethe, gripping the edge of the table to keep from making a move I'll regret. I don't want there to be any witnesses when I beat him to a pulp.

But in a move that catches me off guard, Daniel slides out of the booth and onto his feet. He has his coat clutched in one hand while the other is outstretched in my direction.

"Now that you're upset with me," he says, "should we get out of here?"

I'm frozen in place. All I can do is blink up at him for a long moment. Then it dawns on me. "You did that on purpose," I exhale as the cold realization spreads like ice through my veins. "You were trying to rile me up." Saying all the wrong things to get me heated and wet for him, as if my rage is the key to making me want to sleep with him again. "Looking for another hate-fuck, right?"

"I take back what I said. Maybe you *are* smart."

"Fuck you."

With that, I shove my way out of the booth and around him, pulling on my coat and scarf as I storm toward the exit. I can't believe I nearly entertained his tricks all over again, but it's worse this time. I let this man neg me, let him take my precious time, and even let him get under my skin. It's not even his fault, because I'm the one who gave him the opportunity to do it. But now I've learned my lesson.

The cold rush of air hits my face like a slap when I step out onto the sidewalk. I deserve the cruel shock for letting my guard down for a second. I just feel…used.

"Selene. Wait."

I tuck my chin into my scarf and stride down the sidewalk toward my hotel, ignoring Daniel and the way he calls out for me. Unfortunately, I can't ignore him once he's beside me. In one more long stride, he's blocking my path, forcing me to pull up short.

"Move," I tell him flatly, staring at his shoes and willing them to step out of my way.

He doesn't go anywhere. "I fucked up."

Scoffing, I finally drag my attention to his face and glower. I tell myself my eyes are burning because of the wind and not because I'm on the verge of tears. "You called me stupid and then expected me to fuck you again. In what world is that supposed to work?"

To his credit, he swallows hard, and what looks like remorse shimmers in his eyes. But it doesn't quiet my anger and embarrassment.

When he doesn't say anything for a beat, only works his jaw, I huff out an unamused laugh and attempt to step around him. Just as we're shoulder to shoulder, he curls his fingers around my elbow, pulling me out of the flow of pedestrian traffic and against the metal bars of a closed shop.

"I'm sorry. I shouldn't have said any of that."

There's barely any space between us. Daniel's body blocks the wind and provides privacy from the people who pass by too closely. I should tell him to shove his apology up his ass and then go back to my hotel, but there's something in his expression that keeps me from going far—guilt. He knows just how badly he messed up.

That doesn't mean I won't let him wallow in it, though.

"You're brilliant," he murmurs, dipping his head so I can't avoid his gaze. "Don't let anyone tell you differently."

I tilt my head back and meet his stare full-on. "*You* just did."

"I did," he confesses with no hesitation. "But I thought…"

Grinding my teeth together instead of lashing out the way I want to, I wait. If he doesn't spit it out, they're going to turn into dust.

"I thought that was what you liked," he finally says, the words rushed, as if he's embarrassed to say them. The splotches of red high on his cheeks only confirm it. "I thought that was what you wanted from me. A reason to yell at me. An excuse to let something happen between us again."

That makes my jaw go slack. My poor teeth have been saved, but my chest burns. Because he's not exactly wrong. His methods were horrific, sure, but how can I blame him for thinking that it might work? Based on how we ended up in bed together last time, it seems like a reasonable assumption. My anger was part of what drove me to drag him up to my room. But what he doesn't understand is that it wasn't the only force at play. Years of simmering grudges bubbled up that night—not new jabs that I had to react to in the moment.

"So you thought insulting me was the way to go? I already have more than enough reasons to hate you. I don't need more."

He's tense, and his shoulders are hunched, but to his credit, he still holds my gaze. "I know. And I didn't mean any of it."

"Yes, you did," I counter. "You wouldn't have said it if there wasn't some semblance of truth."

Daniel draws in a breath and gives a sharp, honest nod. Then, somehow shocking me even more, he says, "You do miss the obvious sometimes, but what I said was cruel."

Heated anger courses through me again, and I squint at him. But as much as I don't want to, I respect him for telling the truth instead of placating me with lies. "That's one way of putting it."

He angles in a little more, the hand on my elbow drifting up my arm. "You're right to hate me," he says quietly. "But I meant it when I said I wish I hadn't left you. Out of everything, that's the biggest truth."

Despite the way my heart rate accelerates with every inch his hand moves upward, I refuse to let him see that he's getting to me. "Now you're back to the sweet words," I say, suspicious, eyeing him for any hint of deception. "Which one is it? Insults or flattery?"

But I find no untruth in his expression, not even when he murmurs, "It's whatever you want, Selene. It's your choice. All of this is."

I bite the inside of my cheek, hating how sincere he sounds. I want to stay angry, to justify walking away, but I'm still rooted to this spot, caged in by his warm body. "This is a weak apology." I shoot for indifference, but even to my ears, it sounds like I'm considering moving past this misstep.

And the truth is, I can see his remorse. It soaks through my jacket and into my skin where he grips my arm. He doesn't want me to walk away until this is cleared up. But he'll let me go in a heartbeat if I tell him I never want to see him again. And the ache swimming in his dark irises is proof that he absolutely means it when he says he wishes he'd stayed the night.

He seriously messed up, yes. And yes, I'm well within my rights to walk away and ignore him for the rest of forever. But I'm coming around to the idea of giving him another chance. After all, a lesser man wouldn't have apologized, wouldn't have admitted his wrongs. Maybe—even for someone I don't particularly like all that much—I can find it in me to move past this and start over. And maybe we can have the conversation we should have had in the first place, without egos and misunderstandings getting in the way.

"I'm trying my best," he says, pulling me out of my thoughts. Cautious relief seeps into his eyes when I don't make a move to bolt again. There's even a hint of a wry smile on his lips, like he's trying to get us back to the playful banter—the kind I can get behind. "But I seem to remember that you don't like apologies."

Damn it. He does listen. And that alone proves that he's attempting to do this my way, even if he doesn't know exactly what that looks like. He's…trying.

And that's more than any man has ever done for me.

"Even so, do you think you can find it in your heart to forgive me?" he asks.

The question catches me out. The smart thing would be to say yes, I forgive him, and then go on my way and never speak of this night—or our other one—again. It should be the end.

As I'm starting to realize, though, I'm not very smart when it comes to Daniel.

I want to make the same mistake again. To give him another chance. And give myself the opportunity to explore what could have been if he had stayed. I owe it to us both. And, most importantly, I deserve another world-shattering orgasm after that fuck-up.

Before I can overthink it, I put my hands on his chest and push up onto my tiptoes. I drag my lips up his jaw, smirking at the way he stills under my touch. Because now I know I have the upper hand. And I don't plan on giving it back tonight.

"No," I murmur in his ear. "You're going to have to work for it."

CHAPTER 15

Unlike the last time Daniel accompanied me back to my hotel room, I don't let him touch me until we're inside and the door is shut behind us.

All the way here, I twisted away every time he tried to reach for me. I didn't even speak to him, just let him follow behind me and ask questions. It didn't take him long to figure out what was happening and where we were going.

And when he did, he shut up.

Now, though, our coats are shed, and my back is to the wall as he corners me. There's a question in his eyes. He wants to know if he's allowed to touch me yet. When I nod, he doesn't waste time closing the distance and pulling me against him.

"I didn't think we'd ever make it here," he rasps as his hands greedily roam over my waist and hips, like he's truly been dying to touch me and yet resisting the urge. "Now I can apologize to you properly."

The way he seems intent on caressing every inch of me is flattering as fuck, because keeping my hands off him during our walk here was excruciating. And it was obvious he felt the same based on how many times he tried to grip my elbow or snag the sleeve of my coat to keep me close. I'm clearly not alone in this strange attraction.

But before this can go further, there are still questions that need answers.

"Wait," I say, splaying my palms on his chest to push him back a little. "I need to know what we're doing."

His heated gaze flicks over me, taking away the last bit of chill from our walk here. As nice as it is, it's not enough to distract me from the discussion we need to have. "About to get you out of those clothes, I hope."

"That's not what I—" I take a deep breath to level myself. A snarky comment isn't going to help us any. "I mean, what is this? I want to get that straight. Is this another one-time thing? Or is this going to be some sort of…friends with benefits situation?"

"We're not friends, so it's not that."

He's right, and had he been the one to ask me the question I would have replied with the same thing, but I'm not interested in sparring right now. "Daniel, come on, I just—"

"Hey." He brushes my fingers from his chest and steps forward, cupping my face in his hands, all pretenses dropped. "It's whatever you want it to be. Like I said, all of this is your choice. Do you want to sleep with me again?"

"Yes." I wouldn't have let him follow me back here if I didn't.

"And you want to keep this casual?"

The answer should be obvious, but I respond anyway. "Considering we don't really like each other, I don't think there's any other option here."

He huffs out a laugh and drops his hands from my face. "I guess not."

"And this has to stay between us," I remind him, squeezing his bicep to emphasize my point. "I know Naiad is pretty relaxed about most rules, but I don't think they've ever had employees get involved like…this."

"I won't tell anyone at the office."

"They all know I hate you, so I doubt they'd believe you if you did," I point out, a saving grace in this situation.

He makes a disappointed sound and shakes his head. "Come on, Selene, I just said you were smart. Don't prove me wrong so quickly."

I frown and drop my hands to my sides, taken aback. "What are you talking about?"

"What was the most popular trope on the app last month?" he asks.

"Enemies to lovers," I answer without missing a beat. "What does that—" I cut short, the relevance of it dawning on me before I scoff. "That's *fiction*."

He presses closer, letting me feel every inch of him. And God— there's so much. "Then what do you call this?"

"Enemies fucking." I shoot him a warning look. "Don't try to compare us to a romance novel." *Don't make this about work.*

He chuckles and dips low to brush his lips over my racing pulse point. "Should we call this pure erotica, then?"

My eyes flutter shut at the way his words, combined with his touch, flood me with desire. "That seems like a safer bet."

He's kissing me hard a moment later to seal our agreement, and it's a weight off my shoulders that we're on the same page about this. It's clear we're compatible physically, that we're drawn to one another, even if there's no emotional aspect to it. No, that's a lie, there *is* an emotional aspect—but that emotion is animosity, and I'm perfectly fine with that kind of attachment.

Daniel takes a step back, pulling me with him. I follow willingly, desperate to keep my mouth pressed to his, but that connection disappears as he shifts us. I tumble onto the mattress when the backs of my knees hit the bed, and I'm left a little winded. By the force of his movements and the fire in his eyes, I know this won't be a gentle encounter. And I can't wait. How many days can I expect the bruises to last this time?

He makes quick work of pulling off my boots and tossing them to the floor. Eagerly, I help him out by unbuttoning my jeans and peeling them down my hips. He takes over then and drags them the rest of the way over my legs. The mattress dips as he kneels on it and pushes my knees apart to inspect the snaps of my bodysuit. His gaze drags up to mine for a moment, his expression full of dismay.

"Always something complicated," he murmurs, two fingers dipping under the fabric, between the snaps and my sheer panties. With surprising ease, the snaps come undone with satisfying pops.

"Complicated, maybe, but you know what you're doing." That's as close to a compliment as he'll get from me.

I sit up and pull the bodysuit off over my head, then let it float to the ground before taking his face in my hands and forcing his lips back to mine. He sweeps his tongue over mine, hot and pressing, but he pulls away a moment later, splaying a hand above my breasts to keep me back.

"*Selene*," he says, teasingly scandalized, giving me a very thorough once-over. "Did you wear this just for me?"

I peer down at my body, remembering the black lingerie and the roaring tigers. "I don't do anything just for you."

"Of course not." The words are condescending, like always, and yet they send a thrill through me.

After one more long look of admiration, my lingerie joins the rest of my clothes on the floor, and soon, all of his top the pile. I run my hands over his shoulders and down his chest and abs until I'm gripping his cock. When he groans in response, I can't hold back my grin.

"I thought you said I'd have to work for it." He's breathless, no matter how hard he tries to hide it.

Sliding my hand slowly up and down his length, I say, "You are."

I let go abruptly and push him onto his back while he's distracted.

Without hesitation, I snag the condom he set on the bedside table and rip it open, then pinch the tip and roll it down his thick erection. He's hot and heavy in my hand, and I'm wet from the anticipation alone—and our verbal brawl. But I have one caveat for tonight.

"You don't get to come until I do," I say. "Twice."

He grips my hips as I straddle him and hover just above his cock. "I'd never dream of it," he breathes out, drinking in every inch of my body. "Take what you want."

So I do.

I sink onto him, slow and steady, remembering just how much I have to take. The ache between my legs is all-consuming, and it only grows as he fills me completely, inch by solid inch. I take a moment to focus on where we're joined, blown away by how well we fit together, even though I'm stretched near to breaking.

"You just going to stare, *mi amor*?" Daniel asks with a note of amusement in his voice. The endearment is once again dripping with condescension. "Or are you going to use me?"

I exhale a shuddering breath, still adjusting to the feel of him. "Shut up."

To emphasize the words, I drag my nails down his chest, savoring the sensation of his muscles tensing under my touch. It's only then that I move. In a slow rhythm, I lift my hips just enough to create that delicious friction before lowering back down. The low, throaty sound of pleasure he makes only spurs me on. I want to hear it again—over and over.

But this isn't about him. It's about me taking what I want, just like he told me to.

I brace my hands on his solid pecs as I ride him, letting my eyes fall shut as I lose myself. His hands roam over my ass, squeezing and caressing, while he murmurs words I can't quite make out. I don't bother trying to. I don't care what he has to say.

I can't remember the last time I felt this free, this unobstructed by the worries that usually hold me back from crawling into bed with a man. With him, I don't have to pretend to be something I'm not. He knows I'm not fragile and doe-eyed; he's seen the wildfire that burns in me and isn't turned off by it. It's the perk of fucking a man who knows I don't like him on a deeper level, or even at all. I'm attracted to him physically, attracted to the chemistry between us, but it's nothing more than that.

I open my eyes when he moves his hips beneath me, attempting to meet me thrust for thrust, to get more out of this than I've allowed. "Don't you dare," I pant, halting my movements and pinning him down. "Don't you fucking dare."

When I circle my hips, seeking a new, deeper angle, Daniel hisses and throws his head back into the pillow.

"Selene," he murmurs, his voice strained as his fingertips dig into my thighs. "You keep doing that, and I won't last."

I tip forward until we're nose to nose and plant my hands on either side of his head, keeping up my steady rhythm. "You better. I'm not there yet."

But I'm close, so close. When he slides his fingers into my hair and wraps the dark strands around his fist, he pushes me so close to the precipice I'm teetering on the edge of. I move in quick, short movements, grinding against him, overwhelmed by the friction on my clit.

I lower my mouth to his and kiss him hard, muffling my moan. He takes that opportunity to tangle his tongue with mine, desperately, like we could consume each other. It's wet and messy and nothing short of glorious. I'm like a ticking time bomb about to explode, and when he groans against my lips, that same needy sound that I wanted more of, I let go and let the flames consume me. And I burn all the way down.

Vaguely, I hear myself exhale his name as I ride the wave, slumped against his chest. I'm still pulsing around him when he sits up and bands one arm around my waist. Then he throws me down on my back and drives into me hard.

"My turn," he says, hooking my legs over his shoulders.

There's no mercy in his thrusts. This is payback. It hurts in the best way possible, but I don't want gentle. Not from him. This is nothing but hate and revenge, and it feels so goddamn good. I arch my back and take it.

I'm building up again, this second wave coming from somewhere deeper. The need is less sharp, less keening, but no less exquisite, and I can't help the loud moans that leave my lips in response to it. If the neighbors complain, I won't be surprised.

In hopes of warding it off, and, if I'm lucky, making this more difficult for Daniel, I tense beneath him. But he doesn't ease up. If anything, he drives into me harder, pushing my knees to my chest and hitting the place that makes me beg for release. But I can't. Because that feels like giving in to him. And I refuse to lose to this man.

As if he knows what I'm doing, he nips at my earlobe. "Don't be stubborn, Selene," he murmurs, his breath hot on my skin. "Let go."

I turn my face away, unwilling to acquiesce. He doesn't get to tell me what to do. This is my night. I'm here to take what I want, not to sit back and let him give it to me.

More breathless words—about how difficult I am, how I should give up, give in—spill from his lips. Then his hand is between us, pressing on my belly as his thumb finds my clit. It's torture in its purest form.

"Let go, baby."

Those words, and the intimacy behind them, catch me off guard. They're a plea. A command I can't defy.

And with that, I lose all control. The world explodes behind my eyes, then slowly knits back together. The ability to breathe, to speak, to think, is lost to me as I clench around him. In response, his hips stutter one last time, and his cock pulses, but I'm so lost in the high that his words barely register—a whisper of what a good girl I am. The moment is magnificent, even if it is a loss.

But if this is what losing to Daniel feels like, I don't mind doing it over and over and over again.

CHAPTER 16

I still haven't caught my breath by the time Daniel returns from the bathroom and slides into bed next to me. He lies on his side, propped up on one elbow, and runs his broad palm down the center of my chest, between my breasts, and comes to a stop on my stomach. My belly swells and shrinks with each inhale and exhale, and his hand moves with it.

"Did I hurt you?" he asks, dragging his hand back up to cup my neck.

I shake my head, not sure if I can form words yet. "No," I finally manage to say after a few more seconds of steady breathing. "But isn't that the point of a hate-fuck? That it's rough? Isn't that why you were so determined to piss me off?"

"Maybe," he concedes. "No regrets, right?"

I tilt my chin up so I can take him in. His dark eyes are guarded as he scrutinizes me, like he's waiting for me to shove him away and tell him to get out. Not surprising, considering how badly he messed up earlier. He's being cautious now.

I don't know how to navigate this post-sex moment. Right now, this man isn't the Daniel who makes my life hell, and I'm not the Selene who wants nothing more than to sucker punch him. We're just two people in bed together with no other history and no baggage. We might as well be strangers in the dark.

"No," I say, not an ounce of doubt in my voice. "No regrets." I cover the hand he has on my throat with my own and pull it to my breast. I don't care if he can feel my heart racing under it. "But I'll still hate you in the morning. Don't worry."

A hint of a smirk pulls at the corner of his mouth, then he dips down and presses his lips to mine. His kiss is languid and unhurried, and he swirls his thumb around my nipple, letting it harden under his touch.

I whine in disappointment when he pulls back, dragging his lips across my jaw.

"So, for now, you don't hate me?" he asks, running his knuckles down my ribs and back up again, making me shiver. "Surprising."

"I might start to if you keep teasing me like that."

His fingers drift down to my hip, bringing goose bumps to the surface as he does, then over my thigh—though he doesn't dip down to where I'm still sensitive. "I'll keep that in mind." He pulls his hand away and sits up. "I should go before that changes."

I drape an arm over my chest to cover myself, suddenly too aware of what we've done and who exactly is in my bed. We're strangers no longer. The spell has officially lifted, and reality settles in like a heavy storm cloud.

You fucked your evil coworker. Again. Round of applause for your supposed brilliance, Selene.

Despite the discomfort creeping in, I study the tattoo on his shoulder. In the low light, a few elements are identifiable: a rose with more thorns than petals; a cross embedded in it all; cursive Spanish script that I can't quite make out. It's like a peek into what lies beneath the charming exterior of the man I work with. Though it's not enough to make me feel any less awkward about this shift between us.

I know I shouldn't say it, but that doesn't stop me. "Didn't you say you wished you hadn't left me alone in bed last time?"

His brow lifts, but he gives nothing else away. "Are you saying you don't want me to go?"

I shrug, pulling my knees up and pressing my tender thighs together. "Just reminding you of your own feelings."

Daniel shifts so he's propped up beside me again, leaving the tautness of his muscles on full display. "I meant to ask," he says. "How many days are you in the city for?"

"I leave tomorrow after work," I answer, relaxing a little at the change in subject and the way he's settled back in.

"Short trip."

I nod. "I typically only come up when I have meetings with the bosses, or if something special is going on. It's not exactly a quick commute."

"So why not stay longer?"

"Because I prefer working from home," I admit, "rather than being forced to sit at a desk surrounded by a bunch of people."

His grin is sharp, like he's in on a secret I'm not. "You mean you don't want everyone witnessing the strange faces you make while writing?"

Heat creeps up my neck and settles in my cheeks so quickly I have to turn away. There's a reason writing is a solitary endeavor. I don't mean to make the expressions I'm describing on the page, but sometimes it just *happens* when I'm trying to confirm that I've described it correctly. "You noticed that?"

Daniel laughs as he returns to tracing patterns on the skin over my ribs. "I've seen *all* of you in production do that. My favorite is when you stop typing all of a sudden and stare into space for a few seconds before furiously starting up again."

That clarification brings with it a wave of relief, enough that I find the courage to turn back to him again. Because I'm not weird. Or special, for that matter.

"We're writers," I say, as if that explains all the silly things we do. "We have our quirks."

"You certainly do."

Figuring we're back to being Selene and Daniel of Naiad Novels, I ask him, "Are you coming into the office tomorrow?"

"I haven't decided yet. Depends on when you let me leave."

My cheeks grow warmer. "You're not my hostage. You can go."

The truth is, though, I wouldn't mind if he stayed. Not the whole night—he doesn't need to see what I look like first thing in the morning—but I wouldn't say no to another round before the soreness really sets in.

God, I've already had two orgasms and I'm greedy for more. Is this what happens when a dry spell is broken? If so, maybe I should have let it continue, because I've never felt so sexually needy in my life.

Or maybe it's sex with Daniel in particular that turns me into a fiend, always ready for my next score, loath as I am to even consider that. But there's no denying that the man knows how to coax my body to beautiful heights.

Whatever it is, I know once I'm home, my vibrator is going to get the workout of its life.

As if he can read my thoughts, a knowing half smile lifts one side of his mouth.

"No," he says, bringing his lips to mine and slipping his fingers between my thighs. "I think I'll stay a little longer…"

CHAPTER 17

As expected, I'm sore.

Riding dick should be considered the world's best thigh exercise, because mine hurt like I ran a half-marathon. I probably should have stretched last night before going to sleep, but oh well. Live and learn.

I shower and investigate myself in the mirror. He was kind enough not to leave hickeys this time, but there are finger-shaped bruises all across my hips and ass. Even my tits have a few. I smile at the sight and turn to look over my shoulder to get a better view of the ones on my lower body.

Welcome back, missed you.

After dressing and putting on a little makeup to disguise that I didn't get much sleep, I bundle up and grab my work bag, then head out into the freezing morning. I stop by the Jewish deli down the street for breakfast and scarf down a lox bagel and an iced coffee before continuing on my journey. Fifteen minutes later, I'm stepping out of the elevator on Naiad's floor.

Most of the New York–based production team is here, which means I have to dole out about a dozen hugs before I settle a few chairs down from Ella. Just because we're comfortable writing sex scenes in the office doesn't mean we want to be shoulder to shoulder while doing it. Though we do stay close, just in case one of us needs a synonym for penis—or wants to play our game without disturbing the others in the office.

I have at least five chapters to write this morning, so I get right to it, hauling my laptop out of my bag and getting comfortable in my chair. I'm about to pop in my earbuds when footsteps echo off the floor, drawing my attention. Before I even turn to assess the newcomer, a hit of his cologne tickles my senses.

He didn't leave my hotel room until well after midnight, so I'm a little surprised to see Daniel here. But I'm…pleased. It *should* make me nervous, this reminder that we're coworkers doing something we absolutely shouldn't be, but the forbidden aspect of it is thrilling.

I offer a slight incline of my head in greeting as I put in my earbuds, careful to keep my expression neutral. No smile. No indication that anything has changed between us. In this office, we're ambivalent toward each other—except for when he pisses me off. We'll have to see how long it takes him to get there today.

"Morning, Selene," he says as he pulls out the chair directly across the table from me.

I raise a brow in question as he grabs his laptop from his bag. He's not actually planning to work near me today, is he? Because never once have we set up less than ten feet from each other.

Down the long table, I can feel Ella squinting at us. She and I are close friends, and yet we've still left plenty of space between us. She's also well aware of how deep my hatred for Daniel runs. Clearly, I'm not the only one shocked by his proximity.

A Slack notification dings in my ears, pulling my focus from the confounding man in front of me. The message is from Ella, a simple: *WTF?????*

It's quickly followed by: *Does this man not know what a dangerous choice he's just made?*

To which I reply: *It's like he WANTS to get his ass kicked.*

Ella snorts, and I do my best to hide a smile. I don't dare look at her. If I do, I'll lose it, and then Daniel will know we're talking about him. I'm not sure I actually care if he does, though. What's the worst he could do? Report me to HR for being a gossipy bully? Yeah, right.

I make the mistake of looking up from my screen then and accidentally lock eyes with him. The cadence of my heartbeat immediately picks up, thumping hard as flashes of last night come back to me. Just from this look, I can practically feel his hands all over my body and the slickness of his overheated skin against mine.

With those images fresh in my mind, I blink, desperate to hold on to my composure and yank my focus away from him. I need to show him that his undivided attention doesn't affect me. But I find myself holding his gaze instead, my stomach tightening.

A ghost of a smile tugs on the corner of his mouth as he breaks the contact first, sitting forward in his seat so he can shrug out of his leather jacket. When it's off and draped across the back of his chair, he runs a hand up his right arm, lifting the sleeve of his black T-shirt. It's just enough to give me a glimpse of the ink underneath before it drops—a reminder of what I said upon seeing it for the first time.

True, I don't know you.

You'll get to, he replied. Yet I don't know him any better now than I did then.

I force myself to focus on my screen, determined to ignore him. I have shit to do.

But when he moves again, the motion draws my eyes back up, and I'm entranced as he runs his fingers through his loose curls. I'm struck with another memory, this one of him hovering over me and the way his hair tickled my cheek as he whispered filthy things in my ear.

And then it hits me. I know what he's doing. The man is taunting me. Teasing me. Torturing me.

You evil bastard.

Two can play that game.

Without thinking twice, I grasp the hem of my chunky knit sweater and pull it over my head, revealing the white tank top underneath. In my defense, it truly is hot in this building. It's either freezing or sweltering, no in between, and today is the latter. After tossing my sweater into the empty chair beside me, I run my fingers over my collarbone and then turn to Ella.

"What do they have the heat set to, a million degrees?" I complain.

As expected, Daniel's perusal sears every inch of my newly revealed skin. I don't even have to look his way; the intensity of his inspection is like a heated caress.

He hates how my oversized sweaters hide my tits? Problem solved. There's only so much hiding my tank top can do, especially stretched over an emerald green lace bra. He can eat his heart out.

Ella groans and nods, pushing up the sleeves of her shirt. "It's unbearable. I might go stick my head in the freezer for a bit."

"I might strip down and stand on the roof," I say, turning back to my computer—and Daniel.

She snorts at that and returns to typing, leaving me to raise a brow in challenge to the man across the table. He stares back, unblinking, then drops his gaze to his computer, and his fingers move quickly over the keyboard.

When a notification sounds in my ears, I know exactly who it's from. I click open his message.

Green suits you.

Four hours later, I have my sweater back on, and I'm sitting across from my manager, going over dates and finalizing deadlines. My calendar is overflowing with them, but that's the job.

And is it slowly killing me? Hell yeah. Will I do it all anyway? Of course, because I accept nothing but the best from myself, no matter the toll it takes.

"I think I'll start coming into the office twice a month," I tell Jim as we're wrapping things up. The idea has been lingering in the back of my mind all morning. As much as I like working from home, I miss interacting with my coworkers in person—even Daniel and his dirty tricks. "Or maybe just staying longer than two days when I'm here."

His face lights up. "Yeah, absolutely. We'd love to have you here more often."

I leave his office with a smile, already planning my next trip as I walk back to my table. Daniel has vacated his spot across from where I left my laptop set up. He probably moved to one of the many conference rooms to take a call. Not that I care—I just hope he's not charming anyone else into a shitty contract.

Honestly, the break from his scrutiny is a relief. Sitting across from him for the past few hours has been nerve-racking. It's been years since I felt uncomfortable writing and editing romance in front of *anyone*, but having to brainstorm scenes while the man who made me come several times last night is right in front of me was uncomfortable, to say the least. And it's only partially because I used our activities as inspiration for one of them.

Thankfully, I've wrapped up all the steamy stuff and have moved back to the drama this serial revolves around. Another hour flies by, resulting in two more chapters written, but Daniel hasn't returned. If his leather jacket wasn't still draped across the back of his chair, I would assume he left for the day.

When Ella suggests we finish out the rest of the workday in our favorite itty bitty conference room so we can chat shit, scroll through Pinterest for "inspiration," and complain about the things we've written today, I jump at the opportunity. *This* is why I can't wait to spend more time in the office. It has nothing to do with a set of deep brown eyes and a cocky half smile I can't get off my mind.

By six, I've booked my return trip two weeks from now, and I'm already giddy about my next excursion to the city. For convenience alone, moving here would be wise, and it was something I had started to consider before lockdown, though I put it on hold when the whole company went remote. But New York is expensive as hell. Not to mention all of my family is in Baltimore and I'm not sure I'm ready to leave them. For now, I don't mind the three-hour commute.

After packing up my stuff, saying goodbye to Ella, and waving to the rest of the production girls in the main office space, I swing by the kitchen to refill my water bottle in preparation for hitting the road.

When I round the corner, I come face to face with Daniel. He's leaning against the counter, holding a steaming mug against his chest. I don't acknowledge him. That's how I've always behaved in the past. I just go about unscrewing the top of my bottle and grabbing the pitcher of filtered water from the fridge. We stand next to each other at the counter as I pour, facing different directions.

"You leaving soon?" he asks when my water bottle is half full.

I don't look away from my task, determined not to spill. "In a few minutes."

"You coming back next month?"

Startled by his question, my hand jolts and a drip of water runs down the outside of my bottle. Is he asking as a coworker? Just making casual conversation? Or is it the inquiry of a man who wants to know if we'll be doing what we did last night again?

"Actually," I say, keeping my voice even as I set the pitcher on the counter, "I'll be back in a couple of weeks. I told Jim I'm going to start coming up here twice a month. Since the company's paying for it, I might as well."

From my periphery, I catch the way one of his brows raises a fraction. But that's his only reaction. The rest of his expression remains unreadable. "Is that so?"

"Yeah." I breeze by him with my chin lifted and take the pitcher to the sink to refill. "Sometimes it's nice to work in the office."

"So it's for no other reason?"

I meet his gaze as I turn on the tap. "Nope."

He tilts his head, unintimidated, and a hint of a smile plays on his lips. It's a subtle change, but the meaning behind it is obvious. He's practically laughing at me.

"I'll see you soon, then."

Slowly, he pushes away from the counter as I turn off the tap and shift toward the fridge. He's blocking my path in the small galley kitchen, ensuring I'll have no choice but to brush by to get past him. It's a dare.

And he knows me well enough to know that I won't back down.

I turn sideways and subtly push back my shoulders so that my breasts graze his arm as I shuffle past him. "You'll see me in the office, yeah," I clarify, taking pleasure in the way he turns in order to keep his eyes on me.

My words are simple, but I'm hoping he hears the underlying question. *Will we only see each other in the office?*

"Right," he murmurs, scanning my face. "The office."

I stick the pitcher in the fridge and straighten. Those three words don't give much away, but his tone? That makes my stomach flip in anticipation. Because the unspoken message here?

This isn't the end.

"See you in two weeks," I tell him, and this time he steps aside to let me pass. "Bye, Daniel."

His quiet laugh follows me, low and teasing.

"Safe travels, Selene."

CHAPTER 18

Kimmy Petes is finally happy with me.

Now that it's posted on the app—in which Daniel deserves absolutely *none* of the credit for—*Burned by the Billionaire* is a runaway success. It's earned Naiad several hundred thousand dollars in the first week alone. It's a feat, a win for us and for Kimmy.

Kimmy and I, as well as members of a few of Naiad's teams, including Daniel, are discussing the book's success and future marketing plans via Zoom.

One purpose of this meeting is to come up with advertising hooks, so I came prepared with interest-piquing lines for Kimmy to approve. Once upon a time, I would have been mortified to utter passages like *He runs the stack of hundred-dollar bills between my breasts and spreads my legs. His pulsing erection is hot against my thigh. I'm already dripping for him. "Still think I can't afford you?" he growls in my ear. I know then that I'm not just in this for the money. I'm in it for the man.* Now, it's as easy as talking about app updates or scheduling upcoming meetings.

As we're wrapping up—Kimmy dipped out five minutes ago, ever the busy author—Daniel says, "Selene, stay on for a second. I have a question about Kimmy's other books."

I nod. At this point, it makes sense for us to acquire her entire backlist or negotiate a new exclusive series with her. Now that she and I are on solid terms again, it would be a good time to broach the subject.

Once it's just the two of us, I flash him a small smile. This is one of those situations where my hatred dims a little—when I feel like we're working on the same team, the rare occasion he isn't conspiring against me. We haven't spoken since I was in New York nearly two weeks ago, so maybe that's why he hasn't annoyed me lately. He hasn't had the chance to.

"Can you believe how successful this book is?" I ask, still a little astounded. Even though its release got pushed back, it's been our most significant launch to date.

"The numbers don't lie."

Of course, that's what he focuses on. The numbers. The views, the readers, the bottom line. It's why he's in acquisitions and I'm in production; I care more about the impact of the words on the page than about how profitable the work is. The two go hand in hand, though. Without good content, the money doesn't flow.

I let him have that little comment and move on. "Kimmy really outdid herself on—"

"I don't give a fuck about Kimmy," he interrupts. "This was you."

I'm stunned into silence for a moment. He asked me to stay on only to…say something nice to me? I must be imagining things.

"Are you actually paying me a compliment?" I ask, unsuccessfully suppressing a scoff.

He shakes his head. "Why are you surprised?" He says it like *I'm* the idiot for not understanding. "I've already said you're brilliant."

"And oblivious," I remind him.

"You can be both," he counters, leaning back so the full breadth of his shoulders is visible. I imagine the tattoo under his shirt, and my fingers itch to trace it. "But this success wasn't Kimmy's doing. *You* wrote those new chapters, not her."

His compliments do something funny to my insides. Every word warms me another degree. With Daniel, I've come to expect thinly veiled insults and condescending rebuffs, not these outright commendations. It's strange but also welcome; I've seen him behave like this with others, giving to-the-point praise, though he's rarely done it for me.

"Maybe," I concede, not sure I really want to accept his acclaim. Are there strings tied to it? Will it upset the careful balance of distaste we have for each other? "But it's credited to her either way."

"The people who matter know who's really behind it."

I give a fake offended gasp and clutch a hand to my chest. Still, I'm amazed he's doubling down. "Wow, way to insult her readers, Daniel. So rude."

He laughs, and I can't believe how much I like the sound.

"When are you back up here?"

"Monday morning." I do my best not to let myself read into his question.

The moment we had in the kitchen last time left the option for more open, but there's a smidge of worry in the back of my head that he'll shut this down as quickly as it started.

Which is fine. I wouldn't have a problem with that; this is casual, after all. But I won't really know what he wants until I'm standing in front of him and—

"Good," he says, interrupting my thoughts. "Wear something just for me again."

My jaw goes slack, but I recover quickly. I can't believe he's already proving me wrong.

I clear my throat and fight to keep my voice level. "I told you; I didn't wear it for you. My lingerie is for me."

He goes on like I haven't spoken. "I want to see you in red."

"I don't take requests," I shoot back, finding my footing again.

"And who says anything is going to happen?"

Daniel arches an eyebrow. "Is this your way of telling me it won't?"

Unsure of how to respond, I watch him silently. I've yet to admit even to myself that I want to sleep with him again, but it's not every day that an insanely hot man I have off-the-charts sexual chemistry with offers to fuck me senseless more than once with no strings attached.

But the last thing I want to come off as is overeager or like I expect him to drop everything for the handful of nights I'm in the city.

He has a life. That's clear from our Monday morning meetings when Jim makes us take turns telling the team what we did over the weekend. Last Saturday, Daniel went to a film festival with friends and tried a new restaurant in Soho that he claimed had the best ribeye in the state. He gets out and has fun in his free time—unlike me, who spends nearly every waking hour either working or online shopping from the comfort of my bed.

So where do I—a random girl he's hate-fucking—fall on his list of priorities? I'd say above a movie but definitely lower than a good steak.

"You don't already have plans?" I ask him instead of answering.

"I can change them."

My heart races, but I don't dare let him see how he's gotten to me. So I drop my shoulders and sit back, twirling a pen between my fingers in an attempt to quell my nervous energy. "Pussy good enough to cancel plans. I'm honored."

That comment is met with a grin that makes my belly flip. It's the biggest display of emotion I've seen from him since we were naked last. "What can I say? It's worth it."

Somehow, we've slipped into an alternate universe. One where this is a normal conversation. Never, in the two years we've worked together, have I had even an inkling that we'd wind up here.

"Stop being nice," I scold him, fighting a smile of my own. "I might start hating you less."

I don't know what to do with the feeling blooming in my chest. Despite my best efforts, the disdain I've held for him for so long is waning. While most of that can be attributed to the orgasms he's provided me with recently, the compliments and his willingness to make time for me—okay, correction, make time to fuck me—are doing something to my heart.

"We can't have that," he murmurs, playing into my teasing. But then his expression sobers and his attention drifts, like he's looking at another window on his screen. "Should I tell you that I'm in the middle of negotiations for another book you'll have to work on?"

I freeze. He's joking, right? But then my computer pings, notifying me of a new email. Stomach sinking, I click over to it. Sure enough, the email is from Daniel. The subject reads *Manuscript – Bonded to the Baby Daddy*.

This certainly isn't the first email like this I've received from him. It looks like another erotic romance—probably involving BDSM and an accidental pregnancy if the title is anything to go by—that I'll be required to read and subsequently continue.

Panic seeps into my chest, dousing any warmth for him that had begun to manifest. "Daniel, I can't take on another project. I'm full up."

He's still looking at the other window on his screen, cooler than I'll ever hope to be. "Take it up with Jim. That's not my problem."

I bristle at his brush-off, and a snarl threatens to pull on my upper lip. "Oh, you bas—"

But Daniel ends the call before I can finish the insult.

I let out a strangled scream and slam my laptop shut. This man may fuck me better than anyone ever has—and probably ever will—but Jesus fucking *Christ*, he's going to be the death of me.

CHAPTER 19

I've worn something for Daniel, and I hate myself a little for it.

I'm back in New York, and today, I put actual thought into my outfit for once. Instead of my usual leggings and an oversized sweater, I'm wearing a cute skirt and a top that makes my tits look great but still isn't *quite* inappropriate for the office. And yes, my lingerie is red as requested…and I packed a few of my other favorite sets. A girl's got to have options, and I wouldn't mind if he saw them too.

I'm like a high schooler getting dolled up in hopes that I'll bump into my crush in the hallway. It's fucking mortifying, and yet here I am.

Despite our conversation the day he dumped a new project on me—one I'm trying to wheedle my way out of with Jim—I've still found myself thinking of Daniel in moments when I shouldn't. On the train yesterday, I couldn't stop images of what might happen this time from floating through my mind. Would we hook up in my hotel room again or go back to his place? Would it be as good as our last two encounters, or has the excitement worn off? Would it be prefaced by him insulting me again in an attempt to rile me up for more hate sex?

The fantasies always come to me quick and easy. Maybe it's a perk of being a writer. But it's also a pain in the ass because I tend to set myself up for failure. The idea of men is almost always better than the reality, though Daniel seems to be an exception. So far, he's lived up to all of my expectations. Maybe because the bar is in hell.

The last two weeks have moved by at a snail's pace. My vibrator has truly been getting the workout of its life. It's charged and tucked away in my suitcase as a contingency plan in case nothing happens between Daniel and me, but I can't imagine it won't, especially since he literally said he'd change his plans for me. I won't call it romantic, but I can admit it's…considerate.

I'm hoping to get confirmation from him when he comes into the office. Maybe a quick *is this still happening?* if we brush by each other in the hall or end up in the kitchen at the same time. But when the minutes tick down and our morning meeting is set to begin and he still hasn't stepped off the elevator, my stomach sinks.

Disappointment hits me as I get up and move closer to Ella, where she, Nikki, and Zoe are crowded around her laptop. Half our team is working from home today, as is the norm, so the Zoom meeting is full of little boxes. I lean an elbow on Ella's shoulder and peruse the slowly loading video feeds.

And there he is. Daniel is set up at his desk at home, sipping the coffee I imagined he and I would chat over in the office kitchen. He knew I'd be here, practically made plans to see me today, but chose to work from home. Damn this hybrid work.

And like an idiot, I'm mad about it. Because, I realize now, I've actually been looking forward to seeing him.

Ew, gross.

The meeting starts as it always does, with a weekend catch-up, then we move on to a discussion about what each of us is working on today. I peer over Ella's shoulder when it's my turn, telling the group I'll be editing chapters of *Burned by the Billionaire*. The story is updated daily, along with three others assigned to me. In all, I'm responsible for the production of twenty-eight chapters every week. And if I have to take on *Bonded to the Baby Daddy* as well, I'll likely die from exhaustion. If

Daniel deigns to show up at the office today, I *will* punch him in the gut for bringing this misery upon me.

He's next up to speak. "Bunch of calls today. Closing some deals," is his vague response.

I only know what happens in those acquisitions calls because of my own deal with Naiad. Daniel was wildly charming and said all the right things to garner my interest. It wasn't until I read the fine print on the contract that I discovered the devil hiding behind those honeyed words. As I always do when I think about it, I fume. But then I remember the other things he can do with his tongue, and the hate dials back a notch or two.

I try to keep myself from watching his little video box on the screen and wave to the rest of my coworkers when the meeting is ending. Ella exits out of Zoom and swivels in her chair, glancing between Nikki and Zoe and me.

"Which one of you wants to help me figure out the logistics of this orgy?" Ella asks.

None of us blink.

"Is this the firefighter orgy in *Fire to Flame* or the chefs that run the secret sex club?" Zoe questions.

"It's for *Bone Appétit*." Ella waggles her brows. "And the chefs brought their knives."

I put my hands up and take a step back. "That's out of my realm." I pride myself in my ability to write just about any consensual kink or type of sex, and I'll never kink shame—but there are things I prefer not to venture into, even to help a friend. "Best of luck, babe."

She sighs, then turns to Nikki and Zoe, smiling in that innocently sweet way of hers. "Do either of you know anything about pain kink?"

I snicker as I settle into a seat at another table. With my laptop set up, I dig through my bag for my earbuds and click on one of my many playlists. But before I can press play, I find myself pulling up Slack,

Daniel's name looking entirely too enticing.

I shouldn't, but I've been doing a lot of things I should avoid lately. So I click on our thread of messages and start typing.

Are you coming into the office today? The second I hit send, I regret it, and I consider unsending the message before he can see it. But before I can act, he's typing.

Wasn't planning on it.

It's blunt, no explanation offered. I should leave it at that, my one query satisfied. That way I won't come off as an obsessed stalker, desperate to know his whereabouts. Which I'm totally not.

I'm not.

Oh fuck, am I?

Even if nothing happens between us this time, or ever again, I'd still like to talk face to face. Is that bad? It would be a hit to my ego, but I'd rather be shot down in person than be strung along—to be given a definitive answer as to whether this has met its end instead of waiting around to see what he does next. We haven't made any plans, minus some vague lingerie requests and offers to change plans, but does that really mean anything?

What does it even *matter*? I can't be thinking about this right now. I have too much work to do to let this consume my thoughts.

But, because the universe is conspiring against me, the first chapter I pull up includes a hot and heavy hookup in the billionaire's office. The couple has just finished an argument that has the potential to ruin their relationship. But before either can walk away, the hero has the heroine bent over his desk and he's pushing up her skirt and—

Heart racing, I scan the room. I can't work in the main office space today. Not on this.

"I'm gonna go work in one of the conference rooms." Pushing out of my chair, I shoot a smile at the still chatting girls, then unceremoniously gather my things.

"We'll shut up soon, I promise," Ella says, likely thinking I'm distracted by their discussion.

"Don't worry about it." I shake my head and flash them all a tight smile. "Have fun with your knife play."

Then, without looking back, I hurry off before they can convince me to stay. I take refuge in one of the secluded conference rooms down the hall near the elevators. When I'm settled, I press the heels of my palms against my forehead and suck in deep breaths to clear my mind. When I feel like my skull has been sufficiently punished, I reopen my laptop and shake out my hands.

I'm here to get shit done, not worry about whether a particular man is going to show up—no matter how much I might want him to.

———

I'm halfway through what I need to get edited today when there's a knock on the door of the conference room. I look up and blink a few times, trying to transport myself back to the Naiad office instead of Finsbury Tech Inc. headquarters, the setting of *Burned by the Billionaire*, and find Nikki popping her head around the doorframe.

"Hey, you wanna go get lunch with us in a bit?" she asks.

It takes me a second before I nod. "Yeah, give me like a half hour. I'm crazy behind on edits."

She groans. "Don't even talk to me about those. I'm planning on leaving early today just so I can do them from the comfort of my own bed."

"If I work from my hotel, I'll fall asleep in about five seconds flat," I tell her, though I wish I could crawl into bed right now. "I'm staying here until at least six."

"Don't even blame you." She pulls back from the door. "Come find us when you're ready."

I manage to finish out another chapter before I leave the conference room, glancing around the main office space to see if Daniel has shown up. There's no sign of him, and I hate myself a little more for even checking.

After lunch, I head back to my little space, doing my best not to scan the office again on my way, and hunker down. Zoe and Ella come in and check on me a few times to make sure I don't need anything—like a cup of tea, a snack, or a pep talk to get me through the rest of my work—but around four, my coworkers start to file past my door on the way to the elevators. Zoe is the last to leave around five-thirty, and invites me to dinner, but I decline. I still have too much to do if I'm going to make my weekly deadline.

I choke back the panic that bubbles up, just like it does every time I think about what my days will look like if I'm forced to take on the new project. I already spend most of my waking hours staring at Word documents, battling such bad eye strain that even taking a week off from screens wouldn't help. I might collapse from stress if it ends up on my plate.

Shaking off the negative thoughts, I remind myself that adult life can't always be sunshine and rainbows. I just have to keep pushing.

Once I've successfully shoved the self-pity away, I buckle down again and get back to edits. Down the hall, the elevator dings, but I don't look up from my computer screen. Zoe has only been gone a few minutes, so it's probably her coming back for something she forgot.

I only have a few more chapters to edit today, and I don't want to slow my momentum again. Unlike Nikki, once I close my laptop and leave the office, that's it. My only plans for the rest of the evening involve dinner and my hotel bed.

It's the sound of the conference room door opening that finally gets my attention. And my breath catches in my throat when I drag my gaze away from my screen.

"What are you doing here?" I ask Daniel after a moment, hoping he can't see the way my heart beats wildly in my chest. "You said you weren't coming in." And it's nearly six o'clock.

"I said I wasn't planning on it," he replies smoothly. He drops into the seat across from me and leans back in the rolling chair.

Watching him watch me, I wait for a more in-depth explanation but get none. Typical. "Workday's practically over," I point out.

"I didn't come here to work."

Heat creeps through me at the meaning behind those words, even though I'm determined not to react. I could always argue that the whole reason for coming to the office is to work, but instead, I tilt my head to the side and stare him down.

"So you came here for me." I don't phrase it as a question, just a fact, taking a play from his book.

His eyes are dark, unreadable as he assesses me. "You're being very bold."

Hell yeah, I am. I've spent too much time worrying about him today, wondering if he would appear and what his expectations are. This feels like my last chance, the final opportunity to get the answer I've been waiting for.

"You bring that out in me," I tell him, doubling down on the boldness.

"I'm honored."

"You should be."

For a long moment, we simply stare, daring one another to make the next move. It won't be me, though. The ball is in his court. He's the one who showed up at the end of the day, presumably just for me. If he wants something, he'll have to take it from me.

I nearly stop breathing when he stands and stalks around the table.

I peer up at him, not about to move, lest I lose this slight upper hand. But when he dips down to brush his lips over mine, then drags them across my cheek to my ear, a shudder races through me, reminding me that I never had the power here.

"Close your eyes."

When all I do is narrow them, Daniel repeats the words, my name a warning whisper on the end.

With one more glance up at him, I do as he says.

I wait. For what, I don't know. Daniel's heat dissipates, and I hear his feet move across the floor, but the scent of his cologne lingers in the air.

I remain in darkness for what feels like an eternity, even though it can't be more than a few seconds.

What's taking him so long?

I get my answer when his hands rest on my knees. But the only way he'd be at that angle is if—

Gasping, I open my eyes, finding myself staring at the tabletop until I push back just enough to spot him under it.

"What are you doing?" I blurt, gripping the armrests of my chair so tightly I'll probably leave indentations.

Below me, Daniel is unfazed, his touch drifting higher up my thighs to the hem of my skirt. Suddenly, I'm thankful I ditched my itchy, annoying tights this morning, but the other part wonders if I should have kept them on.

"You know exactly what I'm doing," he says, eyes meeting mine.

And there it is—the dare. He knows I want this, and he's challenging me to work up the strength to turn him down.

In theory, I could. I don't love how I've been subject to his whims, like he assumes I'm sitting around waiting for him to show up.

And I should turn him down. I should get up. I should scoff and walk away with a sway to my hips while telling him *you can't have me.*

Except I don't want to.

"This could get us both fired," I whisper, but I don't pull away. "Are there cameras in here?"

He slides his hands higher, the pace excruciatingly slow, until his fingers dip beneath my skirt. "No."

"Are you sure?"

"No."

"*Daniel.*"

His fingers wander toward my inner thighs, fully under my skirt now, and stroke the soft skin there, making me wetter with each swipe. "I thought you liked breaking the rules."

I swallow hard, flustered. "Not all of them," I hedge. Because this is a terrible idea.

"What about this one?"

My stomach clenches. Naturally, my body is more than ready to break a thousand rules if it means he's going to make me feel so fucking good. There's no doubt that he will.

And the image of him on his knees under the table, pushing up my skirt? This will be ingrained in my memory for the rest of my life. I've read about this kind of stuff—hell, I've *written* it myself—but that's fiction. Romanticized. In real life, this shit doesn't happen.

"Daniel," I say softly, cupping his cheek. "You don't have to do this."

His only response is the curl of his fingers under the edge of the red lace of my underwear. The pair I wore just for him. I get the exact reaction I want when I lift my hips and move to the edge of the chair.

"You fucking live to torture me." His voice is a low murmur as he pulls my panties down my legs. But there's no mistaking the meaning, even if I can't make out the Spanish words that follow.

I gasp and grip the edge of the table when his warm breath hits my exposed skin and he pushes my thighs farther apart. I don't fight him. I'm still unsure we should be doing this here, even though I want it—badly. But Daniel has me splayed out in front of him in no time.

With his mouth poised just above where I want him most, he

peers up at me through his thick lashes.

"Yes or no, Selene?"

"Yes," I breathe as I drop one shaking hand and push his curls back. I want to see all of him as he does this. "Yes, please."

I was so wrong to think I had any power over him. This man will always have me begging in no time.

The corner of his mouth quirks up. "So polite," he commends.

Before I can tell him to cut the shit, his mouth is on me and my sharp inhale echoes off the high ceiling.

While the anticipation alone was enough to leave me pulsing, the way his tongue flicks over my clit and his fingers grip my thighs send me dangerously close to screaming out my release almost instantly. Just like the night of the holiday party, he brings me to the edge before slowing, dragging me back again. It's an up and down, a give and take, a mountain that keeps growing and dipping until there's nowhere else to go but to the top.

"*Fuck*," I moan, gripping his hair a little tighter with one hand while the other slaps down on the table. I don't know whether I want to pull away from the building pressure or grind against his face.

I choose to pull away, to seek a reprieve, but Daniel clutches at me, and as if he's punishing me for trying to back off, he gives my clit a harsh lave of his tongue, making me hiss. Then he's back to that consistent pressure, bringing me higher.

I drop my head back and blow out a breath toward the ceiling, reminded that we're still in the office. But I don't even care. Daniel could do this to me anytime, anywhere, and I'd thank him for it. This man so easily takes the control that I do my best to hold on to tightly. If it weren't so satisfying, it might be terrifying.

I gasp when he slips a finger inside me and crooks up gently. Knowing I can't hold out for much longer, I relinquish my hold on his hair and place that hand on the table with my other, bracing myself as he adds another finger. This time, I can't help but rock my hips, savoring the pressure building in me. I'm close, so fucking close…

And then he's pushing me over the edge. The room around me falls away as deep pleasure pulses through my body. It's so good I practically want to tell this man I love him—or at least what he manages to reduce me to.

He places featherlight kisses on the inside of my thighs as my legs tremble and my lungs heave and I float back down to earth. And somehow, when the world around me comes back into focus, he's standing right next to me.

Daniel wipes the corner of his mouth with his thumb, pulling his full lower lip to the side as he does. "Let's go," he says. "Workday's over."

CHAPTER 20

Right now, I'd follow this man anywhere.

My tights are back on, my skirt is covering my thighs again, and now I want nothing more than to drag Daniel to my hotel room. There's no way I'm done with him for the night.

But when we step out of the Naiad office building and he turns in the opposite direction of where my hotel is located, I frown.

"Where are we going?" I ask, taking a few quick steps to keep up. For a moment, I panic and assume I've misunderstood his words back in the office. He said *let's go*, but he never said we were going somewhere *together*. Maybe I'm just—

"We're going to dinner," he answers simply.

I'm relieved by the *we* but thrown by the rest of it. "Dinner? Why?"

"I'm hungry. And I doubt you've eaten yet."

He's right, and I'm starving, but we've never had dinner together before, even as mere coworkers. "Is that a good idea?" I press, turning to him without slowing my pace. "What if someone sees us together?"

He doesn't look at me when he responds. "Do you not get dinner with the girls when you're here?"

"Yeah, but that's different. We're actually friends," I point out. "You and I—"

"Hate each other."

"*I* hate *you*," I correct, though the hate has dimmed considerably in recent weeks. But I keep that tidbit of information to myself. I don't need him thinking I like him. In this situation, there are no deeper feelings allowed, even friendship. "People might think it's strange if we're out together."

I swear he rolls his eyes. "No one is going to see us," he says, resting a hand at the small of my back to help me dodge a group of tourists who refuse to budge from the middle of the sidewalk. "And if they do, who gives a fuck?"

Try as I might to deny it, the man has a point. What does it matter if we're seen together? If it turns out that an explanation is necessary, I'll just say it was nothing more than a business dinner on the company's dime. That's believable enough.

"Okay, fine," I tell him. "Take me to dinner."

———

A short walk later, we're seated at a small table in a softly lit but colorfully decorated Cuban restaurant. The place smells incredible, the air thick with warm spices. And there's a bolero song playing over the speakers, reminding me of the holiday party. To think a dance between us has led to all of this is nearly unbelievable.

"Where did you learn to dance?" I find myself asking as we settle in. It's something that's been on my mind for weeks now, and it's the first thing I've said to him since I agreed to join him here, but it feels fitting.

Daniel sets his menu on the table and leans back in his wicker chair. "My grandmother was a dance instructor in Cuba." He must see the question in my eyes—he's from Mexico, isn't he?—and elaborates. "My mother's family is Cuban. They immigrated to Mexico when she was young."

Weirdly, I like getting a little peek into his life. It's one I never expected or even wanted until now. "Did your grandmother keep teaching after that?"

He shakes his head. "Not professionally. But she still choreographs dances for parties and weddings. And, of course, she taught all of her grandchildren." He glances away and lifts a hand to signal our server, even though I've barely had time to look over the menu. "I know you love your gin and tonics, but the mojitos here are great."

The distraction technique is obvious, but I still warm at the small detail he's remembered about me. "I'll have one then."

Daniel orders for the both of us. I'm taken aback at first, ready to chide him for thinking it's his right to do so, but then our server smiles and promises it's their chef's specialty. I nod, but that doesn't stop me from side-eyeing Daniel. I'll let a man make decisions for me only if I'm convinced he knows better than I do, and with this new information, I suppose this is one of those situations.

When the server leaves us, Daniel and I sit back and assess each other.

His expression is unreadable, as always, so when he says, "I thought you didn't take requests," I need a moment to wrap my head around the meaning of his words.

Finally, it dawns on me. The lingerie. He asked for red, and I provided. He's only seen the thong so far, but later—if we ever get there—he'll see the unlined lace bra as well.

I have no comeback, no clever explanation, so I go with the truth. "I made an exception. And I look good in red."

There's a flash of something in his eyes, but it's gone so quickly that I'm certain I've imagined it. "You look good in any color."

Another compliment. I can still count on one hand how many he's given me in the years we've known each other, but most of them have come over the past few weeks.

"You don't need to flatter me, you know," I say. I go for nonchalance, even though the matter-of-fact compliments get to me more than any other type of praise. "I'll still fuck you without it."

In other words, I don't want him to try to charm me. This is supposed to be a purely physical entanglement. Pretty words and overt flirtation will only complicate things. I *do* expect him to be polite and get me off again tonight, hopefully more than once, but that's it. It has to be. Otherwise, I worry my feelings toward him will shift even more than they already have. And I'm steadily veering into dangerous territory.

"Good to know," he murmurs as the server returns with our drinks—a mojito for me and rum rocks for him. "Won't stop me, though."

I swirl my drink, watching the mint leaves float through the rum, lime, and soda, wishing I could get a better read on him. What is he going after here? I take a long pull from my straw and will my curiosity to settle.

"I still don't know why you went after me at the holiday party," I finally say, knowing I'll never get this out of my head otherwise. "You knew I hated you. It was a pretty big risk to proposition me, and yet you did anyway. So what was it about me that made you do it? Why me, out of all the other women there?" I level him with a hard stare. "And don't you dare say *you're not like other girls*."

He sips his drink, then sets it down gently as he meets my gaze full-on. "You're not like other girls."

"I'm going to punch you."

He laughs, fully relaxed in the face of my threats. "You'll figure it out eventually. What made *you* put enough of your hate aside to let me taste you?"

Heat surges through me. The man says these things so casually, like it isn't supposed to immediately conjure up the image of him on his knees in front of me, both in my hotel room and back in the office.

I take another pull from my straw and clear my throat, preparing for more honesty.

"I've come to realize that I…don't dislike you as a person," I admit, avoiding his eyes. This is huge for me to say, and it already feels terribly embarrassing. God, I should have kept my mouth shut. "But working with you is still a nightmare," I quickly tack on.

"I don't fully dislike you as a person either," he replies. His tone is full of humor as he throws my words back at me. "Would you like me better if we didn't work together?"

"Infinitely."

It's a knee-jerk answer, because truthfully? I *would* be fonder of him if I wasn't on the receiving end of his business bullshit all the time. He's hot as hell, intelligent, well-read in romance, surprisingly funny when he wants to be, capable of getting me off multiple times in a row, and is just cocky enough that I'm still attracted without being put off. He could be my dream man…if we didn't work together.

But I don't have any plans to change that. And I'm certain he doesn't either. So it looks like we'll be coworkers for the foreseeable future, which means there will always be that undercurrent of distaste between us. Besides, whatever we have going on now will fizzle out soon enough. I'll just enjoy it while it lasts.

Daniel gives a murmur of acknowledgment and runs a finger around the rim of his glass. "I'd like you better too."

I roll my eyes. It's not like I'm the problem in our working relationship. *He's* the one who insists on acting like an ass each and every time we interact. I just match his energy because I refuse to let him get away with his usual shit.

Our conversation wanes when our food arrives, though the tension between us remains. It's ever-present, but there's nothing awkward about it or our silence.

When our server returns to check on us, Daniel orders two mojitos, forgoing his straight rum. While he was right that I'm usually a gin girl, I'm starting to see the appeal of his favorite spirit the more I drink of it. I know from a quick google search that his favorite brand is upward of four hundred dollars a bottle, which is way out of my price range. But of course, our acquisitions manager can afford it.

By the time the table has been cleared and we're nursing a third round of drinks, I'm just relaxed enough to bluntly ask him, "Are you coming back to my hotel?"

Daniel looks away and lifts a hand to signal to our server that we're ready for the check. "What do you think?"

I frown as he slips a card out of his wallet and hands it to the server without bothering to look at the bill. In response to my direct question, I expected a direct answer, but true to form, he can't even give me that.

"What's that supposed to mean?"

He watches me, wearing an expression that looks suspiciously like pity. "You can't be *that* oblivious, Selene."

"You keep saying that about me," I snap, unable to help myself. "But what the fuck am I missing here?"

Infuriating me further, Daniel chuckles and shakes his head. He drags a hand through his dark curls, then drops his elbow to the back of his chair. He's completely at ease while I'm coiling for a potential strike. "Yes, I'm coming back with you."

He doesn't explain past that. He just thanks the server when the man comes back with his card, tips 30 percent, and then stands, motioning for me to do the same.

I huff and shove my chair away from the table, snatching up my coat at the same time. In my frustration, I struggle to get it on. And like he did at the holiday party, Daniel helps smooth the wool over my shoulders, though this time when he lowers his hand, it lingers on my hip.

I turn back to him, ready to step away, because I'm still annoyed.

But when our eyes meet, a bolt of something shoots through me, and it's not anger.

"You're not allowed to touch me yet," I scoldingly murmur, but I don't knock his hand away. "We're in public."

"Then you're not allowed to look at me like that," he counters.

"And how exactly am I looking at you?"

"Like you want me to fuck you against the wall in the bathroom."

I consider it for a second, letting flashes of how hot and fast and rough it could be flit through my mind. "I wouldn't be opposed."

Daniel blows out a breath, like he's trying to keep his composure. Or maybe he's just fed up with me. "I didn't think you were like this."

"Like what?" I ask, though I'm not sure I really want to know the answer.

"Shameless."

I raise a brow. "Is that supposed to be an insult?"

"The furthest thing from it. Let's go."

I almost want to reach for his hand as we leave the restaurant, but by my own rules, I can't. That doesn't stop him from brushing his knuckles against mine and stealing glances that make me burn from the inside out.

I can't help but think about him under the table with his hands on my thighs and his face between them. That action is more flattering than anything he says could ever be—words count for less than actions do, even for a writer.

It takes an eternity to reach the hotel. Inside the elevator, we stand on opposite sides. I could reach out to him now that we're alone, but I won't be the one to make the first move, no matter how much I want this.

But Daniel seems intent on making me wait. That said, if I was staring at him like I wanted to fuck him in the bathroom, he's now looking at me like he wants to hit the emergency stop button and take me right here. Somehow, we maintain a modicum of self-control and keep our hands to ourselves the whole way up.

Without waiting for him, I step out of the elevator and head down the hall to my room. I can feel the impatience rolling off him as I pause to pull out my key card and tap it against the sensor. Daniel steps up behind me, and when the telltale beep of the lock sliding back sounds, he pushes the heavy door open and nudges me inside.

"Fucking finally," he says, and then his hands are cupping my face and his lips are on mine.

We steal kisses as we shrug out of our coats and drop them to the floor without a care. He lets me push him against the wall and explore the planes of his broad chest. Vaguely, as I catalog every ridge and valley of his abs, I wonder how the fuck this incredibly irritating man can make me want him so badly.

He trails his fingers up from the base of my spine, eliciting a shiver from me. He's teasing me again, but that's fine. I want him to make me beg for it. There's something I need to do first, though.

I push up the hem of his T-shirt, and he helps me yank it over his head. Then it's falling to the carpet and his hands are curling around my waist, hitching my shirt higher on my torso. I ignore his attempt to remove my clothing and undo his belt, then move to the button of his jeans. I manage to pop it open before he pulls back.

"What are you doing?" he asks, amused.

"I have to reciprocate how kind you were to me at the office," I murmur, pulling down his zipper and reaching for the waistband of his boxer briefs. I want to feel the weight of him in my hand, to taste him like he's gotten to taste me. It's only fair.

Before I can get my hands on him, he wraps his fingers around my wrist. Now when he looks at me, his humor is gone. "You don't have to do anything you don't want to."

"I do want to." I press up on my toes and brush my lips across his stubbled jaw. "And is this a good time to tell you that I don't really have a gag reflex?"

His grip on me tightens for a moment before he lets go, like he's been burned. "Fucking hell, Selene. Do you want me to come in my pants?"

I lick a path up his neck. "I'd rather you come in my mouth."

"*Selene.*"

I bat my lashes at him, feigning innocence. "What?"

His gaze is dark and heavy, and with any luck, I'm about to get exactly what I want.

"Get on your knees."

CHAPTER 21

If there's one thing I can't complain about, it's the view on my way down. Daniel is easily one of the sexiest men I've ever seen, and while I'll never admit it to him, what I'm about to do feels like a privilege.

I hook my fingers into the waistband of his boxer briefs and drag them down with me as I sink to my knees. He's already hard, and despite having seen and felt him so many times, my breath still catches in my chest at how big he is—how thick. He's damn near perfect. If I wasn't reaping the benefits, I'd be furious at the luck this man has.

For a moment, I'm intimidated by him and what I'm about to do; it's been a long time, and while I can talk a big game, I can only pray I live up to expectations.

With my hands on his thighs, I tip my chin up, waiting for his next instruction. I don't dare touch him until he tells me to. I'll give him what he wants, give him that illusion of power, even though we both know he'll be at my mercy.

He grips the base of his cock and locks me in his gaze. "Open your mouth."

I do as he commands.

His breath hitches. *Good.*

A moment later, the head of his cock brushes my lips and circles. I flick my tongue out for a taste, and I'm immediately desperate for more.

"Show me what you want to do, Selene."

It's that patronizing tone, the dare, the *I bet you won't do it well*, that makes me drag my nails down his thighs and look up at him through my lashes. I'll accept his challenge. And I'll make sure he never forgets it.

I brush his hand out of the way and lick from base to tip without hesitation, feeling his surprise. If he thought I was being bold at the office earlier, then he's in for a shock.

Wrapping my hand around him, I give his length a long, languid stroke before lowering my mouth to him again. I only take the tip, letting my hand do most of the work. If he's allowed to torture me, the least I can do is give him the same.

When my hair falls forward into my face, he sweeps it back and gathers it in his fist behind my head, making sure to tug a little, though not enough to pull me from his cock.

"You look so good like this."

In answer, I slowly swirl my tongue over the head. And in response, his grip tightens in my hair. He knows I'm not looking for compliments, though I can't deny that it spurs me on. If I'm going to be on my knees for him, the least he can do is tell me how pretty I look doing it.

I cup his balls, giving a soft squeeze as I slide my lips farther down his shaft. His hissed breaths only serve to encourage me. I'm entirely too pleased by the noises I'm eliciting from him.

"*Fuck*. I should have let you do this sooner."

He's right. He should have. But he hasn't given me the opportunity before. Daniel isn't a selfish lover, another point in his favor, but if he doesn't walk away from this without taking more of what he wants, then I haven't done it right.

He groans and throws his head back when his cock touches the back of my throat. But a second later, he's staring down at me from under heavy lids, like he doesn't want to miss a moment of what I'm doing.

"You can take it all, baby. Come on."

I let my other hand wander up the taut muscles of his abdomen, and there's a slight tremble against my palm. I'm getting to him, even if his voice remains steady. I can make that last bit of control disappear, though, and I succeed when I take in another inch.

If my mouth wasn't so full, I'd smile at the Spanish curses that fall from his lips. They're too fast and slurred for me to translate, but his tone is universal. When I pull back and leave him untouched, tormenting him the way he's done to me so many times, his swearing only grows louder.

"You're a sadist," he tells me through a pained laugh. His hold on my hair loosens a little in what I assume is pure disbelief.

With a wicked grin, I run my hand up and down his slick length. "Like I said, I had to reciprocate the kindness you've shown me."

He stares down at me like I've simultaneously ruined his life and shown him the secrets of the universe. "Oh, you fucking—"

He doesn't get to finish the sentence. I take him back into my mouth, not bothering to hold back, pulling another groan from him. I'll give him what he wants now that he knows what it feels like to be on the receiving end of his oh-so-special treatment. His grip on my hair tightens again, and then he pushes my head down a little, though not enough to make me want to pull back. It's considerate and yet just hot enough that it has me moaning. The responding roll of his hips only excites me more.

Part of me is tempted to edge him, to pull back and demand that he fuck me if he wants that release. Except, I'm not that cruel—and I want to see him lose control this way too.

"I'm close," he warns, giving me an out if I want it.

But I don't. I grip his hips and take him as deeply as I can manage.

"That's it," he rasps, clutching the back of my head as he thrusts. "That's my girl."

When he comes with a shuddering exhale, I swallow it all, a step further than what I promised him, and the look in his eyes makes it all worth it. There's a reverence to it, a worshipping, and I bask in it as I sit back on my heels and rest my palms on his thighs like the cat who got the cream.

And I suppose I am.

With his arms under mine, he hauls me to my feet. When I'm slumped against his chest, he bands one arm around my waist and traces my swollen lips with a thumb.

"Where did you learn to be so filthy?" he asks, his voice low and rough, his breathing still ragged as he recovers.

I smirk against his chest. "You know what I do for a living, right?"

"Don't pull that," he scolds. "There are plenty of people out there who can write those words but will never follow them up with the same actions." He drags his lips up my neck. "There's nothing wrong with that, but…"

"You're glad I'm not like that," I finish, pulling back so I can study his face.

His expression is a mix of relief and desire. "So fucking glad."

I don't expect him to kiss me. Some men can't handle tasting themselves on a woman's lips, but Daniel doesn't seem to care. It's another thing I can't help but admire about him—his lack of fucks when it comes to truly trivial things. He never lets it stop him from getting what he wants, and it's clear now that he wants me.

"Do you think you have it in you for more?" I ask him once he pulls back a little. Now that we're back on an equal playing field, I want to be indebted to him again.

His hold on me tightens, and he slips a hand around to cup the back of my neck so I can't avoid his gaze.

"Anything you want, Selene. I'll give it to you."

CHAPTER 22

"You want to go again?" Daniel murmurs against my lips.

He tastes like mint and rum, like the mojitos we had at dinner, and his kiss is just as sweet. Every inch of me is tender, and yet there's nothing I want more. I somehow manage to nod. We've been lying here for the past fifteen minutes, recovering from our last round and kissing lazily, like there's no need to take this anything but slow tonight.

Between him going down on me in the office, my reciprocation, and then the hard and fast fuck from behind on the edge of the mattress, it's amazing that neither of us has had our fill. But I'm still beyond turned on. It's like an addiction; I've had plenty, but I still want more, and he has no qualms about getting me high time and time again.

His fingers drift down between my legs, and I open for him. He circles my clit and makes a sound of approval against my mouth, then pulls back just enough to murmur, "You're still so wet for me."

I roll my eyes, but my breath catches. "You act like I can control that."

He runs a finger down my seam, and it takes every ounce of control I have not to sigh and arch into his hand. "You didn't deny it's because of me."

Why would I? It's a fact. But instead of answering, I slide my hand up into his hair and brush my lips over his. "Just fuck me, Daniel."

He lets me kiss him for a moment before pulling back with a familiar glint in his eye. "So demanding." Leaning over the edge of the bed, he searches for something on the floor. But then he pulls himself back up and drops his forehead to my shoulder with a curse.

"What's wrong?" I ask, cupping his jaw.

He sighs. "We're out of condoms."

I could tell him I'm on birth control, that I'm desperate to feel him without anything between us. But then I remind myself of the facts. I don't know this man all that well, and getting pregnant isn't the only thing to be cognizant of.

Which is why I packed a box of condoms.

"There are more in my suitcase." I nod to where it's set up across the room. "Left side."

He rolls off me with one more bruising kiss and strides across the room. I slide my hand between my thighs and close my eyes while I wait for him to dig through the clothing that's likely covering the box. I miss his touch already, and I'm too on edge to wait. After a moment or two, when he hasn't returned and I'm desperate for more than my hand, I roll to my side, ready to urge him to make it quick.

That's when I see him holding my vibrator.

Fuck.

There's a slow smile blooming on his face, like he's discovered all of my secrets and he has every intention of wielding them over me.

"Why did you bring this?" he asks, amused eyes flicking between me and the palm-sized pink device meant for perfect clitoral stimulation.

I suck in a deep breath, refusing to be mortified by this. There's absolutely nothing wrong with having and using sex toys, and there are plenty more in my bedside drawer at home. But damn, *why* did he have to find this one?

Eventually, I clear my throat and say, "Because I wasn't sure if this would happen again, and I knew seeing you would make me…" I don't know how to finish that sentence with anything other than *so goddamn horny*. "Look, a girl has needs."

"You think of me when you touch yourself." It's not a question. It's a pure statement, one that he's daring me to refute.

"Yeah. I do." My face is on fire, but what else is there to say? He knows.

And yet my answer still makes him close his eyes and tilt his head back. His throat works as he murmurs, "*Mierda*, Selene."

"What?" I challenge. "You know damn well you're hot, you bastard. And the things you do to me—" I cut short before I say something I'll regret. "I don't think there's anything wrong with a fantasy, or—"

"Stop talking."

I scoff. "Excuse me?"

"I *said*, stop talking," he repeats. His voice is tight as he shifts onto the bed again. Far more naturally than they should, his hips slot between my thighs and press me open harshly.

I wrap my legs around his waist without thinking twice, eyes flicking down to his steadily hardening cock.

Tossing the condom onto the pillow, he braces himself with one arm and drops his face to my neck. The kiss he presses to that sensitive spot below my ear is soft, but then he roughly scrapes his teeth along my skin, pulling a hiss of surprise from me. Still, I shudder with desire, and an inferno rushes through me. I'm a little pissed but incredibly turned on by what he's doing to me.

"You're being an ass—"

"Shut up," he says against my jaw, cutting me off. "Just shut up."

"Don't tell me what to—"

And then his mouth is over mine, silencing me. But the faint buzzing that fills the air steals anything else I could have said. I gasp when he grazes the vibrator over my clit and nearly scream when he brings it back up and presses down, leaving me unable to escape from the jolt of pleasure. My head presses back into the pillow as my spine arches, fully possessed.

"Never tell a man he's who you think about when you're alone," he murmurs. "It will go to his head."

I want to speak, to tease him in return, but I can't form words. The pressure builds faster than I anticipated when he slides two fingers into me. Between his touch and the vibrations, his name is all I can utter. A desperate, breathy plea for release.

He swallows it as he kisses me again, hard and punishing. Like that single word was enough to remove the façade of control he had.

His cock is hard and hot against my thigh. Precum leaks from the tip, painting my skin as his fingers work in tandem with the vibrator. I gather just enough wits to reach down and touch him, but he bats my hand away, then pins it above my head as he increases the intensity on my clit in punishment.

"You aren't in charge here," he growls against my ear, and it only sends more lightning to my core.

I buck up into his hand, wanting him deeper, wanting more, and he rewards me by adding a third finger. I groan, luxuriating in the way he stretches me. And when he curls his middle finger up and presses down on my clit, I'm done for. I come hard, pulsing around his fingers. Wetness drips down my thighs, mixing with what he's left on my skin.

I'm still coming down as he pulls the vibrator away and turns it off. He drops it beside me and shifts up onto his knees, grabbing the condom. He rips it open and rolls it on, giving himself a long stroke as he stares down at me, his eyes darker than ever.

I've barely come down from my orgasm, and I still want him. I don't even know how that's possible. But the sight of him—all long, hard lines and narrow hips that I already know fit perfectly between mine—has me craving more.

My walls still haven't settled, but I spread my thighs and place one wrist over the other above my head. I'm open for him, his to take.

"Fuck, Selene," he breathes out as he covers my body with his and pins my wrists again with one hand while gripping his cock with the other. "You make me crazy."

I'm dizzy with power and the knowledge that I can make this man feel like that. It's an accomplishment worth bragging about. I want to tease him about it, to grin sharply and bat my lashes, but all I can do is beg him for more.

He doesn't go easy on me as he pushes inside, all the way until I physically can't take any more of him. We both moan and take a moment to adjust. His is muffled in my neck as he bites down, sure to leave a mark. I won't cover it up tomorrow.

"Show me just how crazy," I say in shallow gasps.

He withdraws and slams into me harder, over and over and over again in slick rhythm. It's desperate and possessive and I take it without complaint, closing my eyes and giving myself over to him. His grip on my wrists is tight, making it impossible to escape, not that I would dare. He told me I could have whatever I want, and it's this—the chance to let go and let him use me however he desires.

The sound of our skin meeting is nothing short of vulgar. The pleasure-slurred words he breathes into my ear are even filthier. Some I understand, some I can only guess, but there's no mistaking him when he tells me to never think of anyone but him.

"Only me," he whispers.

In this moment, I can't imagine ever wanting to. Right now, the only one in my little world is him. He's all I can feel, smell, taste. He's all I need.

He lets my wrists go and slides his hands under the small of my back to lift my hips to him, and that's all it takes for me to come apart under his touch. His voice guides me through it and brings me back on the other side when my hazy vision clears.

Backlit by the city lights, his hair is damp and swept across his forehead, and his expression is one of exhausted amusement. For a moment, all I can think is that he can't be real. That he's nothing more than an apparition. But when he drops low to kiss me hard, to murmur more against my lips, there's no denying it.

Daniel Santiago is all too real. And I'm falling headfirst for him.

FEBRUARY

CHAPTER 23

I'm at dinner with Carly and her boyfriend, and I don't know how much more of their romance I can take.

The affection they have for one another doesn't typically bother me. They clearly love each other, and they seem to know the other better than they know themselves. And the little things they do for each other, consciously or not, are a testament to the depth of that love. Most days, it keeps my belief in romance alive and thriving.

Tonight, it makes me sick.

I try not to watch them snuggle closer as I lift my wine glass and knock back what's left of the Shiraz in one gulp. The temptation to signal for another bottle is strong, but it's probably in my best interest to just get out of here and sulk in peace.

Before I can tell Carly as much, though, Justin picks up the dessert menu. He declares that the chocolate mousse cake here is amazing, and if we leave without trying it, he'll never forgive us. I usually adore Justin, but tonight I want to drive my fork through his eye.

I push my chair back before I can give in to the urge. He doesn't deserve it, and Carly would be furious. Truthfully, the man has beautiful eyes. It would be a tragedy if he lost one.

"I'll be back," I mumble as I stand. "Just heading to the bathroom."

"Oh, I'll come with you," Carly says, taking her napkin from her lap and dropping it next to her plate.

Pretending I don't hear her, I spin and weave through the tables of the quaint Italian restaurant before she can protest.

I just need a moment alone to chill the fuck out. Neither Carly nor Justin have done anything wrong, and I don't want to take my frustration out on them.

I've had too much to drink, I'm horny after two weeks of no sex, and all I can think about is falling into bed with Daniel. We hooked up two nights in a row the last time I was in New York, squeezing in as many rounds as we could manage. By that Wednesday morning, I was nothing short of wrecked. I was so sore that I had to trade the jeans I pulled on that morning for leggings, despite the temperature being below freezing. Needless to say, I shivered and winced the whole way to the office, though I splurged on an Uber to get to Penn Station after work. It was a lesson learned. Now I know that there's such a thing as too much rough sex.

Right now, though, I wish I'd bottled up some of those orgasms to save for this dry spell, because the self-induced ones I've had to settle for don't come anywhere close to measuring up. I want to feel the weight of him on top of me, the heat of his skin. I want to trace the patterns of ink on his shoulder, to run my tongue over every inch of him.

But I can't, and I'm furious about it.

I shove my way into the bathroom and lock myself in a stall, then close my eyes and breathe. When Carly comes in, her heels clicking against the tile floor, I consider bolting. But if I do that, she'll abandon her plans to stay at Justin's tonight so she can come home with me and press for answers about why I took off so suddenly.

Blowing out a breath, I yank out a few sheets of toilet paper from the dispenser and dab at my forehead, feeling like an overheated mess. Honestly, I'm embarrassed for myself. Witnessing the love between my best friend and her wonderful boyfriend should make me happy, but instead I'm…bitter. Jealous. Overwhelmed by the realization that I want that kind of relationship too.

I've been fine as a single woman for years. Sometimes my job makes me want a partner, someone who will worship the ground I walk on and whom I can worship in return. But most of the time, it makes me realize just how much work relationships can be.

The thing about writing stories that show every beat of a couple's journey—including after the original *happily ever after*, when they've been together for ages—means that I have to create drama between the characters in order to keep the story entertaining for the reader. Not everything can be smooth sailing forever. Every couple will run into their rough patches and tough spots, but it's *how* they get through them that makes the story.

But that's fiction. It's romance with a capital *R*. With it comes a blatant promise that everything will work out in the end. That the characters will get their permanent happily ever after—when they finally get to *the end*. It's not always like that in real life. And typically, that reminder is enough to keep me happy being unattached.

Except I'm starting to wonder if that's still what I want.

"You okay?" Carly asks from the stall next to mine, pulling me out of my thoughts. "You've been a little broody all night."

Of course she caught on. We're the kind of best friends who practically share the same one brain cell most of the time, and there's no getting anything past her. That doesn't mean I won't try.

"Just getting a headache," I tell her, dropping the paper now covered in golden-tan foundation into the toilet. "I'll be fine."

I flush to keep the conversation from continuing, then unlock the stall door and head to the sink. As I wash my hands, I avoid my reflection in the mirror. I can't bear to look at myself, to see in my eyes what I've been trying to deny all night.

I miss Daniel.

The thought almost makes me gag. I can't believe I miss *him*. Not just the life-altering orgasms he's been responsible for, but the man himself. What the fuck?

Something shifted between us the last time I was in the city—on my side, at least. The possessiveness he showed, the physical adoration, the praise he lavished upon me, all left my head spinning. Professionally, I still hate him; that's a given. But personally, though it pains me to acknowledge, I'm starting to feel attached to him. Possessive in my own right.

Except that's not allowed in no-strings situations. We agreed to casual. At my insistence, nonetheless. So I can only hope that this is a fleeting feeling, that he'll reignite my rage toward him soon and dull my obsessive crush.

Thank God I don't have his phone number. If I did, I probably would have drunk texted him already and blabbed all my secrets. Our only modes of communication are Slack and email, and I'm not foolish enough to contact him from an official work account on a Saturday night.

"Seriously, babe," Carly says, using her no-nonsense voice as she joins me at the sink. "What's going on?"

I nearly snap at her that I'm *fine*, but I manage to hold back. Carly doesn't deserve to be my punching bag.

I'm tempted to tell her the truth—that I'm obsessing over a guy that I shouldn't be, pissed that I can't be with him right now, and struggling with how to feel about it all.

And it's a wonder I haven't broken down and filled her in. If there's anyone I could confess this to, it's her. We don't usually keep things from each other.

But this? I want to keep it to myself. It's going to end sooner or later. She'd never judge me for fucking around and catching feelings for a man I can never be with, but I'll feel the mortification of it anyway.

So instead, I groan and complain about how I can't get out of this new project at work. Because I *am* pretty upset about it, and it's one more reason I'm so conflicted about what I'm feeling for Daniel. He's making my life at work miserable while simultaneously making me feel so incredibly wanted.

The last time I felt this way about someone, I ended up screwed over and brokenhearted. I'll never say I'm jaded; I believe in love and romance, and I believe there's someone out there who will love me for me one day. But opening myself up to that after being hurt and unwanted for so long terrifies me.

"Let's get back to the table," I tell her as I dry my hands. "I have a feeling Justin will eat all the cake by himself if we give him the chance."

Carly laughs, and I motion for her to lead the way out, forcing myself to smile until her back is to me.

I need to get myself under control. Daniel may make it clear he's the one in charge in bed, but I can't let him take over any other parts of my life.

Too bad I kind of want him to.

CHAPTER 24

"He's such a *dick*," Nikki grits out, slamming her coffee cup down on the table.

I'm almost obtuse enough to ask who she's talking about, but there's only one answer. Daniel. She's just left a meeting with him and Jim to discuss the new projects they're dumping onto her plate soon. Based on her reaction, she didn't get good news.

It's Monday morning, and I've been awake since dawn, stressing about how today will go. It took entirely too much restraint to keep from sending Daniel a message on Slack when I got into the city last night. Somehow, I managed to hold back, and I've kept my distance this morning, even though we're both in the office today. Considering he disappeared into a conference room the second our morning meeting ended, it's been a relatively easy task.

As much as I want to, I can't deny it anymore—I'm into this man more than I should be, and it's going to hurt to pull myself back out.

"What did he do this time?" I ask her as I open my next round of edits on my laptop. The fan immediately kicks on as my overloaded device tries to manage the copious documents loading.

She grumbles as she throws herself into the chair next to mine, sulking like a toddler. I can't blame her; I've had the same reaction to the shit Daniel pulls too many times to count. And while I might have a very small crush on him (gross), I'm not about to defend him over something he's likely done wrong.

"The timeline he gave me for this project is completely unrealistic," she rants. "I can't launch a continuation in less than three weeks. Like, I know we're trying to make a return on our investment as quickly as possible, but he doesn't understand the sheer amount of *effort* creative work requires. All he does is look at the fucking numbers and shell out money to these authors for rights to their books without thinking about the work our team will have to put into them. And since *Daniel* believes it can be done, so does Jim. I've got no one in my corner on this."

She lets out a strangled scream as she pulls her laptop closer, looking like she wants to throw it clear across the room. Her workload is just as heavy as mine—maybe even more so now with what Daniel has handed over to her. "God, I'm tempted to go sock him in the fucking jaw."

I've been there before. As production leads, we're responsible for pretty much everything required to get a story up and running—and continued—on the app. That process, when done correctly and given the proper attention, takes months. So expecting her to launch this project in a matter of weeks is outrageous.

"He's such a condescending prick, and he doesn't care about anything except the bottom line," Nikki says. "I'm genuinely shocked you haven't fought him yet, considering the shit he's put you through."

I'm pretty shocked by it too. Business-wise, Daniel and I are still pure enemies. But personally…I don't know what we are. All I know is that I want him in my bed tonight.

"Unfortunately, I realized I'm no match for him." I sigh. "He's kind of…big." If only she knew in how many ways.

"Let's tag-team him," she offers, lifting her fists like a professional fighter. "You hold him down, I'll pummel him."

I snicker, about to tell her that I'll start planning the ambush, when a whistle rings out. Behind us, Ella is gripping the doorframe to the nearest conference room, leaning just far enough out to get our attention.

"Come here," she says in a stage whisper. "I have gossip."

Nikki and I exchange a quick glance before we're pushing out of our chairs and giggling as we hustle into the conference room with Ella. Zoe is in there as well, smirking like she's already been let in on the secret. If I wasn't curious before, I certainly am now. We're an office full of writers; we thrive on drama.

"Spill," Nikki demands, rubbing her hands together. "I need a distraction to keep me from fighting Daniel."

Zoe shoots me an amused look. "Isn't that *your* job?"

"I'll take the help," I answer, though the idea of anyone else laying a hand on him doesn't sit right with me. I want to be the only one to touch him. Fighting or otherwise.

Ella motions for us to lean in. "The gossip I have is about him," she whispers, looking directly at me.

My stomach drops. Oh God, she *knows*. She knows about Daniel and me and what we've been doing.

But there's no way. She wouldn't have pulled me into the room with Nikki and Zoe to expose me. She's a good friend; she wouldn't put me on the spot like that. And how would she have even found out?

Are there cameras in here? My own words come back to me. The flash of Daniel on his knees, his lips on my skin. If there really were cameras…

"I saw Daniel out on a date over the weekend."

Nikki makes a sound of interest beside me. "Oh shit, really?"

After that, white noise in my head threatens to drown everything else out.

Daniel. On a date. Out with someone else when I was home in

Baltimore, fantasizing about the next time I'd see him.

It's a punch to the gut. A blow I have to be careful not to react to. But the air has been knocked from my lungs and the little voice in the back of my head is saying *I told you so*.

I absolutely should not feel betrayed. Number one, I have no claim to him. This is nothing more than hate-fucking when it's convenient for us both. And number two, like Ella said, this is gossip. There's a chance it's not true.

"You're sure it was a date?" I ask when I manage to find my voice, but the words are scratchy in my throat.

She nods like a bobblehead. "Oh, for sure," she says, and my stomach sinks even further. "She was *all* up on him. The girl practically had hearts in her eyes. I was kind of embarrassed for her, to be honest. Like, whatever, I'll admit he's kind of cute, but that asshole is not worth the trouble."

I swallow back the bile inching into my throat. "Did he seem into it?"

In my periphery, Nikki shoots me a pointed look, but I ignore her. Ella merely shrugs, oblivious to the reasons behind my line of questioning. "I don't know. I can't read the guy," she answers. "It wasn't like he was pushing her away or anything. But that isn't even the juicy part."

It's hard to brace for the next blow, though I try.

"I'm pretty sure I recognized the girl," Ella continues conspiratorially. "She works for JotNote."

Nikki gasps at our competitor's name, thankfully shifting her attention from me to Ella. "*No*. He wouldn't."

"I definitely think he would," Zoe pipes in. "That guy would do anything to get ahead. He's willing to fuck all of us over with our workloads in order to do it, so what's a little sexy corporate espionage?"

"Unless *she's* the one getting information out of *him*," Ella counters.

I can already see the ideas forming in her head. We're creatives through and through; the plotlines come to us with the slightest spark of inspiration.

"Maybe she's pretending to be in love with him so that in their moments of pillow talk, he'll accidentally spill what we're working on and JotNote can steal it." Ella's eyes go wide. "But then he finds out and is heartbroken, and—"

"That man is a closed book," Nikki interrupts before Ella can weave a whole novel for us. "She probably doesn't even know where he works." Her eyes cut to me, but my head is spinning so fast that I barely have time to make sure my true feelings don't show on my face. "What's your take on it?"

My take is that I don't want any of this to be true. I want it to be pure fiction because this can't be the way things between Daniel and me end.

"He better be the one getting information out of her," I finally say, relieved that my voice doesn't waver even though my heart is up in my throat. "JotNote is right behind us on the charts, and if they get just one new hit story, it's over for us."

There's a communal grumble of annoyed acceptance. We're not the only good fiction app on the market anymore. Our competitors are growing too close for comfort, and we all know it. We've shown the book world that our serialized model works, and now everyone else wants to get in on it, including the company that shares its name with a rainforest.

I don't actually give a single fuck about that right now, but it's a good way of shifting the conversation away from Daniel. If we keep talking about him, I'm afraid I'll say something I can't take back.

More than that, though, I'm afraid I might be falling for a man who's already in a relationship.

But for the time being, I have to believe it's just gossip. All wild imaginings and fictionalized scenarios.

As the girls debate which of our competitors could surpass us first, I pull out my phone and open the Slack app, finding Daniel's name near the bottom of my contacts. Our chain of messages is short, but I add another.

Can we talk?

───────

Daniel hasn't responded to my message.

In the two hours since I sent it, I've only managed to edit a handful of chapters. If I don't get my act together, I'll fall behind and have to make this up later, but I can't focus. Dread sits heavy in my stomach, churning and threatening to come up and out. As much as I want him to respond, I don't know that it will ease my anxiety any.

But I have to know. I can't stay in this limbo, unsure of whether our arrangement has come to an unceremonious end and whether I've been complicit in cheating. The guilt will eat me alive if I don't get to the bottom of it.

When the girls invite me to lunch, I beg off, claiming I have too much work to do to take a break. The truth is that I can't take any more of their gossip; if I have to listen to another word about Daniel's supposed date, I might lose my mind. I also don't want to miss the moment Daniel steps out of the back conference room, the only one without a wall of windows—the same one we were in when he went down on me just a few weeks ago. Right now, that feels more like a lifetime ago.

Like a lovesick loser, I've been counting the moments until I could see him again, while he clearly hasn't thought twice about me. He told me to never fantasize about anyone but him, only to be off with someone else. It feels manipulative. It feels like I've been tricked.

You don't even know if it's true, the angel on my shoulder scolds. I should probably listen to her. I'm hurting my own feelings by overthinking and jumping to conclusions. But, as humans, that's what we do when we don't have all the answers—we fill in the blanks based on the limited information we have. Whether they're filled in with something good or bad is all based on personal experience.

And with my history of men and cheating, it always skews bad.

What feels like eons later, the door to the conference room swings open and Daniel steps out. His laptop is resting on his palm, and his eyes are glued to it as he moves to one of the tables on the opposite side of the room, away from everyone else.

I wait until he's settled before I pull up Slack on my computer and scroll through my messages to see if he's responded yet. My heart squeezes when there's nothing new from him, though I shouldn't be surprised. I've been anxiously listening for the grating notification sound that hasn't come.

Still, I stare at his name, waiting for the three dots to pop up beside it to indicate that he's typing. It's not like I've asked a difficult question, so why hasn't he at least given me a simple yes or no yet? Is it really that hard?

Maybe he opened the message and got distracted before responding. Should I message him again? Or will that make me look desperate? Do we even *really* need to talk?

Jesus, that's a stupid question. Of course we do. Otherwise, I'll never rein in my focus and get shit done. And there's a lot I need to do, most of it put on my plate by him in the first place.

Before I can overthink further, I push back my chair, smooth out my sweater, and take a deep breath. Then my feet are moving, taking me past all the communal tables to where Daniel is seated with his back and laptop screen angled toward the wall.

Do I have any idea what I'm about to say? Absolutely not. But I can't blurt out something like *hey, do you have a girlfriend you've been cheating on with me for the past couple of months?*

So when I find myself standing next to his chair, I clear my throat and ask, "Can I talk to you about the Donna Pascoe deal later?"

It's a weak excuse to talk—the deal we have with Donna is all but settled, and I'm not even working on the project, but it's the best I can come up with, and it won't draw suspicion from anyone who might be listening.

I hate the way my voice shakes as I say it, but what I hate more is that his attention never leaves his laptop. I swear he even shifts away from me slightly, like I'm already being dismissed.

"I don't have time," he says distractedly. The brush-off stings a little more than it should.

Biting my bottom lip, I watch him for a moment, clinging to hope that he'll at least glance up at me and suggest we talk about it tomorrow, but his concentration stays firmly on his screen as he furiously types. And when I ask him if he wants anything from Starbucks, since Jim is about to make our usual afternoon run, all I get is a vague head shake.

I figure I might as well be direct at this point. So, keeping my voice low, I ask, "Are you coming over tonight?"

"No," he replies, *still* not looking at me. "I'm in the middle of something important. I'm going to be here late."

Rooted to the spot, I watch him, waiting for him to say more. This is the man who once told me to steal all his time, that he'd make it for me if I wanted him to.

My breath catches when he finally looks up. But his eyes are distant, and there's an annoyed crease to his brow. "Is there something else you need?"

The terse, impatient question shocks me out of my stupor, leaving me to shake my head and turn away. I've been shut down and rejected. But at least I have my answer.

This is over.

MARCH

CHAPTER 25

I'm going back to the office, and I'm dreading it.

I've never felt like this before. I've always looked forward to seeing my friends and coworkers. Sure, I've been nervous and jittery about it in the past, but I wish I'd told Jim I couldn't make it this month. Or ever again. At this point, I'd like to avoid the Naiad office at all costs, especially one particular employee there.

Nothing happened between Daniel and me on my last trip. After his brush-off, I finished my workday, then went back to my hotel and waited—waited for a Slack message, a knock on my door, a fucking carrier pigeon, literally anything to tell me that he hadn't been serious. But, of course, I got nothing.

When I went into the office the next day, I did everything I could to avoid him, mortified by my behavior and my clearly unreasonable expectations. I moved tables any time he got close, took an extra-long lunch with the girls, even sat in a meeting that had nothing to do with me because it would keep him away.

An hour before the end of the day, a Slack notification dinged in my headphones, and my heart dropped to my knees when I saw it was a message from him. I spent five minutes debating whether to open it and finally clicked with far more force than necessary when my curiosity got the best of me.

All it said was that he had time now to talk about the Donna Pascoe deal. Nothing else.

I didn't bother to reply. I just shut my laptop, called out to the girls that I was leaving for the day, and swept into the elevator before the last of them could say goodbye.

Daniel wasn't in the office when I came in the next day. I hated myself for planning a longer stay in hopes of having more time with him. How stupid I'd been.

I didn't even acknowledge him when he finally showed up around noon, keeping my music loud and my eyes firmly on my screen. But ten minutes into ignoring him, I had a message. Anger flared through me as I opened it, growing more pissed off as I saw what it contained: a link to another bar with a time to meet following it. All I could think was *the fucking nerve of this man.*

Again, I ignored him, and when Nikki suggested all the production girls meet for dinner after work, I enthusiastically agreed and made sure he heard. Yeah, I technically stood him up, but at least he got a little warning.

I didn't bother going up to the office a second time last month, but when Jim inquired about my plans to come back, I grudgingly told him I'd be there the first week of March. And now here I am, sweating like a sinner in church and on the verge of puking in the elevator of Naiad's building.

When it finally stops on our floor, I have to drag myself out. I head straight for one of the smaller conference rooms, mumbling good morning to the various people I see along the way. Unfortunately, before I can ensconce myself behind the glass walls, Jim steps into my path.

I force myself through the usual office pleasantries, wearing a fake smile as I tell him about my weekend. The upbeat persona slips a bit when he asks what my plans are for my time in the city. If Daniel and

I were still hooking up, I would have plans—not that I would tell Jim that, but I almost hate that it's not a lie when I admit to him that I have nothing going on.

He lights up at that and launches into a glowing review of a new restaurant a few blocks north of here that I absolutely *have* to visit. I try my best not to tune him out, but when the elevator doors open and Daniel emerges, everything around me fades.

I don't know how it's possible, but he somehow looks even better than I remember. His hair is a little shorter, like he's gotten it cut recently, but it still curls and sweeps in that unruly way I've come to adore. There's nothing special about the black T-shirt he's wearing or the subtle gold chain around his neck, and yet I can't keep myself from drinking in his sharp jaw, the lines of his throat, or the way his biceps fill out his sleeves.

His skin's a little tanner, a gentle golden brown, like he's gone somewhere warm in the past few weeks and let the sun worship him. I wouldn't know, considering we haven't talked and he never shares more than he has to about his life in our meetings. Like Nikki said, the man is a closed book—but I can't get over how he showed me a few chapters before slamming it shut.

Over the last month, I've come to realize that he may not actually have a girlfriend, and he may not have been out on a date, but the mere idea of either scenario has put this whole situation into perspective for me. Our...*entanglement* was never meant to last for long. Those secret liaisons would have had to come to an end at some point. And if I've been complicit in cheating, then it's good that it's already met its conclusion.

I don't think Daniel would do something that shitty, but I don't actually know him. I really don't. He could be like any one of the fuckboys I dated in college who claimed we were exclusive while they were screwing someone else behind my back. Or like my most recent ex, and the most serious partner I've had, who had a long-distance girlfriend the entire time we were together.

Daniel may be different, but I don't want to press my luck. It hasn't been very good in the past.

I force myself to tune back into Jim, refusing to watch Daniel walk by behind him. Daniel's eyes are on me, though. I can feel them, dark and piercing and...questioning.

I'm relieved when he disappears from my line of sight and into the main office space. Another second, and I might have combusted.

"Anyway," Jim says, finally ending this roundabout speech. "You should go while you're here. It's so worth it."

I swallow and nod, trying to find my voice. "Yeah, absolutely. I will."

"Do you have meetings today?" he asks, frowning a little as he looks between me and the conference room door I was heading toward before he stopped me. Usually, we only camp out in conference rooms when we have story planning meetings or calls with authors, things we wouldn't want to bother our coworkers with. But if we're just writing or doing edits, we sit in the main office space.

I can't lie to him. He already knows my schedule—he's the one who makes it, after all—and he's well aware that I'm just editing today. "No, I don't," I tell him. "I just needed some quiet time to concentrate on my edits. I've got a lot of them this week."

"Oh, come on in here and work with us," he goads, extending an arm to usher me toward the long tables. "We hardly ever get to see you. I promise everyone will keep it down."

It's difficult to bring a smile to my face. "Great."

Jim walks behind me, practically herding me to one of the empty office chairs. And since I have the best luck, it's the same table Daniel has settled at. The only saving grace is that he's sitting at the far end, though it's not far enough that we can't lock eyes.

WORK FOR IT

Which is exactly what happens as soon as I drop into the chair.

I look away as quickly as I can manage, but the damage is done. My heart is racing, my stomach is on the floor, and I'm hot all over—whether it's from embarrassment or regretful desire or a combination of them both, I'm not sure.

Ducking my head, I busy myself by pulling out my laptop and my headphones. A few people pop by to greet me as I get situated, wrapping loose arms around my shoulders and inquiring about how I've been, but I can barely reply or return their embraces.

Finally, once I've said hello to the last of them, I put on my headphones and turn my music up as loud as I can bear, determined to get into the zone and ignore Daniel's presence.

It works at first. But I've just started the second of the chapters when a Slack notification dings in my ears. I reluctantly swipe out of my document and pull up my messages, expecting to see a company-wide news blast or a silly joke from one of the other production girls. But instead, I'm staring at the little red number next to Daniel Santiago's name.

I hesitate to open it, but then I hear his voice in the back of my head. *Don't be a coward, Selene.* The everlasting challenge. Even if there's nothing left between us, his influence lingers.

Drawing in a deep breath, I hover my cursor over his name. On an exhale, I click. At the bottom of the screen is another link to a restaurant and the question: *7 p.m.?*

This time, it's a question. In the past, he's given me a time and expected me to show up. But this is an actual request, probably because he knows there's a chance I'll ignore him again. He wants confirmation that I'll be there.

I click out of our messages.

He won't be getting shit from me.

Somehow, I manage to find my groove. Sitting low in my seat, headphones on, music blaring, I tune out everything around me—including Daniel's general presence—and get my work done.

He hasn't sent more messages or tried to get my attention again, but every so often, I can feel him staring. Whatever. Let him stare. Let him think about how he fucked up and dwell on why I want nothing to do with him.

I eventually have to break my concentration for a trip to the bathroom. I'm careful not to look Daniel's way as I get up. I avoid my own reflection in the mirror as I'm washing my hands too. There's a chance I could see my fragile heart reflected back at me, which won't help me keep my resolve. I can't let anyone, not even myself, see how weak I am inside.

On the way back to my workspace, I'm stopped by Jim once again.

"Selene, would you mind doing the Starbucks run?" he asks with a glance at his watch. "I've got a meeting I forgot all about, but I promised everyone a caffeine fix."

Pulling out my phone, I smile. "No problem." I scan the room as I tap on the Starbucks app. "Who wants what?"

Immediately, I'm hit with a succession of rapid-fire orders, and it takes all my brain power to get them inputted correctly.

"Take Daniel with you," Jim calls out as he hustles toward one of the conference rooms. "He has the company credit card in case we forgot something and can help you carry everything."

That is *not* what I need. "No, it's all right. I've got—"

But Daniel is already brushing past me as he moves toward the elevators. I can't even protest to Jim again because he's already shut the door, and his glass-wall-muted-but-still-booming voice is brightly greeting the person on the other end of his call.

I have two options. I can get on that elevator with Daniel, ignore him, and bring back the drinks as promised. Or I can sit my ass back down and let him do the run alone. The order is already submitted and paid for, so all he has to do is listen for my name to be called and then cart back twenty-ish drinks on his own.

As much as I want to go with the second option, it'll raise questions I'm not interested in answering. They'll come the moment I sit down after being specifically asked to do the run. But what's worse is if Daniel returns with only half the drinks because he couldn't carry them all on his own, or if he comes back with coffee spilled all over him and a tray full of ruined drinks. Either way, everyone will be mad at me for interfering with their afternoon treat.

Shit. I guess I care more about my coworkers than my own mental health, because I'm already walking to the elevator.

Daniel has an arm extended to keep the doors from closing on me, leaving me to slide along the opposite side to avoid touching him as I step in. Once I've pushed myself into a corner, he drops his arm and hits the button for the lobby, then slowly turns toward me as the doors shut.

And just like that, I have his full attention.

"Are you coming to dinner with me?"

I give a noncommittal murmur. I have nothing to say.

My breath hitches as he shifts so close I can feel the heat rolling off his body. It has my head spinning, but I refuse to let him get to me again.

"That's not an answer," he says with what I swear is a note of disappointment in his voice, like he can't believe he has to interrogate me.

Well, fine. I'll give him a direct answer if he really wants one.

My eyes snap up to his, boldly meeting his gaze. "I don't think that's a good idea."

Somehow, Daniel is undeterred. "You've already done it once," he counters.

"One time too many," I shoot back, and thankfully, the elevator doors slide open before he can respond.

I push around him and step into the lobby, then I'm shoving through the doors and out onto the busy street. I'm only a handful of steps down the sidewalk, but Daniel catches up to me easily.

"Okay, what is up with you?" he demands, his brows drawn together as if he truly can't understand what's going on. "Why are you avoiding me?"

"I'm not avoiding you," I say coolly, not bothering to move until he gets out of my way. Disinterest is better than giving him the anger he loves to elicit from me. "I've just been busy."

Daniel, however, doesn't hold back. No, he shows me exactly how close he is to the edge. "Bullshit. I've given you space since you clearly don't want to be around me, but I'm tired of being in the dark. What's wrong?"

The emotion in his expression and his words knock me back. He's so good at maintaining that calm façade, but right now, it's like he's dropped it completely and stomped on it.

"There's nothing wrong," I say, folding my arms over my chest and lifting my chin.

"Is it something I did?"

I stay silent, not trusting myself to speak.

Daniel blows out a breath and dips his head so I'm forced to meet his eye. "Is this about how I said I didn't have time to talk the other week?" he asks, a little quieter this time. "Are you upset about it?"

I bristle, and I can't stop my tongue this time. "I'm not upset about any—"

"Because I shouldn't have brushed you off like that," he continues on, ignoring my interruption. "It's been a stressful few weeks, and I took it out on you. It was shitty of me, and you didn't deserve it. But it was just work. Nothing personal—nothing you did."

That's how it always is. Just work. Just the shit we do for a living getting in the way of behaving like normal human beings to each other. As long as we're employed by the same company, that won't change. It's another reason this could never turn out well. Maybe if we weren't coworkers—

Well, what? What would be the difference? Would I actually try to pursue a relationship with him? Would we be dating? Or would we still be stuck in this strange hookup limbo with no attachment and even less communication?

"Come *on*, Selene." He moves half a step closer, forcing other pedestrians to funnel around us, but he doesn't seem to care. "What is it really? Talk to me. Please."

Damn it. He's not going to leave me alone until I explain, and my resolve is slipping a little more with each passing second. Besides, lack of communication got us into this mess in the first place; nothing will improve unless I help break this cycle.

"It's not just about that," I grudgingly admit after a few more long beats of silence. "Look, Ella saw you out on a date, and *then* you brushed me off. So I took the hint. I'm not trying to interfere with your love life, okay?"

Daniel freezes and his jaw goes slack. He stares at me so hard I can practically see the synapses firing in his brain. "*That's* why you're avoiding me?"

I cross my arms tighter. I don't appreciate his tone, the disbelief that lives behind his words. "It was my mistake. I should have asked if you had a girlfriend or were seeing anyone or—"

His surprise fades as I speak, that careful neutral falling back into place. "I don't have a girlfriend. Clearly, you do hate me if you think I'd cheat on someone I was committed to."

His voice is sharp now, like instead of rolling off his back like all the rest, this insult has hit him dead-on.

The urge to backtrack, to explain myself, bubbles up, but I choke it down and hitch my chin higher instead. "Like I've told you before, I don't know anything about you or your life."

But his response brings me a sick rush of relief. Things must not be serious with the woman he was out with. At least I haven't played a role in breaking up a relationship.

Still, is that what he's looking for? A serious relationship? And am I just the one he's fucking until he settles down with someone else?

What does it matter, though? I shouldn't care. If it ends because he wants to pursue someone seriously, then so be it. I won't stop him. That's not my place, and I never expected this to last long. Hell, I never expected more than a one-and-done thing in the first place, but it's lingered out of sheer convenience. And maybe because the sex is mind-blowing.

Okay, and yeah, I'm kind of into him. But I can toss those feelings out in a heartbeat if I need to.

Maybe.

I hope.

I fucking better.

His jaw is tense as the sounds of the city screech in the background. "Then come to dinner with me tonight," he finally says. "Come get to know me better."

Part of me isn't surprised by his insistence. This is no doubt a tactic to keep getting me into bed, especially if he's not dating anyone. I'm an easy choice. But another part, the tiny part that's willing to give him the benefit of the doubt, wonders if this is him trying to change our arrangement. What if he wants to turn it into something with a little more depth?

And if so, can I handle that?

Licking my lips, all I can do is study him silently. Because I honestly don't know.

"I'm trying, Selene," he presses, low and urging. It's not quite desperate, but it's close. "Give me a chance."

I shouldn't. I *really* shouldn't. I should say no, let this end for real. Mend my heart in private while it can still be fixed. That's what I need to do. That's the safest road to take.

But instead, I swallow hard and murmur, "Dinner. That's it. Don't make me regret it."

CHAPTER 26

There's no way I can wait until after work to get more answers out of Daniel. And if he tells me something now that I don't want to hear, I can still back out of dinner.

"So," I prompt as we continue our trek. He's taken up station by my side, blocking me from the cars that breeze by. "Who was—"

"Do you want to know what kept me so busy last month?" he asks, cutting me off like he couldn't hold it back any longer.

I almost stumble at the urgency in his tone. It *is* something I'm interested in. There are far more important topics to cover, but if this gets us talking again, I suppose it's as good a place to start as any.

"What were you doing?" I ask, peeking over at him.

"I was negotiating a distribution deal for your physical books."

This time I do stumble, leaving him to grip my elbow to keep me from falling to the sidewalk. I consider asking him to repeat himself, because there's no way he's finally doing the thing I've been practically begging him to do for the past couple of years.

"Are you serious?" I exhale instead, slowly turning toward him.

He shrugs as he guides me the final few feet to the Starbucks storefront. "You said that was what you wanted."

He can't be telling the truth. I stay quiet as he opens the door and ushers me inside to wait in the mobile order pickup section, searching his expression for any sign of deception. But as far as I can tell, he's not lying.

"Did the analytics finally hit the threshold you were looking for?" I question, still suspicious of his motivations. If he's doing this, it can't solely be because it's something I want. "Is the demand you've been looking for finally there? Is that what made you move ahead with it?"

"I did it because you asked for it," he answers, as if it's as simple as that. "I said I would give you whatever you wanted, didn't I?"

The air escapes my lungs at that admission. He *did* promise it, but I never once thought it had to do with anything outside of my sexual desires. But he remembered. And he's holding himself to that promise outside of the bedroom.

I think I might pass out.

"Don't get too excited yet," Daniel warns, but my heart and my head are already floating into the clouds. "The negotiations aren't done, and I still haven't decided on a distributor. It's going to take at least a few more weeks to finalize things before we sign any contracts. But it's all in the works."

Forget passing out. I think I might puke up hearts and stars and rainbows all over his shoes. I swallow hard to keep it down. "Why didn't you just tell me?"

"Because I wanted it to be a surprise. I didn't want you to worry about any part of it."

"So you acted like a dick instead?" I comment dryly, still trying to figure out how to take in a proper breath. I refuse to let him know how much this means to me until he has properly groveled. "I shouldn't have expected any different."

The corner of his mouth lifts. "Maybe you do know me."

I have to fight to keep from returning the smile. This man will *not* win me over so easily. "Doesn't excuse your behavior, though."

He blows out a breath. "I know," he admits with a regretful grimace.

"I'd just gotten out of a tense meeting with Jim when you came up to me. I spent hours trying to convince him to make this happen, and then you nearly saw everything I was working on. I'll admit, I panicked a little. I was trying to get you to walk away before you figured out what I was doing, but I clearly shoved a little too hard. I'm sorry."

I make a small sound of acknowledgment, not quite accepting his apology but recognizing it. "You didn't answer my question about the sales. Did that play a role?"

"No. You didn't come close to hitting the threshold Naiad was looking for. I'll show you the numbers when we get back to the office. It's why Jim and I nearly got into a fight before I finally got him to agree."

Well, that's a blow, because I've always considered myself to be a pretty successful writer. But if the sales weren't good enough and he was willing to go to battle with Jim over this…

Jesus Christ, he really *is* giving me what I want.

"Isn't that risky, though?" I push. "If the numbers don't make the case for publishing, and someone higher up at the company asks why you did it, what are you—"

"Selene," he interrupts gently, his dark eyes glinting with amusement. The asshole is practically laughing at me. "Whatever fallout there is, I'll handle it. Just enjoy this."

I scoff and roll my eyes, but I can't ignore the way my stomach has twisted into knots—the good kind this time, though it's still a sensation I don't want to feel in regard to Daniel.

But this is something I've wanted for so, so long. I've been nagging him for ages, only to get the same canned response every time. *Wait until sales of the e-books justify going through the trouble of producing physical copies.* And, yeah, he's probably breaking the news to me now to get back into my good graces, but it still feels like an incredible gift. He's right. I *should* enjoy it. I've finally gotten my wish—though I'm torn between loving and hating the fact that Daniel is responsible for making it happen.

Before I can dwell on it, a barista calls my name from the pickup counter, where dozens of drinks await. We move up together, briefly arguing over who's going to take what. I can't help but admire how large his hands are, how he can rest an entire cardboard drink carrier in his palm and still manage to hang bags full of pastries from his thumb. I, on the other hand, am forced to press a single tray against my chest to keep it from falling.

"Give me those," he insists, easily taking the drinks I'm cradling precariously in my arms. Somehow, when we exit, he's carrying three-fourths of our order. It's chivalrous, no doubt, but it's yet another thing endearing me toward him.

Damn this man.

He even manages to open the door as we leave and nods for me to walk out first as he holds it. Another blow to my grudge against him. When we get back to the Naiad building, I make sure to cut in front of him to grab the door before he can, ignoring the pointed glance he shoots me when I do. But he doesn't protest and even lets me hit the button in the elevator for our floor.

"Are we good now?" he asks as the doors close.

I take him in as I consider. Caution is key here because I don't want to give him false hope. We have so much more to talk about.

"I'll decide after dinner," I finally say. "Should I meet you there?"

He shakes his head. "We'll go over together." Before I can ask how exactly he plans for us to do that, especially without getting caught by anyone we know, he continues, "Just stay late. Everyone will be gone by six-thirty."

I'm still a little hesitant. Getting caught by a coworker would involve a lot of explaining. "Are you sure?"

"Absolutely."

I don't feel his confidence, but I nod, nonetheless. After what I've learned today, I'm intrigued to hear what he says tonight.

I've been counting down the hours.

Daniel and I sit at our table like this is a normal day for us both. I do my best to avoid staring at him, no matter how tempting it is, and he plays his part by keeping his head down and concentrating on his work. Seeing him so focused makes me want to do the same, like we're competing to see who can get more done. That said, I try not to get *too* much done so that if anyone asks why I'm not leaving now that it's six o'clock, I don't have to lie when I say I'm not finished.

At six-fifteen, Jim finally waves goodbye to us. He teases us about not working too hard, and in response, we flash him tight smiles. We both know damn well that he expects each of us to perform at least three times a reasonable amount of work. If I didn't love the creative aspect, I would have quit months ago.

I wait a beat after I hear the elevator doors shut, then peer over my screen and whisper, "Is everyone gone?"

He nods and closes his laptop. "Give it another minute, and we'll head out."

As Daniel stands and shrugs into his leather jacket, I put my computer in my bag and tug on my sweater. After a busy day of edits, I probably look a mess, so I mumble that I'll be right back and slink off to the bathroom. Under the harsh fluorescent lights, I wince at my reflection. My hair is messy from being up in a bun earlier when I was neck deep in edits, and my eyeliner is a little smudged. I do my best to rectify the situation by dragging my fingers through the loose waves and swiping under my eyes.

But before I can go any further, I force myself to stop. Why am I bothering to put in any effort? I wouldn't mind looking like this usually.

WORK FOR IT

It's actually pretty standard for me after a long day of work. And I'm just having dinner with a guy I'm still not sure about. Honestly, I should be showing him my absolute worst to see what he does.

I push out of the bathroom and head back to where Daniel is waiting with my coat and bag in hand. When I try to take my coat from him, he shakes his head and motions for me to turn around. I huff, but I'm not in the mood to fight, so I follow instructions and slide my arms into the sleeves, letting him pull it up and over my shoulders. He's careful not to let his hands linger, but his touch still sends electricity shooting through me.

Just like on our trip back from the coffee run, Daniel guides me with a gentle hand, holds doors, and keeps me shielded from people on the sidewalk. The farther we walk, the more apparent it is that this behavior is second nature for him. It pains me to admit, but I think Daniel might be a *gentleman.*

He's proved that, outside of work, he (mostly) isn't the worst person on the planet. He's still on my shit list for what he pulled last month—and I still don't know the story behind the girl Ella saw him with—but he's slowly moving into my good graces.

Daniel gently grips my elbow as we descend the steps to the subway. I really don't think there's any risk of me falling, but I don't shake him off. Secretly, I'm comforted by the security it provides.

He lets go when we swipe through the turnstiles, allowing me to go first and following close behind. The platform is crowded when we reach it, and I nearly jump when he grabs my hand to lead me through the crowd. He shoots me a glance over his shoulder like he's asking me to trust him. So I take the risk and wrap my fingers around his in return.

We come to a stop toward the end of the southbound platform. Daniel drops my hand and deftly moves to keep me from becoming a victim of a group of rowdy tourists, but when I'm out of danger, he doesn't take my hand again. Instead, he slips behind me and wraps an arm around my waist.

My heart races, and I pray he can't feel my pulse. Because *what exactly is going on right now?* His chest presses to my back, and he splays his hand protectively over my stomach. The position is entirely too intimate for a public setting. Even though the platform is so crammed that I doubt anyone would give us a second glance, I can't bring myself to relax into his embrace.

"Next train is in five minutes," he says, his lips at my ear.

I'm close to freaking out, but he sounds perfectly calm. Like this is a normal Monday night for us. In another world, maybe it would be. In this one, though, I'm worried about getting caught.

I think about pulling away, but he speaks again before I can. "Relax," he murmurs. "No one here knows us. Just talk to me."

He's right. Being in Midtown means we're almost constantly surrounded by visitors to the city, and if the *I Heart NYC* shirt-wearing people around us are any indication, we'll probably never see any of them again.

I clear my throat. If we have a few minutes to wait for the next train, we might as well talk. Hopefully that will ease my nerves.

"So." I take a breath. "You don't have a girlfriend."

He tenses a little, like I've insulted him by continuing to insinuate that he may have cheated. "Obviously not."

I press a little more. "No relationship in general?"

Daniel turns me in his arms, enough so that he can stare at me in a way that makes it very clear he would never stoop to that level. But I need more information.

"Ella said you looked pretty cozy with the girl you were out with," I elaborate. I want him to understand where my concerns are coming from. "That she seemed into you."

"Sounds like Ella's imagination was running wild."

"Daniel. Come on."

He blows out a breath and squeezes me a little tighter, like maybe he's afraid I might bolt when I hear what he's about to say next.

"I've been on a couple of dates with that girl in the past," he confesses.

I wince before I can remind myself that it shouldn't matter to me.

"But it was never serious." He's quick to clarify, his tone firm. "She and I aren't dating. We aren't in a relationship. And I don't have feelings for her."

But do you have them for me? Is that why you're doing all of this? I want to ask the questions, but I bite my tongue instead.

"I hadn't talked to her since December," he continues. "Then she invited me to a screening for a movie based on a book JotNote produced. I didn't think it was a date, since I'd made it clear I wasn't looking for a relationship the last time we went out, and she didn't care for that. So when she texted me, I thought it was just a friendly invitation. Or a chance to rub JotNote's success in my face."

"But it wasn't just friendly," I prompt.

"Not for her." He meets my eyes. "But there was nothing from my side. I hugged her goodbye at the end of the night and that was it."

I nod, and relief trickles into the cracks of my heart, but that only makes it beat harder for him. "Okay."

He squeezes my hip with one hand and grasps my chin with the other, forcing me to look at him. "I haven't slept with anyone but you since the holiday party, if that's what you're worried about."

It is. No matter how many times I tell myself I shouldn't care, I still do, even though I'm not *allowed* to care. "You can sleep with whoever you want, Daniel." And I'll go on continuing to avoid thoughts that involve his life outside of the time we spend together.

His brow raises, but his eyes remain steadily on me. "Are *you* fucking anyone else?"

"No, of course not," I say quickly, then reconsider my answer. I don't need him thinking it's because I want some sort of commitment from him, so I add, "I don't have time to even go out and look. But I just didn't expect the same from you. It's not like we're—It's not like we're exclusive or anything. Like we said, this is casual. I just wanted to be sure you weren't cheating on anyone."

I clear my throat again, knowing I need to lighten this conversation before it gets too heavy. "Besides, aren't women constantly throwing their panties at you?" I joke. "I can't imagine you wouldn't have had the opportunity to crawl into bed with someone else."

"Opportunity, yes. Desire, no."

Okay. Clearly my attempt at humor isn't working, so I drop it. This time, my words are serious. "You're really saying you've only had sex the few days a month I'm here?"

"It's always worth the wait. You're the only one I want." He kisses my temple, lips lingering. I don't even care that we're in public. I think I *want* the attention. I want these people to know this man has somehow picked me and isn't ashamed of it. "And like you, I have my fantasies in the meantime."

"Don't say things like that," I murmur, dizzy from the impact of what he's told me. "It might go to my head."

I can feel his smile. He recognizes his own words thrown back at him. "Let it."

I don't think twice when I lean into him, savoring the way he holds me closer.

"How badly do you want dinner?" I ask him over the sound of the approaching train.

"Why?" he asks. The wind around us picks up, ruffling his hair.

Because I want to feel more of him, to reassure myself that this is real. "I'm just not that hungry."

"You need to eat. It's been a long day."

He hasn't gotten my hint, or if he has, he's more concerned with my well-being than getting me into bed. Does that mean this man… cares about me?

Crazy idea. Not possible. Unbelievable.

The train pulls to a stop, and we wait as some of the current passengers disembark before we join the masses cramming themselves into the cars. Again, he and I are pressed to each other, my back to his chest. There's not enough room for me to reach out for a handrail, but I'm not worried about falling.

Daniel's got me.

CHAPTER 27

I don't really want to be out at dinner right now, but I'm glad to be with Daniel.

He lets me order for myself this time, but not before giving me his top three recommendations. I don't fight him on it, simply because he does seem to know what I like. I choose one of the dishes he suggests, and I'm not disappointed one bit when it arrives. Even the wine he picks to pair with it is perfect. He's a man of many talents, semiprofessional sommelier being one of them, apparently.

He pours the last of the wine into my glass as the server clears our plates. I'm pleasantly warm without being drunk, so a little more won't do me in. Once he sets the empty bottle down, he picks his own glass up, though he doesn't take a sip yet. He's too busy watching me.

For the past hour, he's been like this—quiet and assessing. He's answered all the questions I've asked, about timelines for my physical books and all the way to what he does for fun on the weekends. He even responded to a joke about having more dates lined up with girls who work for our competition by unlocking his phone and sliding it across the table to me.

"No dating apps," he said, inviting me to swipe across the screen. "No dates on my calendar."

I pushed his phone back to him without a peek, but the message was clear. He trusts me to look. Wants me to know I really am the only one. "You don't have to prove anything to me."

"No, I don't have to," he agreed. "But I will. I want you to know."

"Why?"

It was the only question he didn't answer. He took a sip of his wine instead. From there, I turned the conversation back to safer topics, or as safe as talking about work could be.

We've just finished shitting on the latest movie JotNote produced and silence has fallen between us, but it's not awkward. There's tension, as always. The kind I shouldn't welcome yet absolutely do.

Maybe it's the quiet or maybe it's the wine, but I find myself again asking the question that's been on my mind since our first night together. Last time, his answer was vague; I'm determined to get the real story this time.

"You never did tell me why you went after me."

Daniel finishes off his wine, leaving the silence to hang a little longer. A faint hint of red lingers on the rim of the glass as he places it on the table. When I look up at him, I find the matching shade on his bottom lip. I want to kiss it off.

"I did say you were interesting," he reminds me.

"That's not enough of a reason to fuck someone you hate," I counter.

"You think I hate you?"

I hesitate, because the answer is an obvious no at this point. He wouldn't be making this much of an effort if he did. And I can't say I hate him either, even if my feelings toward him sway in the *intensely dislike* direction every so often.

"I don't know," I lie. "Do you hate me, Daniel?"

He's quiet again as he takes a moment to scan the restaurant around us. A few beats later, he says, "I remember the first time you came into the Naiad office. You were wearing what was possibly the most hideous sweater I've ever seen. It had all these ugly little hearts on it."

His confession surprises a laugh out of me. "Oh my God, you're such a dick," I say, covering my amusement with a scoff. "That sweater was cute. You just have boring taste in fashion."

A ghost of a smile touches his lips as he shakes his head, still not looking at me. "You're missing the point, Selene. I wouldn't have remembered what you were wearing that day if I hadn't been paying close attention to you."

"It sounds like the sweater alone was enough to make an impression," I say dryly, swirling the remaining wine in my glass.

"*You* were the one who made the impression. The ugly sweater just made it stick."

I roll my eyes at his continued insults. "What exactly are you trying to tell me? Do you hate me or not?"

"I hated you immediately," he answers, his eyes snapping to mine. The intensity in them makes me want to draw back a little. "I thought you were brash and annoying. You made my job even more difficult, and all I wanted was for you to shut up every time you opened your mouth to demand something else."

"Be very careful with what you say next, Santiago." I can already tell I won't like it. "There's still wine in my glass. It could end up in your face."

He doesn't even blink at my threat. "I knew you were a great writer and added value to the company, but my God, every day I wondered if you were worth the hell you brought into my life."

"Funny, I felt the same way about you," I drawl, back to swirling the wine, prepared to toss it if need be.

"Turns out you were absolutely worth it." He leans in and plants his forearms on the table, leaving me unable to escape his gaze. "I started to realize how brilliant you are over the summer. You have a way of dealing with authors like no one else can. You're the only person who can keep these stories going for thousands of chapters without complaints that they're boring. You always expect the best of yourself and everyone else, no exceptions, even if it nearly kills you to do it. And despite your terrible taste in sweaters, I've been attracted to you since the first second I laid eyes on you."

My heart thuds hard and fast as I take in his words. "But you hated me," I point out. "What does it matter if you were attracted to me?"

"Because I finally realized my attraction was beginning to outweigh my hate."

Once again, I could say the same thing about him. I wouldn't be sitting here tonight if my hate for him hadn't waned. But I have to protect my heart. I have to make sure all of what he's saying is real before I let him in. What he's done and said so far has cracked open the door, but I'm waiting for him to push it all the way open and step inside.

"So you realized I wasn't so bad over the summer," I lay out. "But you didn't make a move on me until the holiday party."

At that, a little of his intensity fades, then a spark of humor reappears in his eyes. "I've been calling you oblivious for a reason."

I freeze and think back, searching my memory for moments when Daniel might have hinted that he was into me. There's only one recently that comes to mind.

Steal all of my time, if you want.

But before that, before we returned to the office, were there other clues?

A memory hits me hard. Back in June, when we were still negotiating terms with Kimmy Petes and spending six hours a day brainstorming ideas, Daniel sat in on a few of those meetings. Usually, only production team members joined, but to my absolute annoyance, Daniel insisted on involving himself.

Since Kimmy was almost always late to our meetings and the other production girls didn't bother to join the Zoom call until Kimmy was ready to start, I was often the only person in the room for the first few minutes…until Daniel appeared.

Kimmy had gotten snippy with us the day before, worse than she usually did, going so far as to insult my abilities to create a captivating storyline. I wasn't looking forward to spending another full day with her, and I'd been psyching myself up to keep a straight face every time she shot down one of my ideas.

My exhaustion must have shown, because the first thing Daniel said to me that morning was, "Don't lose sleep over someone who isn't as talented as you are."

I snorted at his words, sure he didn't mean them. Or if he had, it was only for the benefit of the company—he didn't want me walking away from such a huge project lest Naiad lose money because of it.

Then there was the entire month of July when he randomly put a series of one-on-one meetings on my calendar. Those half-hour chats had been a waste of my time. Daniel used them to check up on my progress regarding the stories I was working on so he could report back to their respective authors. I had gone along with the check-ins until I complained to the other production girls about it, hoping to commiserate with them, only to find out that none of them were being forced into the meetings like I was.

"He's not our boss," Nikki pointed out. "He has no right to demand those kinds of updates from you. He can wait until our weekly team meeting for that information. Why's he singling you out like that?"

"Because he hates me," I replied, then pulled up my calendar and declined the invite for next week's one-on-one. He didn't send another after that.

Then in August he— Well, it doesn't matter what he did. I see the pattern now.

"You've been trying to get my attention this whole time." I say the words, but my brain hasn't caught up yet. It's still too twisted by the realization.

"Like I said," Daniel murmurs. "Oblivious."

I adjust in my seat, trying to ignore how flustered I suddenly am. "Or you were just too subtle," I huff.

He shrugs, frustratingly at ease, while I'm over here barely resisting the urge to fan myself. "It worked eventually."

I drain the rest of the wine in my glass and slam it down. I *have* been oblivious, and I only see what he was doing now because he forced me to stop and think back. "All those times I thought you were being condescending and smirky," I say, trying to fit all the puzzle pieces together in my head. "Were you flirting with me?"

"Not all the time."

So I wasn't completely clueless. That makes me feel a little better.

"Sometimes you really did annoy the hell out of me," he finishes.

"But other times…definitely flirting?"

Daniel clasps a dramatic hand to his chest and tilts his head back. "Finally, she notices."

I scowl and nearly flip the table as I shove back my chair. "Oh my God, Daniel. That wasn't flirting. That was trying to start a fight!"

He drops the theatrics and stares me down, but his hand stays over his heart. "Same thing for us, no?"

I take a moment to consider that. "You know what?" I grudgingly admit. "True."

It's so fucking true. It's like we don't know how else to act around each other. But can we learn? If not, this is bound to spiral into some sort of toxic nightmare we'll never survive.

But haven't things already changed? We still throw barbs at each other, and I don't see that ever ending, but we know when we've gone too far and when to walk it back. We're learning about each other and the boundaries we can push. That's normal for any type of relationship, sexual or not, even for people who used to truly hate each other. Things between us are already lighter, and yet the heat continues to simmer.

I shake my head and run a hand through my hair. After hearing all of this, I don't know where we go from here. It's clear that this is no longer casual—and from what he's divulged tonight, it likely never was for him. I don't think it has been for a while for me either, no matter how much I tried to fight it.

But how do we go from no-strings hookups to bringing our real feelings out in the open?

As if reading my mind, Daniel asks, "Where do we go from here, Selene?"

Already, it feels like he knows me better than I know myself. I'll take it as a sign that we're doing something right. "Why do I have to be the one to decide?"

I throw the question back at him to deflect, even though all I want is to drag him back to my hotel room and have my way with him. From there, though? I don't know, but I'm excited to find out.

"Because, out here," Daniel answers, lifting a hand to lazily motion to the world around us, "you're in charge of what happens. You tell me to leave you alone, I leave you alone." He angles closer, his arms on the table again, and pitches his voice low. "But if you let me take you back to your hotel room, you won't be in charge anymore."

A shiver rolls down my spine at the promise in his voice. God, how I've missed what he does to me, even without a single touch.

"So, what's it going to be, *mi amor*?" he asks. "What do you want from me?"

CHAPTER 28

Daniel kisses my neck as we stand in the crowded subway car, soft butterfly touches that could be perceived as innocent if I didn't know where this was headed. It's blatant PDA, the kind I probably wouldn't allow from anyone else, and something I never expected from a man I thought was cold and incapable of emotion. This public declaration is proof that I was wrong all along.

The people around us have to notice what he's doing, but the best thing about New York is that no one cares. Here, everyone is in their own little world, including us.

"You called me shameless once," I remind him. My words are barely audible over the screech of the wheels on the track and the wind rushing through the narrow open windows. "But I think that title belongs to you."

"Guilty," he says between kisses, the possessive arm around my waist tightening as the train sways.

Every time his lips meet my skin, my pulse quickens. And when his fingers trace patterns on my ribs, my breathing joins the race. Then he backs off, allowing my heart rate to slow and my breaths to even out, until he starts all over again.

He knows what he does to me, and there's no doubt that he's reveling in the power he has over me. This is a man who loves to edge me both in and out of the bedroom. And I look forward to it every time, no matter how much I protest to the contrary.

"You're a tease as well," I accuse, placing my hand over his to keep it from moving.

He smiles. "A tease? Really?" His nose brushes up my jaw until his mouth is at my ear. "How exactly am I a tease, Selene?"

I swallow hard and stand with my feet a little closer together to ease the growing ache between my legs. "Because there are still three more stops before ours, and you have the nerve to touch me like that."

"Like what?" The question is innocent, but the way he presses against my back—and what I feel of him when he does—is far from it.

"You're the worst." I'm struggling to find my breath. "I hate you."

His laugh simultaneously boils my blood and sends heat blooming within me. "I know, baby."

Time slows, drawing out the torture, but once the train pulls up at the last station on our journey, I'm the one dragging Daniel out the doors, up the steps, and onto the packed streets of the city. I don't bother looking back at him; with his hand curled around mine, I don't have to worry about him following along or getting lost in the crowd. And once again, I find myself not caring who sees us.

I only glance at him once we're pushing through the doors of the hotel lobby, taking in the intensity of his gaze on me. "What?"

Daniel gives my fingers a small squeeze as I tug him toward the bank of elevators. "One more chance to back out."

My heart stutters. Why would I want to back out? I thought I made it abundantly clear that I want more—more of this, more of him, more of the sparks we create together. We can't predict whether they'll fizzle out, but for now, I want to fan the flames.

"I'm not backing out," I tell him. "I want this." *I want you.* "Do you?"

For a brief, sick moment, I worry that he's silently trying to convey that he doesn't want this anymore. That he wants an out for himself without having to be the one to say it. It's an outrageous thought, especially considering all that he's declared to me at various points today, but the doubts still linger.

Before I can get too lost in the spiral, I'm jerked back out of it. Because there it is, making its triumphant return—the fucking condescending smile I want to slap off his perfect face.

"Selene," he says, a tinge of disappointment in his tone. "You were doing so well."

I shrink in on myself at the reminder that I've been so oblivious to his advances. How could I have missed so many hints?

I know he can feel my embarrassment, because the smile falls away as he hits the button for the elevator and tugs me to his chest.

The humor in his eyes is gone. All that remains is a glint of worry. "What the fuck do I keep doing to make you think I don't want you?"

I'm still recovering from the brush-off and the alleged date, even after learning the truth. But what it really comes down to are my own insecurities. In the past, I've been led to believe I was wanted, only to discover it was a lie. Or that the desire was conditional. Only if I acted a certain way or played by someone else's rules. They didn't want *all* of me—just bits and pieces or what they could get out of me. I don't know what it's like to be wanted as a whole person.

But he doesn't know that because he doesn't know me, not really. I haven't given him the chance to know me out of fear that this could end at any second and my heart would be crushed when it did.

I open my mouth, ready to tell him that I'm the problem. That my hang-ups are the issue here, but the elevator doors slide open before I can. Without hesitation, Daniel guides me along behind him until we're both inside. He studies me expectantly as I hit the button for the twenty-second floor, then duck my chin, hoping he can't see how red my cheeks are. Thankfully, no one else joins us in the awkward few seconds before the doors shut, giving us the privacy I've been desperate for since we left the office.

Daniel lets go of my hand in favor of cupping my face and forcing me to look at him. "Don't push me away," he murmurs, his gaze searching. "Just let me in, Selene."

I don't know what to say to his pleas—so I simply brace my palms on his chest, push up onto my tiptoes, and brush my lips over his. It's a ghost of a kiss, an open invitation. A whispered *come in*. The door is fully open now; it's up to him to step through. I've already made my choice.

In response, Daniel leans down for a proper kiss, sending relief coursing through me. He slides one hand behind my neck to keep me in place while the other lingers on my cheek. When his tongue strokes over mine possessively, there's no question about who or what he wants.

Heat pools low in my stomach, like it always does when his hands are on me. I run my fingers through his hair, wanting to pull him closer, desperate for more. I crave it. Crave him.

We break apart for breath just as the elevator doors reopen. It takes a moment before I'm coherent enough to guide him in the direction of my room. I fumble in my bag for the key, but before I can get a grip on it, Daniel slips it from my fingers and taps it against the sensor. Then he's pushing down on the handle with more coordination than I could have dreamed of and pulling me inside.

The second the door is shut behind us, he drags me back to him and kisses me again, leaving me simultaneously melting into his arms and shocked by the electric current that passes between us. It steals my breath away as he backs me against the wall, and I nearly whimper when his lips leave mine. I haven't had enough of him, not yet.

"Last chance," he whispers against my ear. "After this, I'm not letting you walk away."

I could say the same to him. There's no way I can give him up now, no matter how dangerous he is for my heart.

Instead, I smile slowly and tell him, "If I can walk after this, then you've done something wrong."

CHAPTER 29

Daniel's laugh makes me feel like I've unlocked a secret treasure.

He rests his forehead against mine, his chest rumbling with amusement as he squeezes the softness of my hips. I wasn't expecting my little throwaway line to get this kind of reaction, but I can't help but grin along with him.

"You're too much," he says so warmly that I nearly melt right out of his arms and into a puddle on the floor.

This moment is more intimate than any touch could ever be. To laugh with a lover is the ultimate test of compatibility, and knowing I can laugh with Daniel, that we can make fun of ourselves enough to do so... Well, I've already been sucked down the rabbit hole, so what's a bit more falling?

I lift my hands to playfully push him back. "I know I am," I tell with a smirk. "But you wouldn't want me any other way."

"You're right. I wouldn't."

He finds my lips again, easily closing the distance I put between us, his kiss sweet and playful. As much as I love the heat and anger and desperation of our previous encounters, this kind of affection makes my heart skip a silly little beat. Like I'm kissing a crush for the first time and learning how glorious it can be. It doesn't matter that we've done this dozens of times already; it feels like a novelty.

"Stop smiling," he murmurs against my mouth. "I know you find me amusing, but you're making this difficult."

"So try harder," I taunt, my heart still doing somersaults. "Make me stop."

At that, he pulls back to look me in the eye. There's a sparkle of pleased surprise in his dark depths. "Look at you," he says, impressed. "Daring me like that. What other moves of mine are you going to steal?"

I curl my fingers into his shirt and drag him to me, rolling my hips against his to tease a little more. "I won't call you a coward, I promise. That's all yours."

His grip on me tightens, making it impossible to break from his grasp—not that I want to. I want to feel all of him, right here, right now.

"Don't worry." His voice is tight, like he's holding himself back. "You won't have to."

His next kiss wipes the grin off my face. It's deep and sensual and leaves me perfectly breathless. It's the kind I write about, the kind that finally shows our heroine just how eager the love interest is to have her in his arms. I've had my fair share of knee-weakening kisses and heart-fluttering touches, but this? *This* is something else entirely.

No one else has ever made me feel this way, and in this moment, I can't imagine that anyone but Daniel ever will.

I reluctantly turn my head to take in a gasp of air. If I'm not careful, I'll implode before we get to the good stuff. Not that Daniel's mouth on mine isn't *the good stuff*—God, it's fantastic—but there's so much more in store for us tonight.

As I catch my breath, his lips trail over my neck and his hands slip beneath my unbuttoned coat and sweater. My muscles tense as his touch ghosts over the small of my back, then slips down to the waistband of my jeans and traces the fabric around until he reaches the button. His eyes flick back to mine, still asking permission every step of the way.

If I nodded any harder, I'd knock myself out.

He starts by pushing my coat off my shoulders and tossing it to the floor. Then he's got my sweater off and over my head. My lingerie is white today, beautiful sheer lace with little swirls like falling petals. Daniel steps back, admiring it for a moment, tracing the fabric covering my nipples, leaving them to harden in his wake. Before I can blink, his touch is on my back and he's unclasping my bra. He doesn't wait for the fabric to fall to the floor before his mouth brushes over one of my nearly bare breasts.

I sink my fingers into his hair and let my head fall back, relishing the way his tongue swipes across my nipple. He starts slow, like he wants to savor every taste of me, as if I'm nothing but deserving of his adoration. When his attention switches from one breast to the other, I hiss as cold air hits the abandoned skin, though Daniel is quick to cover it with his hand, squeezing gently and saving me from the sensation. Always so considerate, this man.

My breath comes in ragged pants, and the throbbing at my core becomes nearly unbearable. And he knows it. There's no hiding the way my chest heaves or how my hips seek out his. I don't bother to temper my eagerness as I fumble at his shirt in an attempt to get it off him.

I'm overwhelmed by need, and yet he moves at an agonizing pace.

"Don't edge me again," I warn him. I want to sound threatening, but my voice is barely above a whisper.

"I wouldn't dare."

As if to placate me, he unfastens the button of my jeans, then drags the zipper down. I let him peel the denim over my hips, a little disappointed when he stops there, but then his hand delves between my thighs and strokes me through my underwear once, twice, three times, before he drags the lace down too.

Once I kick off my shoes and step out of both my jeans and thong, he cups a palm over my pussy and slips his middle finger into me—testing me, teasing me. There's no need for it; I've been wet for him since we were on the subway platform. Dinner was practically foreplay.

I barely recognize the sounds that leave my lips when he pulls away and drops to his knees in front of me.

He wastes no time hooking my thigh over his shoulder to open me up to him. My clit is swollen, the skin glistening with evidence of my want for him. If he doesn't do something about it soon, I'm going to lose my mind.

"Is this all for me?" he murmurs. His voice is distant, muffled by the haze of lust surrounding me.

I force myself to focus again. When the fog clears, he's peering up at me, still absolutely in control.

His smirk turns me on and pisses me off at the same time. I'm so sick of the slow burn.

"You know it is," I groan, lifting my hips off the wall as if that will get him to finally put that mouth to work. "You're the only one who makes me like this."

There's a deep sound from the back of his throat, like a little of that control is slipping. "Be careful when you say things like that, Selene."

He brushes his lips along my inner thigh, placing open-mouthed kisses on the tender skin.

A new rush of fire surges through me, but he's still not where I want him. "Come *on*," I urge him.

He gives a disappointed murmur, the gentle vibration enough to make me gasp. "Say please."

"No."

"Say *please*."

I whine like a child denied her favorite toy. "Do you have to be such an asshole?"

"I don't know," he says, contemplating it as he moves ever closer but stops short. "Do you have to be such a brat?"

My hips buck again in protest, but he pins me to the wall with a hand splayed across my belly.

And the bastard laughs, mocking me. "You're lucky I like this so much."

"That makes one of us," I tell him, absolutely pained but somehow even more turned on. My words are a lie, though. I *do* like this. I love this push and pull. I love that he never makes it easy.

"Just say it," he coaxes, his voice a little lower, his accent a little thicker. "Come on. You can give me that, can't you?"

I could scowl and tell him to go fuck himself, but being together is about give and take, and right now, Daniel is poised to do most of the giving—but only if I allow myself to be vulnerable.

"Please, Daniel," I whisper as he trails a finger up to brush away some of the wetness that's eased down my thigh.

My legs nearly give out when he puts that same finger in his mouth, tasting me without contact. I watch, heart racing, as he pulls it back out and grips my ass.

Leaning close enough that I can feel his breath, he says, "I love it when you beg."

And just when I think he'll offer me some relief, he shifts away again to place more kisses over my hipbones.

I have to bite back a curse of disappointment. Is he serious right now?

His eyes flick up to me, dancing with amusement. "Is something wrong, *mi amor*?"

I'm hot all over from anger and arousal. "You know damn well what's—"

And then the wet heat of his tongue runs up my pussy, seeking out my clit and drawing a surprised moan from my lips. I throw my head back against the wall and lift my hips, chasing more. When he slides a finger into me and crooks up, I nearly collapse.

I grip his hair and pull to get him to slow down, hissed curses leaving my lips. But he adds another finger instead, clearly set on making me come as hard and as fast as possible. After all his slow motions, this change in pace is a shock. Yet it's torture in itself.

"Daniel," I beg, though I don't know what I'm begging for. For release? For him to keep doing exactly this forever? Whatever it is, the only coherent word I can form is his name.

Even if I don't know what I want, he knows what I deserve. His other hand drifts up from my ass to my lower back, forcing me to arch a little more, pushing me further against his face no matter how much I want to pull away. It's too much, too intense, but I can't fight it.

I'm at his mercy. I come undone.

As I descend from the high, too sensitive to bear his touches, I push him away. It's like the world has tilted on its axis as I grip the wall and try to catch my breath. Daniel has stolen every molecule of oxygen from my lungs, and I can't even begin to complain.

On the floor in front of me, he sits back on his knees like a religious man just finishing a prayer. In a way, I suppose he has. His hair is a little more disheveled thanks to my fingers, but his satisfied smile is the same. It's the look in his eyes, though, the intensity of his stare, that throws me further off-kilter.

"You're even more beautiful when you come," he says, slowly rising to his feet.

I track him all the way up, still blinking away the fog. "Why are you still dressed?"

"Why do you always ignore my compliments?"

"Because they're just words." I don't mean to be so honest. It's like I'm orgasm drunk. The filter between my brain and mouth is completely gone. "Sometimes people don't mean what they say. Sometimes they lie to get me to like them. Actions mean more to me."

"I'm not lying." He runs his hands up my arms and scrutinizes me. "Who made you feel like that?"

"It doesn't matter." Not when Daniel's in front of me, proving that he's not one of the bad guys. I push off the wall, my legs feeling like jelly, but I manage to take a step toward him. "Now take off your clothes."

I expect him to resist, to force me to talk about past hurts now that the topic has come up. But instead, he reaches behind him and pulls his T-shirt off in one smooth move. He keeps his focus locked on my face as he undoes his belt buckle, daring me to command him again. I don't bother. Instead, I reach forward to roughly unbutton his jeans and slide my fingers past the waistband of his boxers. I'd rather show him what I want.

He inhales sharply as I wrap a hand around his cock and stroke steadily, twisting a little over the slick head. I'm not the only one who's more than ready for this.

"Ah, ah," he warns, grabbing my wrist and pulling my hand away. "I have amends to make. And I won't be using words." He turns me and nudges me toward the bed. To aid my compliance, he slides a hand up my neck and sinks his fingers into my hair, grasping firmly.

I don't resist. I'm too weak and too satiated. Right now, I'd let him do whatever he could dream of to me.

When my knees hit the mattress, he presses between my shoulder blades to get me to bend over. I brace my forearms on the bed and arch my back, pushing my ass against him. In response, I'm gifted with a satisfying groan. He curls over me a moment later, pulling my head to the side by my hair so he can kiss up my neck, sucking and biting my skin the whole way.

"Spread your legs for me," he says, nudging my feet apart with one of his. "Wider."

I gladly obey, letting my eyes flutter shut at the sound of fabric rustling and the ripping of a foil wrapper. A shiver of anticipation slithers down my spine. When his fingers trace the same path from the base of my neck, I let out a breathy moan. It doesn't matter that he's already brought me to heaven and back—I still want more.

My hands fist in the sheets as he slides into me in one slick thrust. The sudden fullness has me tensing at first, needing a moment to adjust, because every time we do this, I underestimate how much I have to take.

As I breathe through it, he lowers his lips to my ear, murmuring, "Is this too much?"

Cheek pressed to the mattress, I shake my head, swallowing back a sob of pleasure. "Don't stop."

His lips linger for a moment as he kisses my temple. "What was that?"

He heard me just fine, but again, I have to give him what he wants in order to get mine. "Please don't stop," I whisper.

"There. That's my girl."

I moan as he pulls out a little. Then he pushes back in, his strokes steady and shallow as he eases me into taking more of him, but it's not long before he picks up the rhythm. After that first orgasm, I'm even more sensitive to the friction, and with the rough way he fucks, it's not long before the pressure building low in my belly threatens to pour over.

I pant his name in desperation as he clutches at my hips, holding me in place so I can't buck against him like I want to. Need to. My thighs tremble, and a wave of heat sweeps over my body, preparing me for the deep release he's brought me all the way up to.

But as I'm at the precipice, he pulls out.

I gasp, confused and lightheaded. I was *so close*. "No, Daniel, please,

I need—"

My pleas are cut short when he wraps an arm around my waist and hauls me onto the bed so I'm flat on my stomach and covers my body with his. We're skin to skin from shoulder to knee, his breath on my cheek, his lips seeking mine as I turn my head to the side. I whimper against his mouth, almost frenzied enough to implore him to keep fucking me, though I get some relief when his hand slides under my body and finds my clit.

"Trust me," he says, working his fingers in slow circles. "I'll give you what you want."

When he sinks back into me, I moan into the pillow and claw at the sheets. The new angle hits a spot that makes me writhe. His thrusts are slow and deliberate now, nothing like the brutal heat a few moments ago. But this… Oh God, this is somehow even better.

He cradles and surrounds me, stretches me, fills me until I'm consumed by him. His breaths are ragged in my ear, his coaxing gentle, urging me to stay with him through this, even though all I want to do is squeeze my eyes shut and beg him to let me come.

My whole body is heavy, like a storm cloud threatening to burst. With a hand behind my back, I blindly grasp at him, as if that will help me get to where I want to be. But Daniel grabs my wrist and pulls it above my head, pinning it down as he pushes into me with more force than before.

He continues his torturous circles around my clit with his other hand as he drags his lips across my jaw and mumbles slurred Spanish in my ear. The vulgar words and the sound of skin on skin send a rolling shudder through me. I lift my trembling free hand to touch his cheek.

With a tenderness that juxtaposes the way he's pounding into me, he kisses the inside of my wrist.

It sends my pulse up to dangerous levels. My breathing grows ragged as I chase the high he keeps just out of reach. It threatens to ruin me. Break me. And I finally crack when he exhales my name like a devotion.

I want to scream, to verbalize my release, but it rocks me so hard that all I can manage is a whimper that catches in my throat as euphoria pulses through me.

"That's it, baby," he says. "Ride it out. I've got you."

I know he does. I've known it all night.

And I never want him to let me go.

CHAPTER 30

"Do you think you can walk? Or did I fuck you right?"

Eyes half-closed, lying limp on my stomach with Daniel's weight on my back, I smile into the pillow. "I couldn't walk even if I wanted to," I mumble against the fabric, sighing as he kisses down my spine.

His every touch is tender. He may fuck me like I'm unbreakable, but afterward, he's nothing but gentle. Every caress is meant to heal.

"Do you need to go?" I ask. He never stays long, and I thought that was how we both wanted it, but now I'm not so sure.

It doesn't make sense for him to stay over anyway. Showing up at the office wearing yesterday's clothes wouldn't be ideal. He's a man, so I doubt anyone would really notice, but he doesn't seem the type to want to do that. Then again, what do I know?

He shakes his head, his stubbled jaw brushing my skin as he presses a kiss to the small of my back. "No," he says. "I'll stay awhile."

I let out a contented sound, a little surprised but mostly pleased that he isn't leaving.

This isn't just about sex anymore. There's an intimacy now that's caught me off guard. I'm not quite sure what to make of it, or if it will even last, but…I want it to.

The thought scares me more than it probably should, but the last time I opened up to that kind of attachment, I got my heart broken.

Being willing to put myself out there again after years of being happily single would be a big step, and to do it with Daniel, someone I shouldn't be with for a variety of reasons, is a huge risk.

The environment at Naiad is undeniably relaxed, and our HR department is really only around to handle payroll and company events, so maybe it wouldn't be such a big deal. But I can't forget that nagging clause about fraternization.

Not to mention I'm one of our acquisition authors as well. Any favors done for me—like Daniel pushing to produce physical copies of my books without the stats to back it up—could get one or both of us into serious trouble. And could mean losing our jobs.

So is this—whatever it is—worth the risk?

"When do you go home?" Daniel asks, drawing me out of my thoughts as he kisses his way back up to my shoulders.

"Tomorrow after work," I answer, a little disappointed that I can't stay longer. That I can't stay *with him* longer.

"And when will you be back?"

I crack open an eye and turn my head so I can see him in my periphery. "I don't know. I haven't scheduled it with Jim yet. Why? Are you planning something?"

"I just want to know when we can do this again."

I freeze under his touch. What exactly does he mean by *this*? Because, so far, all it's been is fucking, misunderstandings, and weird not-exactly-a-date dinners. Should I expect more of the same? Or will it be something else entirely?

"What does that mean?" I ask.

Not only do I need to know what he wants out of our arrangement going forward, but if we're going to continue, we should discuss the chances we're taking with Naiad. We were careless today, and there could still be blowback. But if we keep doing this, the chances of being discovered will grow exponentially. I have to know if he's okay with facing that.

Daniel sighs against my neck. "How much more obvious do I have to make it for you?"

Here we go again. Another patronizing little comment because I can't read his mind, struggling to process how we went from hating each other to...*this*. I don't know what risks he's willing to take. If he can't be transparent with me, then fine—I'll do it for the both of us.

"You think you've made it obvious?" I challenge him, dislodging him so I can roll over. Once we're lying side by side, facing each other, I elaborate. "Daniel, I'm here once, maybe twice a month. We barely talk between my trips. We've been doing this for months, and I don't even have your phone number. I have to fucking *Slack you* when I want to talk."

I draw in a breath, fighting to keep my composure. "You're attracted to me; I get that. You want to fuck me; I get that too. But other than that? I don't know what you want from me. Yes, you've explained what happened last month, but even so, you made me feel like I was just some lay you wanted to avoid. And I never want to experience that again."

I cringe when my voice cracks a little. I hate being vulnerable like this, but I refuse to keep dragging things out with this man if I don't know where we're headed. "You're here living your own life, and I don't know how I fit into that," I push on. "You've never made that clear. For all I know, one day, you'll show up in a relationship with the girl of your dreams and this will all end. I don't even know what *this* is."

"Why do you think it would be me in the relationship?" he questions, ignoring everything else I've said. "Why not you?"

Because I'm in deep with you already. "I'm not dating around."

"Neither am I."

I groan and cover my face. What am I not saying right? "It's not just about that." I drop my hands and give him a pleading look. "You asked what I wanted from you. But what do you want from *me*?"

He examines me, his dark eyes guarded, unreadable. "Get your phone," he finally says.

Unbelievable. I pour my heart out, and that's all he says? "Are you serious right now?"

"Get it," he insists. "And unlock it."

I huff and push myself up from the bed. I rip off the duvet to wrap around me, wincing at the soreness between my legs. Storming over to where I've left my purse by the door, I curse under my breath. The nerve. I should toss him out, not humor him. But here I am, rustling through notebooks, pens, and receipts until my fingers curl around my phone. I punch in my passcode, then toss the device to him. My anger only grows when he catches it with ease.

"There," he says a moment later as I glower at him from beside the bed. "Now you have my number."

He holds the phone out to me, and I snatch it back. Sure enough, his name is in my contacts.

"Stop doubting me, Selene," he says, dragging my attention back to him. "And stop doubting yourself." He holds his hand out to me. "Now drop the duvet and get back in bed. I'm not done with you."

I'm hesitant as I put my phone on the bedside table, but I do as he commands, letting the white fabric slip through my fingers. Daniel watches as it drops to the floor, eating up every inch of my bare skin.

"Come here, *mi amor*." The endearment doesn't sound like a taunt this time. "Come back to bed."

It takes a beat, but I kneel on the mattress, though that's as far as I go. He has me on my back in no time, pinned by his hips. He's not hard yet, but the feel of him stirring makes me want him inside me again, despite my better judgment.

"If you come to the city again this month, I won't be here. I'll be out of town for the next two weeks." He grasps my chin so I can't avoid his stare. "But next month, I want to have a weekend with you. I want to take you on a real date."

My heart is in my throat. If giving me his number was a tiny step, then this is a massive leap. This is Daniel's declaration. He wants more than a no-strings-attached situation, and he's not afraid of our company finding out about us. And it seems there truly is an *us* now.

I resist the urge to ask *are you sure that's a good idea?* Instead, I swallow back my doubts and tell him, "I'll come up Saturday night. That's the best I can do."

"I'll be waiting." He doesn't let go of my chin as he lowers his lips to mine. He kisses me slow and sweet, then pulls back a fraction of an inch and murmurs, "But I'll give you something to tide you over until then."

When his hand finally leaves my face and traces lower, I know I'm going to be thinking about his touch until I can feel it again.

CHAPTER 31

I can hear Carly in the kitchen when I step into our apartment. I drop my suitcase and purse by the door and call out, "Honey, I'm home!"

She pops her head around the corner, her bouncing curls framing her smiling face. "Perfect timing. Dinner's almost ready. Can you grab the plates?"

I nod and do as instructed, then watch as she plates the lasagna and pulls a tray of garlic bread from the oven. I'm going to cry the day she moves in with her boyfriend.

Dinner in hand, we curl up on the couch and turn on an episode of a show we've watched a million times already. I have to stifle yawns between bites of food, because thanks to Daniel, I didn't get much sleep last night.

Worth it.

Carly throws me a concerned glance when I yawn for what has to be the tenth time. "You always come back from New York so exhausted," she says. "Are you sure you have to go up there twice a month? Seems like a lot for a job that's supposed to be remote."

If only she knew why I've been going up there more often. I still haven't told her about what's going on with Daniel. She's heard my rants about him, and she's talked me off the ledge more than once when I've threatened to commit homicide. So when I do break the news, I expect it will come as a shock to her. I don't think there will be anyone more surprised (other than myself) that he and I have developed feelings (other than hate) for each other.

I'm going to have to tell her at some point, especially if this date goes well and we decide to take things to the next level—whatever that is. But if it goes horrifically awry or if we decide we're not compatible outside of the bedroom…I'll be glad that I never said anything to her.

So for now, I'll continue to keep my best friend in the dark.

"It's nice to see everyone in person." I shrug. "Makes meetings easier too. And if I get to hang out in the city for a few days every month on their dime, I'm not going to complain." I set my plate on the coffee table and pick up my glass of water. "But I'm not going back until April, so you're stuck hearing me complain about sex scenes for the rest of the month."

Carly snickers and stretches her legs out into my lap. "Gee, I'm so lucky. As long as my boss doesn't overhear you shouting about why one didn't have the proper emotional impact again."

I cringe at the memory. I was in the middle of a heated but friendly argument with Nikki about why an arc we were plotting wouldn't have the proper emotional payoff with the sex scene she wanted. I carried my laptop out of my room and padded to the kitchen to refill my water bottle, keeping my rant going as I went—only to realize Carly was sitting in front of her own laptop in the living room, having a one-on-one with her boss.

"I promise I'll never take my meetings outside of my bedroom again."

She grins and snuggles into the couch. "It's good he found it funny, especially after I explained what you do for a living."

"It's a little weird, isn't it?" I ask, laughing as I let my head fall back against the couch cushions. "But it's fun. And it pays the bills."

It's also introduced me to a man I've somehow started to fall for.

WORK FOR IT

I couldn't have written it better myself.

After two more episodes and another piece of garlic bread, I retreat to my bedroom to unpack.

I'm in the middle of dumping all my clothes into the hamper when my phone buzzes on my bed. I scoop it up and open the text my mother sent. She's checking in to make sure I made it home safely and to ask about whether I'm coming over for dinner this week.

The answer to both is yes—I hardly ever miss a Friday dinner at my parents' house. Mostly because my grandmother would kill me if I did. That's why I told Daniel that the earliest I could come back to the city was on a Saturday.

But now that my phone is in my hand and I'm thinking about him, I realize I never sent him my number. We were a little busy after he saved his contact information in my phone, and this morning, my sole thoughts revolved around how I was going to make it through eight hours of work.

I could have texted him at any point, but I didn't want to run the risk of a coworker peeking over my shoulder and seeing his name on my screen. By the time he covertly nodded goodbye to me at five o'clock, the only thing on my mind was making my five-thirty train and getting some last-minute editing done once I'd found my seat.

Now, though, I'm hesitant to text him, and there's no way I'm calling him. It's juvenile, but part of me doesn't want him to know I'm thinking about him late at night, like some teenager pining over her crush. Then again, so what if I am? If anything is going to bloom between us, I have to stop being so hesitant.

So fuck it. I tap on his name and pull up a new message. I type a simple, *Hey, it's Selene* and hit send before I can think twice. When I catch myself staring down at my phone, waiting for a response, I groan and toss the device onto my bedside table. It can stay right there for the rest of the night.

After showering and changing into pajamas, I'm ready to pass out. I switch off the light and climb between my sheets, grateful to be sleeping in my own bed. As much as I love being in New York and my nights with Daniel, the hotel life gets old pretty quickly. I've never asked if we could go back to his place, mainly because I'm sure my hotel was closer every time. And, well, before last night, that would have been entirely too personal.

Besides, if he lives somewhere like Brooklyn or (God forbid) New Jersey, there was no way in hell I wanted to go all the way out there just to have to commute back to Midtown in the morning.

Honestly, though, I should probably know where he lives. Right?

I run through a list of increasingly outrageous options as I drift off—maybe he lives in a penthouse on the Upper East Side, a mansion in Connecticut, or a cave in the sewer where he's king of the rats—but the sound of my phone buzzing on my nightstand pulls me back to consciousness.

I grab for it without thinking, and my heart seizes when I see the name *Daniel Santiago* on the screen.

Go to bed, his message reads. *I know I wore you out.*

I roll my eyes at the nerve, but it doesn't stop me from smiling. Because, as much as it pains me to admit, his smug little comments endear me to him even more.

I think about replying. Something along the lines of he can't tell me what to do. If this were happening in a book I had to write, that text would lead to sexting, and then a steamy dream.

But since this is real life, it's Daniel who messages again, putting an end to things before they can even begin.

Sleep well, mi amor.

CHAPTER 32

When I pull up to the curb in front of my parents' house for dinner, my mother and grandmother are waiting for me at the front door, watching my every move like hawks.

Mama pushes the storm door open and waves me inside while Teta tugs her shawl tighter around her shoulders, complaining in Arabic that my mother is letting in the cold.

"*Habibti*, get in here before you catch your death," Mama greets me, leaning farther out the door as if that will get me inside faster.

"It's not even that cold out," I tell her, but I hurry anyway, taking the stairs on the front stoop of the row house two at a time, just like I've done since I was a kid.

She scowls and practically pulls me into the house by my jacket, scolding me all the way for not zipping it up and wrapping my scarf improperly. "Baba's on his way back from the store," she says after the lecture. "I made sure he got all your favorites to take home."

This is part of the reason I visit at least once a week—they send me home with so much food that I rarely have to do my own grocery shopping. Between them and Carly, I'm always well fed.

Teta looks me over as I shrug off my outerwear. I can see in her eyes that she's about to counter what I was thinking. "You aren't eating enough." She pinches my waist through my sweater, and I nearly jump back. "You need to take better care of yourself. If you don't, you'll have to move home so we can feed you properly."

There's no use arguing with my grandmother. "I'll work on that."

Mama peers over my shoulder through the glass pane in the front door. "Where's Carly?"

"She's having dinner with her boyfriend's parents tonight."

"Such a good girl," Teta hums. Carly might as well be her granddaughter too; sometimes I think Teta loves her more than me. "When are they getting married?"

I shrug. "I don't know. We're still waiting for him to propose."

"He better do it soon," Mama comments as she shoos Teta and me toward the dining room. "Dating for three years?" She scoffs. "I married Baba after three *months*."

Teta agrees with a grunt, slipping her arm through mine so I can help her to her chair. "And what about you? When will you bring someone home to meet us?"

"Teta, come on," I groan. This is an evergreen conversation.

Since the moment I graduated from college, the pressure has been on to find a man, get married, and start popping out babies. When I decided to major in English and become a full-time writer instead of a doctor or a lawyer, I thought *that* would be a spot of contention between us, but my single status is the only thing they ever give me grief about. And now that I'm pushing twenty-six, the pressure is only growing.

"Your mama and I want babies to spoil," Teta practically begs. "Find a good boy and settle down. I keep telling you, all my friends at church have nice grandsons. *Single* grandsons. Good Lebanese boys."

"Does he have to be Lebanese? Baba's Palestinian," I point out as I escort her to her seat at the head of the table.

"Yes, yes, I know where he's from. I studied geography," she says, waving it off as she sits. "As long as he's a good boy who loves his mama, you should date him."

"I'll keep that in mind."

My mother and grandmother blow out matching beleaguered sighs and murmured prayers for me to find a man. If I was hesitant to tell Carly about Daniel, I certainly won't be telling these two until there's a ring on my finger.

Not that...not that I *expect* to ever wear his ring, but still. It's the principle of it all. Yeah. Right.

I'm saved from my horrific thoughts when my phone buzzes in the back pocket of my jeans. I excuse myself from the dining room and step into the hall as I pull it out, sure it's Carly calling since she's pretty much the only one who ever does.

But her name isn't flashing on the screen.

It's Daniel's.

There's no way I can take this call anywhere near my family. They'll ask who I'm talking to, and they'll know I'm talking to a man I like immediately. Despite a lifetime of trying, I've never been able to keep my mother and grandmother from reading my expressions.

Heart in my throat, I bolt upstairs to my old bedroom and shut the door. I pace the room my parents have kept as a shrine to my childhood, staring down at the screen. Do I answer? Do I let it go to voicemail and then text him to ask what he was calling about? Do I ignore it and hope it was a butt dial?

Don't be a coward.

I slide a trembling finger across the screen. "Hello?"

"Hi, Selene."

Just the sound of his voice sends something electric shooting through me. "Hi," I repeat, my voice embarrassingly breathy. "Everything okay?"

Why is he calling me out of the blue after nearly a week of no contact? We haven't spoken or texted each other since I sent him my number, so I can only assume he's calling now because something's up.

"Everything's fine," he answers.

I wait for him to say more, but that's it. Why is getting him to elaborate always a task and a half? "Okay…is there a particular reason you're calling?"

"Just wanted to hear your voice."

If I'd been falling slowly for him before, then that phrase has accelerated the process.

There's a clamor of a crowd in the background. Clearly, he's in the middle of something, but he's taken the time to call me.

Frowning a little, I ask, "Where are you right now?"

"Out."

"Out where?" I press.

"A bar. In Mexico City."

My jaw goes slack. "You're seriously calling me while you're at a bar in *Mexico*?"

"Yeah," he says easily. "I am."

My legs all but give out, and I drop to the edge of my bed. "Don't play."

"I'm not playing."

Laughter, clinking glasses, and conversations in Spanish echo down the line as I let his words marinate. "You really wanted to hear my voice that badly?"

"Is it so hard to believe that I think about you when we're apart?"

Swallowing hard, I tell him, "I guess not."

He gives a soft murmur, amused. "I already know you think about me. Do you miss me?"

I scoff, trying to force myself back to my senses, but I'm drowning. "Don't even go there."

"Ah, so you *do*." His warm voice wraps around me like an embrace. "Don't worry. You'll get to see me soon."

"Not soon enough." The words that escape my lips surprise me, leaving me to hold my breath while he's silent on the other end of the call.

"You really are dangerous," he finally murmurs. "You're going to have me flying back to New York early, aren't you?"

I laugh at that, blushing but empowered. Because I'm beginning to realize that maybe I have him wrapped around my finger. All I have to do is crook it to have him back with me. "Enjoy your night, Daniel. I'll see you next week."

"Like you said, not soon enough." His heavy sigh makes me smile. "Good night, Selene."

"Good night, Daniel."

No matter how much I want to, I won't abuse my power. Just knowing I have it is enough for now.

APRIL

CHAPTER 33

Daniel, hands shoved into the pockets of his coat, is waiting outside of my hotel when I turn the corner of 36th Street. Even though the day was warm, the night is bitterly cold for so-called spring. And yet he chose to wait out here instead of in the warmth of the lobby. I'm taking it as a sign of how eager he is to see me.

I feel the same way about him.

Seeing him now nearly feels like all my dreams have come true. It's yet another indicator that I've progressed past the point of having a minor crush to a major one. I've taken a step down the slippery slope, and there's no going back, even though it scares the absolute hell out of me.

And, okay, I'm a little embarrassed by it too. I don't know how to handle these kinds of feelings anymore. I haven't really, truly fallen for someone in so long. It doesn't matter that I write about it every day; now that it's happening to me, I'm trying not to fold in on myself, trying not to lose my fire. These big emotions are threatening to take over and weaken all the shields I've put up.

It's proving to be a challenge, though, because all I want to do is run in the opposite direction and pretend none of this is happening.

But I keep walking toward him.

He watches as I approach. Then, without a word, he pushes off the wall and follows me through the revolving door. There's no point in looking over my shoulder. He's there, even as I step up to the front desk to check in. I flash a smile at the woman and pull off my gloves, finger by finger, and give her my last name for the reservation.

I still don't glance back as he settles his hands on my hips and presses his own against my ass. It's stupid how flattered I am when I feel the bulge against my back. His enthusiasm matches mine in that respect. I'm already getting wet from the sheer anticipation of what's going to happen when we get upstairs.

The woman behind the counter flashes us a wide smile as she asks if we'd like two keys.

"Yes, please," Daniel answers, his voice low and smooth, igniting a flicker of attraction in the woman's eyes.

The jealousy that shoots through me is unwelcome, and yet I find myself leaning back into Daniel in response to it, smiling at the woman as I stake my claim. While I take the key cards she offers, I slip my free hand around my back to cup Daniel through his jeans, pleased when I feel him growing harder.

I shouldn't behave like this. I shouldn't let the attention of one random woman make me feel like my grip on a man I'm not officially committed to is slipping. And yet here I am, rubbing my palm over his cock in public like I'm unafraid of the consequences.

Keys in hand, I pass one back to Daniel, making sure to let our fingers brush as he takes it.

"Enjoy your stay," the woman says, still staring at Daniel. "Let me know if there's anything you need."

"Thank you," I tell her, tamping down on the sarcasm itching to break free.

Daniel wraps his arm around my waist, grabs my bag, and tugs me toward the elevators.

I still don't look at him as we step into one and head up to the eighteenth floor. It's not until we're in the room with the door shut that he steps in front of me and dips his head to meet my eyes.

"You were jealous," he says, the corner of his mouth pulling up. "You didn't like how she was looking at me."

I scoff as I shed my coat, staring over his shoulder instead of directly at him. If I make eye contact, my lies will be given away. "Why would I be jealous? People can look at you however they want. That's not my business."

"You were jealous," he repeats with a little more emphasis, leaving no room for argument.

As much as I want to, I won't keep trying to deny it. He has a way of always getting the truth from me.

"Fine," I huff, putting my hands up. "I was jealous. You're here with me, not her. I wanted to make sure she knew that, shitty as it was."

"Shitty, maybe," he concedes. "But I enjoyed it."

"So you *like* seeing me jealous?"

"No," he answers. "I like seeing you care."

I don't know what to say for a long beat. Frozen in place, scrutinizing him where he stands, I feel embarrassingly called out. Finally, I settle on, "Fuck *off*, Daniel."

That, for some reason, makes him laugh. Then he's pulling me into him and pressing his lips to mine. At first, I pout instead of kissing him back, leaving him to drop little kisses all around my mouth before pulling my bottom lip between his teeth, tugging and teasing me to open up.

"*Bésame*," he murmurs as he lets go. He hovers over my mouth, close enough that one subtle move would bring our lips together again. "Don't make me work for it."

I say nothing as I focus on the window behind him and bite my tongue.

He frowns and tilts his head. "I've embarrassed you." There's a hint of surprise in his tone. "You don't like the fact that you care about me. I'd go so far as to say you *like* me."

That gets my attention. Snapping my focus back to him, I glare, but once again, I can't deny his words.

"You like me," he repeats, and this time he's almost gleeful. "Oh, no wonder you're embarrassed. What a terrible thing."

"It is." I swallow hard, pushing back the emotion in my chest. "I'm not supposed to like you." And definitely not as much as I do.

"We can still pretend you hate me." His lips dip to mine again, and this time, I let him kiss me, light and lingering. "I won't tell anyone."

"But you know," I whisper. "And that's dangerous."

"It is. I might use it to my advantage."

"I'd rather you not."

"Too late."

He kisses me harder now, staking his claim and letting me claim him in return. It's acceptance of my feelings, of acknowledging his win. He's showing me that he's not the only one with a prize.

"Would it make you feel better if I said I liked you too?" he asks quietly, gathering me closer, brushing against my jaw with his stubbled cheek.

"Only if you mean it," I say weakly, letting him hold me up. I'm fully clothed, but I'm more exposed than I've ever been. The vulnerability aches in my chest. It fucking hurts, but it's the tradeoff for finally allowing him in.

"I like you, Selene," he tells me. "Even if you want to hate me."

This time, when our lips meet, he pushes his tongue into my mouth and coaxes mine forward, deepening the kiss. It's slow and lazy, like we have all the time in the world. I'll happily pretend that we do.

I'm dazed and lightheaded, like I've been drinking expensive champagne, when he pulls back.

"Let me take you out tomorrow."

Blinking, I clear away the spell he's put me under, registering what he's said. "Yeah? For that real date you mentioned?"

"Yeah, for that real date. It's long overdue."

I'd agree, but it's probably best that it's taken us this long. It proves that this isn't a fluke.

"What time should I be ready for this date?" I ask, stroking the back of his neck. "Should I wear anything in particular?"

"Be ready by nine a.m."

I tilt my head in surprise at the early time. Though he did say he wanted a weekend with me, so I suppose he plans to make the most of the time we have.

"And wear whatever you want, as long as you have something on underneath I can fantasize about."

I smile and bat my lashes, feeling a little of my power returning. "Don't I always?"

Daniel drops his head back for a moment and closes his eyes like he's fighting to keep his composure. "And you really have the nerve to doubt that I think about you constantly."

With his hands on my arms, he pulls them from around his neck and steps back from me.

I frown, confused by the distance he's put between us. "What are you doing?"

"Leaving," he says, zipping his jacket back up.

Now I'm truly baffled. What was the point of showing up here if he wasn't going to stay? "You don't…" I pause, fighting to find the words. "You don't want to have sex?"

"Not tonight."

My stomach churns, and embarrassment creeps up my neck. "Did I do something wrong?"

He chuckles and runs a hand through his hair. "Not at all," he admits. "I just want to save it for tomorrow."

The bulge in his jeans affirms that he's not turning down the opportunity because of a lack of desire.

"Why not both nights?" I challenge, because *goddamn*, I'm not sure I can hold out until tomorrow. I've been desperate for his touch for too long.

"Because with what I want to do to you, you wouldn't be able to get out of bed tomorrow," he answers, reaching over to cup my cheek and driving his point home. "If that were the case, we couldn't go on our date."

"Oh, so you're doing me a favor," I say dryly.

"Exactly." He leans in to kiss me one more time, hard and bruising. "I'll see you in the morning."

I whine, catching his hand in mine as he pulls back. "Can't you just go easy on me tonight?"

His answering grin is knee-weakening. "Baby, you know that's not possible. You'd never let me, and after being apart for this long, I can't trust myself not to give you exactly what you want."

"We could just cuddle," I try in one last ditch effort to keep him here with me, even if we both know we're not capable of *just* cuddling. As amped up as I am right now, I'd maul him after five minutes.

He brings our intertwined fingers up to his lips and presses a kiss to the back of my hand, his dark eyes holding mine. "I promise the wait will be worth it."

"It better be," I warn, but all I get in reply is another knowing smile and a goodbye.

I blow out a breath as the door closes behind him.

If this isn't the best date in history, I'm going to riot.

CHAPTER 34

There's a knock on my door at nine sharp.

"Let's go," Daniel says when I open it.

"Good morning to you too, sunshine," I tell him, zipping up my jacket. I've been awake since before six, waiting for the sun to rise and for him to show up.

I don't ask him where we're going. I just follow him out of the hotel lobby and in the direction of 7th Avenue.

"Breakfast first," he says, putting a hand on the small of my back as he guides me toward the closest subway stop.

On the train, we stand close, and his touch never leaves me. If it isn't a hand on my hip or my shoulder, it's his fingers brushing mine. These small moments of intimacy make me want more.

He takes me to a small eastern European bakery nearly a hundred blocks north and orders coffees and pastries with practiced ease, even holding a conversation with the older woman behind the counter. He asks about her daughters who are off at college. She asks him about his sisters, one back in Mexico, one in Spain, and the other here in New York.

"I didn't know you had siblings," I comment as he hands me a steaming cardboard cup. It only drives home how little we know about each other. We're still essentially strangers, despite how connected I feel to him.

"Three sisters," he tells me. "All younger. I can't stand them, but I'd do anything for them."

I nod and take a sip of my coffee as he gathers up our bags and ushers me out of the quaint shop. We arrived at the perfect moment; the line is now down the block and curving into the closed-off street. There are metal chairs and tables set up on the pavement outside the bakery, but Daniel walks past them.

"I know a nicer spot," he says, glancing at me over his shoulder.

I nod again and fall into step beside him, the brisk spring breeze blowing my hair back. Last night was cold, but now that the sun is out, the temperature is pleasant. I turn my face up toward the sky, letting the rays warm my skin. I nearly blush when Daniel takes notice and a hint of a smile lifts his lips.

"I love spring," I admit. "There's something about it that just feels so…fresh. Like a new beginning. What's your favorite season?"

It's a cheesy question, no doubt, but it's fitting for a first date. Despite knowing each other for years, we still have to learn the basics, and this is about as basic as it gets.

"I like spring too," he says, and I'm weirdly pleased to hear that tidbit of information. "More so the later part of it. Those weeks right before summer hits and everything gets disgusting."

"What, you don't like New York in the summer?" I tease. "The unbearable humidity? Sweating through your shirt after walking two blocks? The scent of weed, hot piss, and garbage?"

"Wow, you make it sound like a dream. I might have to change my answer."

The laugh he's fighting makes me grin in reply. So far, this date has proved that we can get along for more than five minutes.

We wander over to the Columbia campus—"My alma mater," he tells me—and set up on a wide concrete bench outside the library.

The stone walkway is flanked by lush green lawns, and the few trees lining the perimeter sway in the light morning breeze. I face him and sit cross-legged, watching as he unfolds a few napkins between us and displays our spread. There are croissants and almond pastries, plus fresh jams and creams. The absolute breakfast of champions.

My fingers hover over the carbs while I debate which to go for first, but Daniel hands me a croissant and nudges a tiny pot of apricot jam my way.

"Start with the best," he instructs, watching carefully as I smear a little of the jam on the end and take a bite. "*Está rico, no?*"

"That's an understatement," I say around a mouthful of buttery, flaky pastry. "This is the best croissant I've ever had in my life, and I studied abroad in Paris." I savor that first bite, forcing myself to take my time, then sip my coffee, working up the nerve to comment on something else I enjoy just as much as this croissant. "I like hearing you speak Spanish." I duck my chin a little, unsure. "Is that weird to say?"

He shakes his head as he dips a piece of his own croissant into the jam. "Not weird at all. It's my mother tongue."

"You sound more…relaxed," I explain. It's mostly for my own benefit, but I want him to know where I'm coming from. "More at home. Comfortable."

"I definitely worry less about fucking up what I want to say when speaking it." He laughs and shoots me a knowing glance. "I'm definitely blunter in English. It's not a language that leaves room for poetry."

"You're telling me," I commiserate. "Sometimes there are phrases in Arabic that I want to use in my writing, but the English equivalent doesn't do it justice."

He takes a bite of his croissant and chews slowly, his attention never swaying from me. "Considering your sales, I think you're doing a good job."

"But still not good enough to warrant having physical copies of my books without receiving inside help," I point out, keeping my voice light so he knows I'm not taking it too seriously. In the end, I'm getting exactly what I want. "Thank you for that, by the way. I'm not sure if I ever said it."

Daniel's dark eyes meet mine and hold. "Even if you did, you don't need to. It's long overdue. And you deserve it. You're a fantastic writer."

"I'm glad you think so," I murmur as I shove more croissant into my mouth to distract from the intensity of his stare. When I swallow again, I say, "How did you end up working for Naiad, anyway? You don't strike me as the romance novel–loving type."

He chuckles and glances away for a moment. "You're not wrong. The genre isn't my favorite," he admits. "I started working at Naiad as a favor to the old CEO, the one who stepped down right before you started. He was a friend from college who asked me to join his start-up. I was fresh out of business school, working at a hedge fund that bored me to death. So I agreed, thinking I'd be there for a year or two to pad my resume. Neither of us knew much about romance, but we both knew it was a huge market, so it was an easy sell." He flashes a wry smile. "Five years later, I'm still there, even though he's moved on to new ventures."

"But how can you buy these books to put on our platform if you don't even like them?" I shake my head. "Shouldn't someone who actually enjoys them be doing your job?"

"Probably," he confesses. "But disliking the genre doesn't mean I can't make objective decisions about the quality of writing and whether a work is destined to sell well."

"At least there's that," I say, lifting my coffee in a mock toast.

He taps his cup against mine. "My turn to ask a question."

I raise a brow, inviting him to do so.

"What made you want to write romance?"

It's a question I get often, but I never quite know how to answer past "I like love. And happy endings."

Of course, there's more to it, like *I write about it because I'm afraid I'll never experience it for myself.* But for now, this is what I'm going with.

"Ah, so you're a true romantic," Daniel says, like he's figured me all out.

"Yeah, I am," I admit freely, and I always will. There's absolutely nothing wrong with that. "I'm also a realist—I know that some of the scenarios in books don't work out in the real world, but some do. It's that hope that makes me a romantic, I guess. The two don't have to be mutually exclusive."

I pause for a moment to gather my thoughts. "Romance doesn't have to be fully realistic. It's a fantasy. It's a chance to explore desires. Discover what I like and what I don't." And what I may never have for myself. "Plus, I…I sort of see it as a service to others. I can bring them a little escape, a little happiness." I shrug, feeling a bit self-conscious, but if I want him to know me, then I can't hide this. "I don't know. It's not just about me, even if sometimes I feel like I'm writing about myself."

Daniel examines me for a long moment, and I try not to grow shy under his gaze. "I like that," he finally says.

I wait for him to say more, but instead, he leans forward and presses his lips to mine, a tease of a kiss that has my eyes fluttering shut and reopening all too soon, wanting more.

"What was that for?" I ask a little breathlessly.

Daniel smiles, his focus steady on me. "You had jam on your lip."

I scoff out a laugh. "And your first instinct was to kiss it off me?"

"I didn't want it to go to waste. It's good jam."

Oh, this guy. Can't even admit he just wanted to kiss me. If I wasn't grinning so widely, I'd play my hand at pretending to be offended.

When we're finished eating, he gathers our empty wrappers and deposits them in a nearby trash can.

"Come on," he says, holding out a hand to me. "Time for our next stop."

I don't hesitate to slip my palm into his. It doesn't matter that he has touched nearly every inch of me already; holding his hand in public feels like a strangely massive step. It's like we've done this all backward: started with fucking and rounded the bases to hand holding. But God, I've got butterflies.

He gives my fingers a squeeze as we walk, glancing down at me with a question in his eyes, as if to make sure I'm still onboard with all of this. I squeeze his hand back in answer and tell him that he better bring me more of those croissants tomorrow, because I'm going to be thinking about them for the rest of my life.

When he laughs, I lean into him a little more, my elbows and shoulders brushing his, and when we stop before crossing the street, he leans down to press a kiss to the top of my head.

All right. Yeah. I'll admit it. So far, this is the best date of my life.

Somehow, the best date gets even better when we reach our next destination.

It takes me a moment to read the worn-down sign, squinting to make out the letters on the frosted window. "A bookstore?" I ask, my heart lifting. "You know this is dangerous, right? I can't be trusted in these places."

Daniel shakes his head and opens the door. "Don't tell me you already have twenty unread books sitting on your shelf and still can't resist buying more."

I cackle as I step inside the shop. "Twenty? Try two hundred." I look around, taking in the narrow aisles full of towering shelves and colorful book spines. "And yeah, I *will* be buying more."

The place is beautiful, with its high ceilings and antique bookcases. They stretch from wall to wall, and up a rickety staircase in the corner is what looks like a cozy reading nook. I hope Daniel isn't in any sort of rush, because there will be no dragging me out of here if I take another step. This is a place I could easily spend hours in.

"This is my favorite bookstore in the city," Daniel says as he waves to the woman behind the front counter. "It's a mix of new and used, so they almost always have something I want."

"Wow," I murmur, dragging my attention away from the books for a moment to take him in. "So you really are a book lover. Every other guy I've dated can barely read."

He smiles at that. "You need better taste in men."

"I'm working on it." Before I let myself dwell on how my taste is now exclusively men named Daniel who work as acquisition managers and aren't exactly the shitheads I thought they were, I grab his hand and tug. "*Yalla.* I want to see if they have a decent romance section."

As it turns out, they have an exceptional romance section. Which is why, two hours later, Daniel is ascending the stairs after depositing my third round of books by the register. I have three more cradled in my arms when he slides behind me and puts his hands on my shoulders.

"More?" he asks, his tone a mix of exasperation and humor. He's been a good sport, putting up with my browsing and the random publishing facts I spout periodically. He even entertains my excitement over finding out-of-print books I've always wanted to read.

I peer up at him. "They have all the new releases I've been meaning to buy."

"If you're not careful, you'll sell them out of their entire stock." He takes a book from my arms and flips it over to read the back cover. "Wow, another billionaire romance. How creative."

I snatch it back from him and tuck the stack against my chest.

"Gotta love a financially stable man."

He snorts. "That's a little more than stable, but all right. Can't really knock it, considering how well they sell."

"True. But if I never have to write another, it'll be too soon."

"No billionaires for you, got it," he teases. "Is there anything else you don't like in your romance?"

"I don't like big love confessions," I answer immediately. "I can't stand when the male character suddenly makes a big speech after doing nothing but grunting and smirking and being a blunt asshole for the entire story. Or when they become the most poetic people on the planet, comparing women to sunshine and the ocean and the greenest grass they've ever seen. It's like, damn, just say you love each other and get on with it."

A rumble of a laugh leaves him as he presses his cheek to mine. "Didn't you say you were a romantic?"

"Not that kind, I guess. I'm less of a *words of affirmation* girl and more here for *acts of service*."

Like how he's started the process of getting my books printed. That's an act of service if I've ever seen one.

"No over-the-top confessions," Daniel confirms, taking the books from me and setting them on a nearby shelf. "Keep it subtle."

"Subtle, but with feeling," I correct.

"Pretty specific." He takes a few slow steps back toward the secluded corner of the upstairs nook where the romance section extends. "Come here."

"Why?" I ask, though I'm already moving toward him. "What's in the corner?"

"Just me," he says, offering his palm up.

I take it and let him pull me to his chest, breathing in the scent of paper and ink and something distinctly Daniel. I tilt my head back reflexively and close my eyes. His soft lips coax mine open, his tongue sure as it swipes against mine without hesitation. His kiss is confident but gentle. He's a man who knows exactly what he wants, yet is willing to take his time. He knows I'm not going anywhere. He knows I'm hooked.

I give a small sigh when he pulls back to press little kisses to my jaw and cheeks.

"Let's go buy your haul," he says against my temple. "And then we'll find another suitcase so you can get them all home."

His teasing makes me grin. I let my head loll to the side in sheer contentedness. "I didn't pick out *that* many."

"You practically decimated their romance section, *mi amor*."

"I can write them off on my taxes. It's market research."

"You're a true businesswoman."

I laugh and smack his shoulder lightly. "Shut up."

I'm practically high on him as we wander back downstairs. I lean against him as he makes easy conversation with the woman behind the register while she rings up my stacks of books. When they're all bagged and she reads my sky-high total aloud, I pull my credit card from my wallet, but Daniel knocks my hand away and taps his own card against the reader.

"Hey," I protest as the machine beeps. "You weren't supposed to do that."

"This is a date," he says, as if that explains everything.

I raise an eyebrow, expecting more. "*And?*"

"And that means I pay for everything."

I'm not the kind of person who will protest when a man pays for a date—I let him pay for breakfast, and if he insists, I'll let him pay for any other meals—but that was several hundred dollars worth of books. Had I known he would be paying, I certainly wouldn't have picked out so many.

"I don't remember discussing that."

"It wasn't up for discussion." He grabs my bags and says goodbye to the smiling woman at the counter, then heads for the door without a glance back at me.

I splutter out my own parting words to her before following after Daniel, still stunned. But knowing what I do about him, there's nothing I can say now other than, "Thank you."

He turns to me when he reaches the door, pleasant surprise on his face. "That was easier than I expected."

"Did you *want* me to fight you?"

"No, but I was ready for it." He pushes the door open and holds it for me.

"I still can," I say lightly as I step outside. "We can throw down. Right here, right now."

Daniel scoffs, shaking his head. "You are truly ridiculous."

"And yet you still asked me out." I shrug, flashing him a smug grin. "Regretting that yet? I'm annoying *and* expensive."

"Good thing I like both those parts of you."

I exhale, trying to ignore the heat creeping through me. "Careful, or you'll never get rid of me."

"That's the plan."

I'm so struck by his words that I nearly lose my breath for a second. At least I don't have to worry about whether he's as into me as I'm into him, because, wow—that's the exact kind of subtle yet direct confession I live for. Man's a fast learner.

I clear my throat, hoping to regain my composure. "Where to next?"

"Lunch now. I'm hungry again after watching you pick out all those books."

I shoot him a look from the corner of my eye. "Is it going to be another place where they know you?"

"I know it surprises you, but people do like me."

"Truly shocking. Impossible to believe."
"Guess I'll have to keep proving it to you."
I'm all for it.

CHAPTER 35

We're sitting at a tiny table in a busy Mexican restaurant, and I don't think anyone but us has spoken a word of English in the past ten minutes. I love it.

"Okay, time for the worst part of any date," I announce, leaning my elbows on the table and staring him down. "The awkward question game."

"My absolute favorite," Daniel says, setting his margarita down in front of him. "Should I start?"

I grab my own drink and tilt it toward him. "Bring it on."

"Why the fuck do you still live in Baltimore?"

I slap a hand to my chest like he's hurt me. "*Ouch*. Going straight for the hard hitters."

He shrugs off my dramatics. "It doesn't make sense. Your job is here. You'd be better off sucking it up and moving."

"Believe me, I know," I tell him, wiping a bead of condensation off my glass with my thumb. "And I consider it more and more every day. But my family's in Baltimore, and I love being close to them. Considering I can work from anywhere and my lease isn't up until the end of the year, I figured staying was my best option. I haven't had much of a reason to leave, anyway."

But now that I'm on a date in New York with a man who lives

here, with a job here—one with a manager who is always begging me to come into the office more than twice a month—and more friends here than in any other city, it's more than just a viable option.

"I think you have plenty of reasons," he says, his gaze steady on me.

And there's another subtle confession. He knows what he's doing.

"My turn." I clear my throat, wanting to get off this topic. "If you didn't work for Naiad, what else would you do?"

"I'd still want to be in acquisitions," he says without hesitation before flashing me a wry half smile. "Just not in the romance industry."

"Valid." I pause as our platter of tacos arrives and wait until the server moves off before motioning for Daniel to throw another question at me. "All right, what's next?"

"Why did your last relationship end?"

I scrunch my nose. I knew a relationship question was in the cards, but I really don't want to talk about my lackluster dating history. "He was cheating on me," I answer, though thankfully the bitter taste those words leave isn't as potent as it's been in the past. "Or, really, *with* me. He had a long-distance girlfriend the entire time we were together. I didn't find out about her until she surprised him with a visit."

"That's messed up," Daniel comments. "Is that why you were upset when you thought I was on a date?"

I give a small nod and take a sip of my drink. "I guess I've just come to expect the worst from the people I fall for." I look away with my own confession and pick up a taco to busy myself. "Anyway, it was a long time ago, so he doesn't matter anymore."

"How long ago?"

I glance up. "That's your third question in a row, you know."

"Humor me."

"Like, four years ago. Maybe a little more. I was still in college."

"And you haven't been in a relationship since?" He sounds surprised to hear that.

"Nope. I've been on a handful of dates, but nothing more than that. Actually…" I pause, wondering if I should really tell him this, but when Daniel raises a curious brow, I lower my voice a little and plow ahead. "The first time we had sex, when I told you it had been a while, I meant that it had been years—not since my last relationship."

He's silent for a few long beats. If he's judging me, I don't care. There's nothing wrong with my spotty sexual history, just like there would be nothing wrong if I chose to have sex more often than that.

"Why so long?" he finally asks.

I shrug. "Other than trying to avoid the plague going around for the last two years? I don't know. I guess I just don't put myself out there. And, yeah, maybe I'm kind of picky."

"But I met your standards?"

I blow out a mock-exasperated breath. "Am I ever going to get to ask you another question?"

"You just did," he counters. "Now answer mine."

I narrow my eyes at him. "Of course you met my standards." I tick off his virtues on my fingers. "You're hot as hell, and I can admit that now that you're no longer my nemesis. You challenge me, but you've learned how far you can take it, which means you have at least some emotional intelligence. And you're a really good dancer."

The last one makes him snort. "Being able to dance is that important to you?"

"Being able to dance *well* is," I correct. "I was a dancer for most of my life. It's in my blood. I need someone who can keep up with me at parties and weddings, or else we can't be together. I won't let a man embarrass me."

He shakes his head. "God, my abuela is going to love you."

"Good to know," I reply without missing a beat, even though my brain is screaming. He expects that I'll meet his grandmother one day? Holy shit. That's…that's a big step. "Okay, my turn again. Where the hell do you live?"

Daniel doesn't hold back a grin. "I can't believe it's taken you this long to ask."

"Oh my God, I know," I groan. "I've been coming up with outrageous options for weeks. Lately, my money has been on a little mud hut in Central Park."

"Mm, so close," he says like a disappointed game show host. "It's actually a hot dog cart on the corner of 6th and 42nd."

"*Fuck.*" I slap the table. "I should have known."

"That's okay, we're all wrong sometimes." He playfully rolls his eyes like he can't believe he's entertaining my shenanigans. "I live on the Upper West Side. I bought a place last year, actually. Three bedrooms with a fantastic view."

I have to admit, I'm a little impressed. Okay, *a lot* impressed. That real estate isn't remotely cheap. I know he makes good money with Naiad, but it's definitely not UWS money. "Mr. Moneybags over here, huh? No wonder you think billionaire romance is overrated. That's just your life."

"Wait until I tell you that I moonlight as a vigilante too," he says, straight-faced. "You want to see my bat cave?"

I put my hands up and lean back in my chair. "Okay, slow down. I don't think we're at that stage yet. I barely know you."

"My apologies." The words are solemn, but the sparkle in his eyes has me holding back a dreamy sigh. "We'll just have to work on getting to know each other."

"I think that's a good idea."

Over lunch, he tells me about his sisters—Martina, Beatriz, and Elena. He swears he loathes them, yet he calls them every Sunday. He thinks his worst trait is that he's impatient. He's twenty-nine, and for his birthday last year, his friends surprised him with a trip to Vegas, and then he promptly got food poisoning on the first night.

He's had plenty of girlfriends in the past, but none of those relationships lasted more than five months—a record we're near to beating with our situationship. He can't stand to have other people in the kitchen when he's cooking. His favorite sport is Formula 1. And he almost lost an eye via a parrot attack when he volunteered at a wildlife sanctuary one summer in college.

"Who *are* you?" I breathed out in sheer awe upon that last revelation.

But Daniel only shrugged. "I have a lot of interests."

In return, I told him the rest of my dating history, my dream travel destinations, the styles of dance I'm most versed in, what life was like as an only child (amazing, highly recommend), and why I think *America's Next Top Model* was peak reality television—a rant that lasted at least twenty minutes.

It's late afternoon by the time we finish our tacos and tequila.

"Now what?" I ask when the server sets the bill in front of Daniel.

He hums as he calculates the tip—30 percent, once again; the guy *must* be a billionaire—then signs his name. "I take you back to your hotel."

My stomach sinks a little in disappointment. I don't want this date to end. It's truly been phenomenal. Like it was perfectly tailored to include everything I love.

But blessedly, Daniel doesn't stop there. "And then I'm going to fuck you until the only name you remember is mine."

I inhale sharply, desire already spreading through me. "And after that?"

"We get Chinese takeout for dinner and eat it in bed. Then we order room service dessert so I can lick chocolate off your—"

I push my chair back with a loud screech. "Let's go."

"So eager."

"I just really like dessert."

CHAPTER 36

I'm bursting with anticipation as Daniel and I make the journey back to my hotel. I briefly consider asking if we can go to his place, but geographically, we're closer to where I'm staying, and the allure of room service dessert is a little too strong to pass up.

When we're off the train, I speed walk in front of him, peeking over my shoulder every few seconds to make sure he's keeping up.

"You wanna walk a little faster?" I ask him, narrowly avoiding running down an elderly couple when I look forward again.

In reply, Daniel takes two large steps and moves ahead, leaving me trapped behind a group of chattering teenagers. "Fast enough for you?" he calls back from five people in front of me.

I flip him the finger but laugh, dodging bodies to catch up. He grabs my hand when I reach him and lifts it to his lips, pressing a kiss to each of my knuckles. I groan, a heavy ache settling low in my belly. We're in the middle of Midtown, surrounded by thousands of people, and I'm so turned on that I honestly want him to fuck me against the window of the one-dollar pizza place.

Thankfully, I have *some* semblance of self-control, but when we're forced to wait for the elevator in the lobby of my hotel, I can't help but press close to him.

"I missed you," I admit as I breathe in the scent of him. "I don't care if that sounds sappy. That was way too long to be apart."

He wraps his arms around my shoulders and smirks. "That's a little forward to say on our first date, don't you think?"

I pull back, but he dips his head and catches my earlobe between his teeth, halting my movement.

"You were always on my mind," he murmurs. "When I was on the beach. Out with my boys. In my childhood bedroom at night. In church with my abuela. It was always you."

I exhale, my heart racing and my need growing. "You better stop talking like that before I come right here in the lobby."

He chuckles and lifts his head, but not before pressing a kiss to my jaw. "That's okay. Let these people know what I do to you. I'll still make you come again. And again, and again."

Before I can melt into a puddle at his feet, the elevator arrives and Daniel guides me in. I stay pressed to him, fantasizing about a time when we can be together more often. For now, it's just a dream, but maybe one day…

We're kissing by the time the doors open again and fumble, desperate for touches, all the way down the hall. I produce my room key from my back pocket and shove it at him, knowing I don't have the fine motor skills to open the door quickly in my state. He thankfully takes care of it in one smooth move, his lips barely leaving mine.

The door slams behind us, and I wrestle out of my jacket as he does the same. Then he's grabbing me again for more heated kisses. I gasp against his mouth as he grips my ass and lifts me. My back hits the wall with enough force to shake the artwork hanging on it. I spread my legs, and he settles between them, the bulge in his pants pressed to me as I hook my ankles together at the base of his spine.

"You gonna fuck me against the wall, Daniel?" I pant, already working the buttons of his shirt.

"I would if you were wearing a dress," he replies, and the next thing

I know, he's striding to the bed and pressing me into the mattress. "You make my life so difficult, Selene."

"I'm so sorry," I mock as he pulls off my shoes. "I should have known better than to wear appropriate clothing for this wea—Oh, *fuck.*"

He's got his hands down my pants now, rubbing his thumb over the lace of my thong, and my hips buck toward his touch. If he ever needs to shut me up in the future, this is definitely a solid method.

"These feel expensive," he notes as the soaked fabric creates friction on my sensitive skin. "How much did you spend on them?"

"Too much," I moan, gripping the duvet.

He gives a thoughtful murmur as he drags my jeans down my legs, examining every inch of my skin in the process. "They were worth it. But I want to see the whole set."

He doesn't have to ask twice. I sit up and pull my sweater over my head, chest heaving and my breasts practically pouring out of the delicate baby blue lace. The replying expletives from him only turn me on more.

"I am the luckiest fucking man," he says, kissing me again, rough and thankful.

I wrap my arms around him, keeping him close, gasping as his fingers move over my pussy. I swear I could come from that alone.

There's no way he'll allow it, though. His touch disappears, leaving me whining and kicking at the mattress with my heels.

"I'm going to need you to fuck me immediately," I tell him, too wound up for anything else. "As hard as you possibly can."

He grunts as he takes over the task of unbuttoning his shirt, forcing me to watch his lingering striptease. "You're very impatient."

"Have you stopped to think that might be because you wouldn't have sex with me last night?" I challenge, pushing the shirt from his shoulders before trailing my hands down his pecs, to his deliciously defined abs, to the button of his pants. "This is *weeks* of pent-up energy."

He lets me touch him, lets me unbutton his jeans and yank down the zipper, all while smiling like he's enjoying the show. "Am I just a piece of meat to you, Selene? After the beautiful date I treated you to today—"

"Oh my God, shut up," I huff, grasping the waistband of his underwear. "It was truly the best date I've ever been on, okay? Like, by a longshot. You made my day, Daniel. I don't think anyone else will ever top it."

He raises a brow at my choice of words, making me replay them in my head.

"Not that I want anyone else to," I tack on. "I can't imagine wanting anyone but you."

This time, the words register the second they're out of my mouth. *Shit.* I practically just proposed to the man. In five seconds, he'll grab his shirt and run, thanking me for the fun times and then never speak to me again. Except…didn't he say something similar to me weeks ago? Maybe this is just—

My thoughts are cut short when he grips my hip and rolls me onto my stomach. I don't even have a chance to ask what he's doing before he's pulling me onto my hands and knees and ripping my thong down my legs. I gasp when he nudges my thighs apart and the cool air hits my slick, heated skin. My need for him is nothing short of ravenous.

"I told you last night that I couldn't go easy on you," he says, his voice rough. "I'm going to make good on that promise now."

At the sound of a condom wrapper tearing open behind me, I garner enough wherewithal to grab the headboard. Half a second later, he pushes into me with one hard thrust. There are stars behind my eyes as he pulls out and does it again, with more force this time, and I can't hold back the scream of pleasure that comes with it. Our date was gentle intimacy, but as he wraps my hair around his fist and pulls, he gives me the fire I've been begging for.

His strokes are deep and steady, angled exactly where I want them and hitting that delicate spot inside me that has my thighs shaking in no time. I'm already panting, but I manage to get out the words "don't stop."

He doesn't. He moves faster, curling over me and dragging his teeth down my neck. It's sure to leave a mark, but I'll be proud to wear it and I'll happily let him give me more.

I can't help the curses that leave my lips as he wraps his fingers around my throat and squeezes softly, then ghosts his fingertips down my body. My hardened nipples sting under the soft lace as he rolls them between his fingers, sending arcs of electricity through me.

He skates his hand down my stomach and lower. A gasp escapes me when his fingers find my clit, circling and caressing, pressing and teasing. I almost knock his hand away because it's too much. It's like my brain is short-circuiting. I can't process the contrast between the way he slams into me and how he tenderly tortures my clit, but if he stops either, I'll lose my mind.

Or maybe I'm already losing it. I'm already a hostage to the sensation, a willing participant in this no-holds-barred storm of desire, so I arch my back and give him all of me.

Every thrust sends me reeling. Every muscle in my body pulls taut. And when he murmurs, "You feel so fucking good," I'm done for.

I cry out his name. My hands slip from the headboard, but he doesn't ease up as I pulse around him. I come so hard I can't breathe. It's like drowning in the ocean. The waves press me under and under and under, and when I surface, the air in my lungs feels like a prize.

Eyes closed, I'm still riding the wave when he pulls out and flips me onto my back again. My head is up in the clouds, eyes half-closed and cheek turning to rest on the pillow, until Daniel's fingers find my jaw.

"Look at me."

I follow his command. Above me, his eyes are dark and intense. The look sends a sharp thrill through me. He holds my gaze as he sinks back into me—slowly this time, carefully. He's given me what I needed, that brutal release, and now he's taking what he wants.

And I'll let him. Whatever it is, he can have it. He can have me.

I cling to him as his hips move, touching every inch of skin I can reach. I trace the swirls of ink on his shoulder, the curves of his biceps, the sharp lines of his jaw, memorizing it all. If there ever comes a day when I can't have him, I want to remember how he felt now—how he made me feel in return, like a goddess worthy of veneration.

As he fucks me, he murmurs in my ear. Sweet words, filthy words, little phrases of adoration in the language he feels most at home in. Every uttered syllable makes me beg him for more. I clutch at him, hoping my gasps and the way I say his name tell him everything I want him to know.

I pant and moan at the slow rhythm he sets, at the way his cock fills me so perfectly and how my belly tightens more and more and more until I'm crying out for release again.

The feeling building inside me is low and heavy. It threatens to consume every atom of my existence. Yet it's somehow still growing. My walls tighten around him, dragging a groan from his lips.

"Stay with me, baby," he exhales in my ear, smoothing back my hair as I writhe.

I want to sob, to plead with him and my body to give me just a little more—and then he does. All it takes is a tiny shift and friction when his pelvis moves against my clit, and I'm there, coming so hard that I can't speak.

I'm limp beneath him. My breaths are ragged and my throat is raw from screaming. Yet I'm greedy enough to want more, and he doesn't stop.

Pressing my head into the pillow behind me, I clutch the sheets. "How are you still going?" I ask breathlessly.

"I just want more of you," he says against my neck, but soon, his strokes stutter. "All of you."

He already has me, body and heart, but instead of confessing the truth to him, I lift my mouth to his, sharing a breath before I fuse our lips. The connection is achingly soft and full of everything I can't say.

A moment later, he drives his hips into mine and keeps them there, and I know then that I'm ruined for all others.

There's no one else for me but him.

CHAPTER 37

I can't sit comfortably, and I've just found a smudge of chocolate in my cleavage, even after two showers. If this is what Monday mornings after being positively railed by Daniel Santiago look like, then I'm here for it.

I feel simultaneously amazing and rougher than hell. Pussy? Destroyed. Heart? Never lighter. Brain? Torn up, twisted up, and absolutely stuck agonizing over how Daniel and I are going to make this work.

Though we talked after our first round of sex—before the main event of room service chocolate lava cake that was eaten off my body—we tiptoed around logistics and where we go from here.

All it took was one date to change everything. Because now? I can't imagine my life without him in it.

Our situation hasn't been casual for months, I know that, but yesterday reinforced it. But we have two problems. First, we're coworkers, and our employer has a no-fraternization policy. And second, we don't even live in the same city. Hell, we don't even live in the same *state*. If we decide to make this official, Naiad policies be damned, we'll have to do the long-distance thing until my lease is up at the end of the year. That's a challenge in and of itself, but one I'd be willing to face if it meant being with Daniel.

For now, though, it's hard enough just getting through the workday.

Daniel sits across from me. We're both focused on our laptops, but it's impossible not to sneak peeks at each other. It's a miracle no one has noticed the way we stare at each other for a few seconds before going back to work. Thankfully, he's only been out in the main office space for the past twenty minutes after spending hours in meetings and conference calls. I don't think I could have kept it together had he been out here all morning, and I'm a little worried about what others might pick up on if we stay like this for much longer.

A reprieve comes when Jim pops his head out from one of the conference rooms and waves to me.

"Selene, can you do the Starbucks run? I'll take my regular," he shouts across the space.

"Only if I can take Daniel and force him to carry everything," I call back, shooting for derision.

It gains a few snickers from the production girls sitting near me, who, so far, seem none the wiser to my little secret. I'd like to keep it that way, but I can't pass up the opportunity to grab a moment alone with him.

"Oh, that's a great idea," Jim exclaims, clearly missing my sarcasm. "Daniel, do you mind helping Selene?"

Daniel sighs in a way that makes him sound perfectly annoyed, then shoves back his chair and stands. "Come on, then," he says, shrugging into his jacket without looking at me. "I've got a call in twenty minutes."

"Wow, what a gentleman," Nikki mumbles beside me.

I shoot her a grin. "Aren't we just *so* lucky to have him here?"

"I can hear you both, you know," Daniel says, his eyes cool as he assesses us.

Nikki leans back in her chair and laces her fingers behind her head. "Yeah, that's the point, buddy."

WORK FOR IT

Even though my antagonism toward him is feigned these days, Nikki's definitely is not. I've done my best to avoid thinking about how my friends will react when they find out I've been hooking up with our nemesis. And that I'm—oh boy, here we go—falling in love with him. The thought makes me want to throw up a little.

To break the tension and clear my own anxiety, I pull out my phone and start taking orders. By the time I hit submit, Daniel is already halfway down the hall to the elevator.

Nikki rolls her eyes. "If you sock him in the jaw on the way, I won't be mad if our drinks are a little late."

I snicker and grab my jacket. "I'll see what I can do."

Daniel is holding the elevator doors open when I finally make my way around the corner. I slip in without a word and stand on the opposite side of the car, and the two of us stare straight ahead. But as soon as we start descending, Daniel crosses the small space and crowds me into the corner.

"Finally, a moment alone," he says, then he cups my face in his hands and kisses me deeply.

It doesn't last for long, but it's enough to leave me breathless and giggling. "Did you like my acting?" I rest my palms on his chest and bat my lashes at him. "I figured I should put on a show to make them think I still hate you."

"I've seen better."

I slap his hard pec. "Rude!"

He grins as he backs to his side of the elevator, preparing for the doors to open on the ground floor. "I appreciate your ability to get me alone, though. Very smooth."

"I tried my best." The doors slide open, and Daniel holds out a hand, motioning for me to step out first. "What have you been working on today?" I ask as we head outside and turn in the direction of the closest Starbucks. "You were tucked away in the back conference room for most of the morning."

"I was negotiating the rights to *Doing It for Daddy*."

I stifle a laugh. It doesn't matter how many times we say these godforsaken titles like *Swallow It All*, *Hot for My Ex-Husband's Brother*, or *Sleeping with the Daddies Next Door*—I will always find them horrifically awkward and hilarious.

"Do you think it's weird how often we all say the word *daddy*?" I ask him. "Like, they need to start listing that in the job description. *Must be able to say the word* daddy *with a sexual connotation without giggling and/or blushing*."

Daniel laughs. The sound warms me from the inside out. "They should," he agrees. "I feel bad for any of our coworkers who call their fathers that."

"Agreed. I'm lucky I never have."

"What do you call him?"

"Baba," I answer. "My family mostly speaks Arabic at home. And I'm guessing yours speaks Spanish, so no *daddy* for you either."

He nods. "Never really had use for the word."

"Not even sexually?" I press, trying not to sound too interested.

He shoots me a curious look. "Is that something you're into?"

"You can't answer a question with a question," I teasingly scold.

"I don't love it," he says, conceding easily for once. "I'd rather hear my name."

"Well, since you were honest, I'll tell you it's not really my cup of tea either."

"Guess we're a perfect match."

My heart trips over itself in my chest. "Guess we are." I clear my throat, trying to settle down again. "Okay, so *daddy* is off the table. What about—"

"Do *not* call me *papi*."

I guffaw at his offense, the sound of it mixing with the soundtrack of the city streets. "Noted."

Daniel holds the door open for me as we step into the crowded coffee shop. We stick close to each other, but we're careful not to touch, even if my body aches to be pressed to his.

"I don't think we can work in the office on the same days," I murmur to him before I can think twice.

He cocks a brow. "Why not?"

"I'm worried I'll give us away," I admit a little sheepishly, wondering if he'll call out my use of the word *us*. There is an *us*, but to what degree?

"How do you think you'd give us away?" he questions, so intent that it feels like an interrogation, but he doesn't seem to mind the way I've phrased things.

I shake my head, embarrassed about being worried. "You know what? Never mind. I'm just being stupid."

"Come on, Selene. Tell me." Our hands brush, and without breaking eye contact, he hooks his pinkie around mine. "Are you afraid you'll forget to say something mean about me? Touch my hand by accident and not be repulsed?"

I blow out a breath and look away, my face on fire. "I said never mind."

"I think you're right to be worried," he goes on. "You haven't been keeping up with your evil glares across the room."

My eyes snap back to him. "I never glared at you!"

"Oh, yes, you did."

"Okay, so maybe I did a time or two," I admit. Because I really did loathe this man at one point.

Blessedly, our conversation is interrupted when a barista calls my name. Daniel once again gathers up the majority of the drinks, leaving me one measly tray, but I know better than to complain about the imbalance. To him, this is equity, and I can't say I mind it.

We don't speak again until we're back on the street, weaving around lost tourists and businesspeople on lunch breaks.

"I wanted to touch you earlier when you were sitting across from me," Daniel says. "I almost got up and wrapped my arms around you."

He's watching the sidewalk ahead, leaving me a chance to look him over uninterrupted. "You don't have to lie to make me feel better."

"I don't lie when it comes to how I feel about you." When he looks down at me, his eyes are full of sincerity.

He's in just as deep as I am, it seems.

"So…" There's a question on the tip of my tongue, but I have to force myself to get it out. "What are we going to do? How are we supposed to be in the office together without giving ourselves away?"

"You're only here twice a month," he points out. "So we don't have to worry about it too often. But no matter what, we'll make it work."

"How?" I question, worry roiling in my stomach. "If HR finds out about this before we're ready to tell them, we could lose our jobs. Shit, even if we *do* tell them, there's a chance we could still get fired."

A hint of a frown touches his lips, and I swear I see a flash of hurt in his eyes. "Are you saying you don't want to risk it?"

"No," I blurt, then suck in a breath to compose myself. "Daniel, *no*. I want to be with you, okay?"

"Good. I want the same."

I guess that's that. We're doing this. "So we…just keep hiding?"

He nods. "The best we can for as long as we can."

I sigh. I don't love it, but I suppose that's the reality of our situation. "I guess that's really all we can do."

His shoulder brushes mine, a subtle move of comfort. It's the most he's allowed to offer me so close to the office. His dark eyes are soft when I meet them, and there's a promise in their depths. "It will all work out, *mi amor*."

It better. Because being with him no longer feels like a want. It's a need.

WORK FOR IT

Five minutes before the end of the workday, a notification pops up on my calendar.

It's a reminder that I have a manuscript edit due tomorrow.

A manuscript edit I haven't even started working on.

"Fuck!"

Down the table, Ella jumps in her seat, clutching a hand to her chest like she's trying to keep her heart from running away. "You scared me," she breathes out, eyes wide. "What's wrong?"

I press my fingertips to my forehead and close my eyes. How the *hell* could I have forgotten about this? I usually stay on top of my deadlines. I keep them written down in a minimum of five places, but this one somehow slipped through the cracks. And now I have to edit a hundred thousand words by tomorrow morning. I'm royally screwed.

"I completely forgot about an editing project," I mumble. "It goes to the proofreader tomorrow and goes live on the app on Friday. I have to get it done tonight."

"Oh, babe," she says sympathetically. She hops out of her chair and rushes over to hug me. "I'm so sorry. Do you want me to help you?"

I shake my head. Ella's workload is just as intense as mine; she doesn't need the extra burden of helping me out of a hole I dug for myself. "That's okay, but thank you. I really appreciate it."

She gives me a tight squeeze, then heads over to close and put away her laptop. "If you change your mind, just text me, okay?"

I nod, already distracted. There's no way I won't be pulling an all-nighter like I'm back in college.

Once Ella leaves, I hurriedly pack my things, knowing I need to get back to my hotel and buckle down. It's going to be a half-assed edit, but at least it will get done. That's all that matters.

I wave goodbye to the last of the stragglers in the office, including

Daniel, who's sitting in one of the small conference rooms. I'll text him to tell him the situation, but there's no way we'll be able to see each other tonight; I can't have anything, even him, hindering my concentration.

Of course, just as the elevator arrives, Daniel slips out of the conference room with his bag slung over his shoulder. "You heading out?" he asks.

"Yeah." I step into the elevator and jam my finger into the button. Once the doors have closed and we're alone, I spare him a glance. "I'm going to be busy tonight. Don't worry about coming over."

"You've got things to do that are more important than me?" he teases. Thankfully, he doesn't seem offended by my brush-off.

I snort, but my anxiety is growing with every second that passes. "I have to edit an entire manuscript by tomorrow, one of the newer ones you acquired. I forgot all about it."

Daniel squeezes my shoulder, his thumb digging into the knot that's already forming at the base of my neck. "Want me to keep you company while you work?"

I blow out a breath and drop my chin. I hate to miss out on any time with him, but he's the biggest distraction in my life. "I should probably be alone," I murmur. "I'm sorry."

"Don't apologize," he says, massaging that spot until the elevator stops and he's forced to let me go. "Do what you need to. When do you go home?"

"Tomorrow after work," I tell him, disappointment sinking in my stomach. "I couldn't get Jim to sign off on a longer visit. Naiad's buckling down on travel stipends, apparently."

"That's okay," he reassures as we step out and wave goodbye to Rolando behind the front desk. "Get the edit done. That's most important."

The thought of not spending my last night here with him makes me want to throw up, but my only response is, "Okay."

I'm dying to at least kiss him goodbye, but we're literally standing outside the office. Instead, I settle for a shaky smile, then I reluctantly turn away.

I love my job. But I've never hated it more.

It's nine, and I've only completed about 20 percent of this edit. Thankfully, the manuscript is pretty clean. I have to break up the long chapters to make them more palatable for the Naiad reader, spice up the sexy bits a little, and expand a few scenes between the love interests, but it could be so much worse.

Still, I'm exhausted. Daniel stayed over until nearly three this morning, and I left for the office just after eight. This fuck-up couldn't have come at a more terrible time.

I'm in the middle of rubbing my eyes to clear away the cobwebs when there's a knock on the door. Sliding my laptop to the side, I frown. Minus hotel staff, there's only one person it could be. My suspicions are confirmed when I look through the peephole.

"What are you doing here?" I ask Daniel after I pull open the door, somehow both surprised and not at his appearance.

He holds up a small bakery box. "I brought dessert."

It's a (literally) sweet gesture, but unless he's here to drop it off and leave, I can't entertain this. "Thank you. But I told you I didn't have time for anything tonight."

"Let me in, Selene."

This is a bad idea, but I step back and allow him to come inside anyway.

"Put your laptop away," he instructs, tipping his head to where it's open on the rumpled bed.

I blow out an exasperated breath. "Daniel, I can't—"

"You need a break," he says firmly. "You worked an eight-hour day and now you're doing overtime you don't even get paid for."

He's right. My eyes hurt and I barely touched the dinner I ordered. And if I'm not careful, I'll end up with a migraine that will take days to get rid of.

"Okay, but we can't have sex," I warn him as I close my laptop and put it on the bedside table. "I'm way too sore to even think about being touched. And if you make me come, I won't be able to stay awake."

He chuckles as he kicks off his shoes. "No sex," he confirms, kneeling on the other side of the bed. "But I *will* be working on that knot in your shoulder and making sure you eat something."

That sounds like heaven, but it won't help me finish this manuscript. "Twenty minutes. That's all I've got."

"Yeah, yeah." He waves a hand. "Now come here. Get on your stomach."

I bellyflop onto the mattress and rest my cheek on my forearms. When I'm settled, Daniel straddles my thighs and works his magic. His hands are warm and strong, and his thumbs dig into the tight muscles just right. God, that feels good. Enough to tempt me into closing my eyes and taking a moment to enjoy it. If he ever decides to give up his career in publishing, he'd make a great massage therapist. Or maybe I'll keep him around to be my personal masseuse. Or maybe…

I wake with a start, confused and disoriented. A glance at the clock tells me I've been out for nearly two hours, nothing close to the twenty-minute break I insisted on. *Fuck*. I'm never going to make this deadline now.

Heart pounding, I push myself up and turn to the nightstand for my laptop. Except it isn't there. In a panic, I scan the room…only to find Daniel stretched out next to me, leaning against the headboard with my computer resting on his lap.

I blink at him for a long moment. Am I dreaming? This feels pretty real, but who the hell knows anymore? "What are you doing?" I ask, my voice scratchy from sleep.

He doesn't look over at me as he types. "Your edits."

All I can do is gape at him. How the hell am I supposed to react to that? Maybe I *am* dreaming. I have to be. "You're not a trained editor," I weakly point out, still stunned.

"Neither are you, technically," he counters.

I huff, but he's right. Naiad hired me for my storytelling abilities, not because I know when to use *lay* or *lie* in a sentence (because I don't).

"Go back to sleep," he says, never taking his attention from the screen.

"I can't. I have to finish this." I motion for him to hand over my laptop, but he doesn't budge. "Dan, please."

"No. You're exhausted."

"I mean, yeah, I am," I concede, throwing my hands up in exasperation. "But that doesn't mean I can sleep right now."

He curls a hand behind my neck and looks me in the eye. "Don't let this job kill you, Selene. Let me help you."

I study him for a moment, letting his words settle. There's a fondness in my heart threatening to surge up and choke me. "You're being so nice," I whisper.

That brings a hint of a smile to his face. "I don't want you having a stroke from stress. You're too valuable to Naiad."

"Naiad. Right."

He raises a brow, questioning me, but I don't pay any attention to it. Instead, I gently push my laptop out of his hands and onto the mattress beside him, then crawl into his lap, my knees on either side of his hips.

"Thank you," I tell him as his arms encircle my waist. "But you shouldn't have done this."

He tilts his head back to look at me. "Why not?"

Because there's no doubt that I've fallen for you now. "Because I'll have to go back and check all of your work. So troublesome."

"My work is always clean," he says smoothly, raking a hand through my hair and pulling ever so slightly so my neck is exposed to him. His mouth is on my pulse a moment later, biting, then soothing. "I think you'll be impressed."

"I'm always impressed by you." The words slip out, unbidden, and my face burns in embarrassment at my admission.

He pulls back and looks up at me, something in his eyes that I can't read, brow dipping. I put my hands to his chest and push off, ready to put a little space between us and pretend I didn't just give so much away. But Daniel moves faster than I can.

He pushes me onto my back, then slides between my hips and pins me to the bed. One hand is still in my hair, and he uses the other to support himself while he hovers above me.

"You mean that?" he asks, and I swear I hear a note of hesitance in his voice.

"Yeah," I say softly. "I do."

The second the words leave my mouth, his lips are on mine. I sigh and relax back into the pillowtop and drape my arms around his neck. We fit so perfectly together that it feels unreal, and I almost can't believe there was ever a time when I wanted to fight him to the death.

"Okay, enough," he murmurs when he pulls back. He gently releases me and moves to the other side of the bed to grab his bag from the floor. "Send me the second half of the manuscript. We'll knock this out together."

"Are you sure?" I ask, sitting up and smoothing down my shirt.

He pulls his own computer out of its sleeve and settles beside me. "Never been more so. We're in this together."

Yeah. That's all it takes.

WORK FOR IT

I'm 100 percent in love with Daniel Santiago.

CHAPTER 38

I wake up with his arms around me.

This is the first time Daniel has ever spent the night, and it's the first time we've done nothing but sleep beside each other.

We edited side by side for half the night, complaining about an author's penchant for overusing the phrase *he ministered at her pussy* to describe oral sex ("What does that even *mean*?" "I don't know, but I'm terrified to find out."). When we finished, all we could do was set our computers aside and pass out, tangled together.

I'm the little spoon, clutched tight to him, with his palm pressed against my belly. He has a knee between mine, and each of his soft breaths stirs my hair. I never want to move from this position, but the clock says it's just after seven, and if he wants to go home to change before heading into the office, then we need to get up. Still, it doesn't stop me from savoring it for a few more minutes, imagining a life where I could wake up like this every morning.

I want it more than I care to admit.

Before I can wake him, he starts to move. The arm around my waist tightens for an instant, then slacks. Instead of pulling away like I expect, he slides his hand down my stomach, strokes my hip and thigh, then works his way back to the curve beneath my ribs.

"I know you're awake," he murmurs, pressing gentle kisses to my shoulder through my T-shirt.

I roll over so we're facing each other and throw my leg over his hip. I press as close to him as possible, meeting his sleepy brown gaze. "You stayed."

A smile pulls at the corner of his mouth. His jaw is covered with more stubble than I've seen before. "I wasn't interested in getting on the train at four a.m." He dips his head to nuzzle my neck, drawing a contented sigh from me. "And maybe I wanted to know what it was like to sleep next to you."

"Thoughts? Comments? Concerns?" I prompt, grinning. "I value all feedback."

"Such a fool," he chuckles.

I run my fingertips up and down his back, savoring the feel of his warm skin under his shirt. "Mm, first I'm oblivious, then I'm shameless, and now I'm a fool? You sure like your derogatory words to describe me."

"They all suit you. And they're always said with love."

With one finger, I trace an *I*, an *L*, and a *Y* at the nape of his neck, then sink my fingers into his hair. "With love, huh?" I question softly with my heart in my throat, searching his eyes, waiting for him to take the words back.

But he doesn't. He doesn't look away, just meets my gaze full-on, long lashes sweeping his cheeks as he finally blinks. "Plenty of it."

He leans in and presses his forehead to mine, doubling down. These are big words, scary words, thrown lightly and landing hard.

"What are we doing, Daniel?" I whisper, so vulnerable that I feel small in his arms.

He presses a delicate kiss to the corner of my mouth. "Making ourselves happy."

It's more than that, we both know it. But for now, this is what we'll settle for. It's enough. Though for how much longer, I'm not sure.

My phone alarm beeps, breaking the moment, and I reluctantly roll away to shut it off. It's time for us to start the day, to face reality—one where we're Selene and Daniel individually, but we can't be Selene and Daniel together.

Yesterday's concerns haven't magically gone away. I still worry that I'll give our relationship away to people who can't know just yet. As we've already agreed, though, it's worth the risk.

"If I wasn't still too sore, I'd ask you to join me in the shower," I tell him as I slip out of bed. I throw both hands up and stretch, my body still attempting to recover from what he put it through.

"Probably for the best that you are. Otherwise, we'd both be late for work." He gets up as well and rounds the bed to kiss the top of my head. "I'm going to run home and shower. I'll see you at the office."

"Yeah," I say as he gathers up his things. "See you there."

He flashes me one last gentle smile before leaving.

I stare at the door for a few seconds after he's gone, just breathing. It's going to be a long day.

Daniel beats me to the office.

It looks like everyone is already here, gathered in the largest conference room around the table. I check my phone. I'm only a couple of minutes late, and there are no Slack notifications on the screen, so I couldn't have missed anything too important.

"Selene," Nikki calls out, leaning around the conference room door. "Get your butt in here."

I drop my bag by one of the long tables and slowly make my way over. Uneasy, I slip into the room with the rest of the production and acquisitions team. I freeze when Daniel moves to me, though he's careful to stand a respectful distance away.

"I have a surprise for you," he says, motioning to the table.

The crowd parts, and I spot it: a large cardboard box.

I eye him suspiciously. "Is it full of snakes?"

Nikki, Ella, and Zoe laugh, but I can't stop staring at Daniel.

"Close," he says, fighting a smile. But the sparkle in his eyes betrays him. "Open it."

An excited Jim passes me a box cutter, and I make my way over to the table. I slice through the tape on the top of the box and gingerly unfold the flaps. And when I peer inside, all my breath leaves me.

The box is filled with books. *My* books.

"Surprise," Daniel says from beside me, a little closer this time. "These proof copies arrived this morning. As soon as you approve them, I'll tell our distributor they can go up for sale. We'll start the advertising push immediately."

I'm speechless. I knew Daniel was working on making this happen, but as I reach into the box and see my name on the front cover, I nearly have to pinch myself.

"I—I don't—" I stammer, staring at the paperback in my hands. "Holy *shit*."

"Holy shit is right!" Jim exclaims, bumping Daniel out of the way so he can pull a copy from the box. "I never thought I'd see these, but Daniel convinced me it was a step in the right direction for Naiad."

"Did he?" I murmur, my eyes finding him again.

Jim nods. "Absolutely. You've got a real fighter in your corner, Selene."

"Yeah," I say. "I'm beginning to see that."

Eventually, after a round of congratulations, everyone files out of the conference room. Mine will be the first of the physical Naiad-published books, but more of our catalog will be rolling out over the coming months. It really is a major development. Not just for me, but for the entire company. We're about to reach a wider audience, and there's definitely risk involved. This new endeavor could tank. But Daniel discussed the positive implications with all of us, and for the moment, my excitement outweighs my trepidation.

Daniel and I are the last in the room. The wall behind us is glass, and anyone could see us if they looked over, but I still stand shoulder to shoulder with him, staring down at the book I can't let go of.

"Thank you," I tell him softly. "Really."

He reaches over to put his hand on mine. To anyone watching, it looks like he's trying to take the book from me. "You deserve this and more."

"Guess we'll have to see how sales go," I say, wishing I could lean over and throw my arms around his neck. "If they bomb, let's pretend this never happened."

He chuckles. "They won't. Like you've been telling me for years, people want your books on their shelves."

"Shit, now I guess I have to write more," I joke, daring to glance at him from the corner of my eye. "My dream is to fill up a full shelf."

"How wide of a shelf are we talking?" Daniel teases. "If it's huge, you better stop talking and get back to writing."

"Let's start with a narrow one. Writing all this other content for Naiad keeps me busy enough."

He watches me, searching. "You plan to keep doing it?"

I nod. "For as long as I can hold out. Stressful as it is, I really do love my job. It kind of feels like a once-in-a-lifetime opportunity, you know?"

"That's true," he agrees. "If by once in a lifetime, you mean you could easily do the same thing at JotNote or any of our competitors."

I snicker and elbow him in the ribs. "Dick. I was trying to be sentimental, but of course you had to ruin it."

"That's what I'm best at." He hands the book back, leaving me to look at him full-on.

And, yep, there it is, my heart skipping a beat. Because I am undeniably head over heels for this man.

"Congratulations, Selene. Enjoy this."

CHAPTER 39

As great as being in the office is, I sure do love working from home.

I've spent the last week writing from my bed, taking meetings while dressed in pajama pants, and doing laundry in the middle of the day. It truly is the dream.

I'm in the middle of a (blessedly cameras-off) Zoom meeting with Nikki where we're plotting out the continuation of *Doing It for Daddy* when something occurs to me.

"Hey, where has Daniel been?" I ask her offhandedly. "I haven't seen him in the morning meeting all week."

It's not out of the norm for him to miss a few of our morning meetings. He's often on calls with authors and other publishing houses, negotiating deals, before the rest of us even check our email in the morning. I didn't think twice about it until now, Monday morning, after a week of him being absent. I haven't even seen him active on Slack now that I think about it.

Not that it really matters. He and I spend the hours after work on the phone and send random texts all day. I still haven't come clean about our burgeoning relationship to Carly, even though I know she's overheard me talking to him. She hasn't pushed me to give her details either.

"You didn't hear?" Nikki says. Her tone implies she's about to spill the juiciest gossip of her life. "Rumor is he quit to take another job. And he didn't give any heads-up, so the bosses aren't happy about it. I'm sure they'll bring it up in the big all-staff meeting on Wednesday, but it's been pretty hush-hush so far."

My stomach drops to my knees. "Are you—are you for real?"

Nikki cackles delightedly. "Hell yeah, babe! We're fucking *free*. No more Daniel Santiago making our lives miserable."

I force myself to swallow back the bile creeping into my throat. "This is the best thing I've ever heard."

"I figured you'd love it. Anyway, what do we think about adding a love triangle to this? Maybe a new daddy. Someone to rival…"

Nikki keeps talking, but I can't do anything more than murmur in agreement at her suggestions. I don't care what happens in this stupid story. Not after what I've just learned.

Hands shaking, I snatch my phone off the bed beside me and type a message to Daniel.

You quit???? I text him. *And you didn't think to tell me????*

My heart races as I wait for him to reply, but as the minutes tick by and Nikki asks if I'm still there, I get nothing back. I have to lie and tell her my internet is being shitty, that I missed half the stuff she just said. I keep waiting for his response as she repeats herself, but it doesn't come. Finally, I force myself to tune in, but my head is still reeling.

Daniel quit without saying a word to me.

He's gone.

Despite my numerous phone calls and desperate voice notes, I don't get a reply until the workday is nearly over. And the response isn't an explanation. No, it's a question: *When are you in the city again?*

Unlike him, I respond immediately. *Are you KIDDING ME, Daniel??? THAT'S what you have to say to me right now?* Then I follow up with *Look, I'm supposed to be there again on Wednesday, but I can come sooner.*

I spend an agonizing thirty minutes pacing my bedroom before my phone buzzes again.

Come sooner, his message reads. *Tonight.*

I'm on the Amtrak website, changing my ticket before I can think twice. The next few trains are sold out, so I settle for the nine-fifteen. It's just after five now. I've got four hours to stew and stress before I even board.

You wanna tell me why you did this without saying anything??? I text with my left hand as my right scrolls down to click *Purchase Ticket*.

I will when you get here, he says. *See you soon.*

I keep myself confined to my room for as long as I can stand, but at seven, I can't take it anymore.

I burst out, dragging my suitcase behind me, not even sure what I packed. There's a chance all I have in there are old gym shorts, an eye cream, and sixteen pairs of socks, but I don't care. I just need to see Daniel.

Carly's sitting on the couch with her feet kicked up on the coffee table and her phone in hand as she scrolls through social media. Our favorite sitcom plays quietly on the TV. She looks up, probably ready to invite me to join her, but she cuts short and frowns when she sees me clutching my purse in one hand and the handle of my suitcase in the other.

"I—I have to go back to New York," I stammer.

I hoped she was in her room so I could just text her on the Uber ride to the train station, but clearly, I have no such luck. Still, I can't let this conversation go on for long; I'm already feeling fragile—any more pressure, no matter how slight, might fully break me.

Her frown deepens as she sets her phone to the side. "I thought you weren't going up until Wednesday for that big company meeting."

"It got moved up to tomorrow," I lie, hustling toward the front door, "so I'm leaving tonight instead. See you la—"

"When will you be back?"

God, what is this, the Spanish Inquisition? Because I certainly didn't expect it. "I don't know," I say, unable to tamp down on my irritation, a dead giveaway that I'm hiding something.

She squints at me, rising from the couch. "What's wrong?"

"Nothing," I lie once again. "Everything's fine."

But Carly sees through me. "No, it's not. Come here, sit down." She approaches slowly, as if I'm a wild animal she's worried might attack. "Honey, what's going on?"

"It's nothing, I swear." I set my purse on the table by the door and grab my jacket. My hands are shaking. "Just my company being a pain in the ass. You know how it is."

"I do," she says softly, taking the jacket from me. "But this isn't that." She hangs it back up and scrutinizes me.

I'm frozen in place, called out and on the verge of cracking straight down the middle.

"Tell me what's up," she urges. She takes my hands and guides me to the couch. "No more secrets."

I follow along like a small child, swallowing hard and ready to deny. "I don't have any—"

"Selene Haddad," she warns as she eases herself to the cushions and tugs me along with her. But there's a hint of an understanding smile on her lips. "You've been keeping *a lot* from me lately. It's time to come clean. Whatever's going on is making you a nervous wreck. So come on. Spill it."

I've hidden all of this for so long, and it's about to come out, but I don't even know where to start.

After a few long beats, I finally manage to admit, "I've been…

seeing someone."

"I know," Carly says gently. "You've done a pretty terrible job of hiding it, but I didn't want to spook you by asking questions. I know how you are. Like a horse ready to bolt at any second."

"You've known me for too long," I grumble. She knows everything about me, but maybe that's a good thing. She knows all about my ex, my romantic hang-ups, my determination to keep my distance from men. She understands better than anyone.

"Keep going," she prods. "You've been seeing someone and…"

"And I…" I drop my chin, unable to look her in the eyes. "People are going to think I'm crazy because of who it is."

"Crazy? Why would anyone think that?"

"Because it's…Daniel." I force myself to take a breath before I pass out. Finally, I drag my gaze to her. "Daniel Santiago."

And there it is, the grand reveal. That I'm dating the man I've very vocally claimed to hate for so long. Everyone is going to think I'm a liar, that I've been deceiving them for years, just going along with the general dislike for him in order to fit in.

Carly is frowning. Her brows are drawn together in confusion, and my heart aches at the sight. I know she loves me and will never be as harsh as my runaway imagination believes, but I'm more concerned about facing her disappointment.

"Your coworker?" she clarifies. There's no judgment in her voice, just uncertainty. "The one I've had to talk you out of murdering several times?"

I wince. The reminder is a perfect example of how difficult it's going to be to convince people that things between Daniel and me have changed. "That's him."

And then the words flood out. The whole story leaves me in a rush before I can even stop to think about what I'm saying. Every moment of it, every feeling. Every doubt and fear and desire escapes my lips.

Everything but what I learned today.

"Oh, honey." She squeezes my hands tightly, the confusion on her face shifting into gentle understanding. "You've been holding on to this all by yourself?"

"Yeah," I say. My voice cracks on the word, and my eyes sting. "I didn't want anyone to judge me. Or tell me I was making a mistake. Or say *I told you* so if it went bad."

"Did it go bad?" she coaxes, running her thumbs over my knuckles. "Is that what this is about?"

"No," I choke out. "No. But he did something without telling me."

"What did he do?"

The first tear rolls down my cheek, easing the floodgates open. "He quit. He left Naiad last week."

The unknowns of it all hit me straight in the chest. He didn't tell me any of this. He left me in the dark, and I was the last person to know. How could I not realize that the man I've fallen in love with no longer worked at the place that brought us together?

And honestly? I don't want him to leave Naiad, not yet, even if it will make it easier to be in a relationship. He's just given me the greatest gift—the first of my books published in paperback—and now he's *gone*? Just…done? Work has tied us together for so long; what are we going to be like without it?

"Oh, wow," Carly exhales, drawing me out of my thoughts. She worries her full lower lip between her teeth. "That *is* big. But…it's a good thing, right?"

"I mean, yeah." It is, despite how up in the air everything feels right now. "Naiad doesn't allow employees to be in relationships with each other. We were planning to hide it for as long as we could…"

"But he changed things up and left the company instead," she fills in for me, and I'm so glad I have this wonderful girl in my life who can finish my sentences. "And you're upset that he kept this from you. That he did it without consulting you first."

"I am." I sniffle, rubbing at my eyes, as if that will stop the tears. But they still drip down my face. "The fact that he quit is—It's not *about* that."

"I get it." She hauls me against her chest and tucks my head under her chin. "You need to talk to him."

"He should have *already* talked to me," I mumble against the soft cotton of her shirt. "He won't even tell me anything over the *phone*."

"I'm sure he has his reasons."

I jut my lower lip out in a pout. "Whose side are you on here?"

She laughs, her chest vibrating under my cheek. "I'm on yours, obviously. But I'm trying to keep you from breaking your own heart." She presses an apology kiss to my hair. "If I ever meet him, believe me, I'll punch him in the gut for doing things this way."

That manages to drag a garbled laugh out of me.

"But I'm guessing he did this for you—for your relationship. So you wouldn't have to worry about hiding."

My eyes well with tears again. I'm so overwhelmed, so happy and confused and *angry*, that I can't process it all. "I hate him," I sob, clinging to my best friend.

"I know," she soothes, though there's a hint of laughter there. "You hate him so much that you love him."

My answer comes out as a sad cross between a whine and a hiccup. "Exactly."

She holds me for a little while longer, waiting out my tears and my mumbled insults and my threats to kick his ass when I see him. Eventually, she helps me sit up and wipes my face. Though her eyes are filled with sympathy, she scrunches her nose at what she sees. I'm sure I look an absolute fucking wreck after that breakdown.

"Let's go get you cleaned up." She gives me a nudge. "Then we'll get your behind on a train to go see your man. Okay?"

"Okay." I rise onto shaky legs. But as she pulls me toward my bedroom, I stop short. "What if I'm wrong?" I whisper. "What if—"

"You're not," she says firmly. This time, she makes sure I can't avoid her gaze. "He wouldn't have done this if he wasn't all in with you. You know that, don't you?"

She's right. Even if my insecurities are trying to tell me otherwise. I just need to hear it from him too.

CHAPTER 40

I spend three hours on the train nibbling my thumbnail, tapping my foot, and checking the time on my phone. Not even listening to music can settle my nerves. Talking to Carly took the edge off in the beginning, but now that I'm alone with too much time to think, the anxiety is back in full force.

Daniel leaving Naiad *could* be a huge declaration. No one leaves the job they enjoy unless they have a damn good reason. And if his reason is not wanting to hide his relationship with me… Oh God, that's a lot. That's big. That's a confession without having to say the words.

That's more than I ever expected.

I'm on my feet when the train pulls into Penn Station, and I practically trip down the steps and onto the platform. I drag my suitcase along behind me on the cracked concrete, making an absolute racket as I go, dodging and weaving around people who are moving too slowly. I need to get out of here, need to be out in the city instead of stuck in its writhing belly.

When the escalator finally drops me in the train hall, I stop and breathe. I can't just storm to the Upper West Side and hope to run into him. I need a game plan.

Now that I have better reception, I pull out my phone to call him.

He better fucking answer this time. If he ignores another one of my calls or texts, I'm going to—

"Selene."

My phone nearly tumbles from my hand at my name. The sound of it rolls off the speaker's tongue with such warm familiarity, yet it doesn't stop my heart from racing. It takes a moment before I can will myself turn toward the voice.

"Daniel," I exhale, so relieved to see him that I almost laugh, despite the furious disbelief coursing through me. All of this is so outrageous. I jumped off a train at midnight to see a man. How embarrassing. "You fucking *asshole*."

He isn't fazed by my insult or the way I storm over to him. I barely resist the urge to kick him in the groin like I've so desperately wanted to do for years now. All my rage has rushed back, replacing the nerves.

"I can't believe you," I seethe, only stopping once I'm in his face. "You quit last week? And you didn't *tell me*? You better have a damn good explanation."

"I do," he says simply. His level of calm just makes me angrier. "I got a better job."

I wait for him to elaborate, but when he doesn't, I throw my hands up. Of course when I need him to actually talk to me, he goes back to his vague little answers. Un-fucking-believable.

"Okay, sure, let's go with that!" I release a heavy breath after my outburst, trying to chill a little. We won't get anywhere if I'm about to burst a blood vessel, and I really don't want to be the crazy lady screaming in the train station. "Why quit so suddenly? Why not put in your two weeks? And why"—my voice breaks—"why not tell me?"

"Because I didn't want you to worry."

Is this man for real?

"A little late for that!" I snap. "What do you think I've been doing for the past twelve hours? Twiddling my thumbs?" I shake my head and press my fingers to my brow, once again trying to convince my blood pressure to come down. "You know what?" I say as I drop my hands, fighting to keep my voice even. "I'm happy for you. I'm sure this new position is better than your old one."

"It is," he says easily, still infuriatingly calm. "I signed the contract today. I wanted to wait until it was official to tell you, but I didn't think it was going to take this long."

I deflate a little, my anger dipping a notch. "I—Okay. But why not share this with me? I could have handled it. I could have kept a secret." I swallow back the lump in my throat. "And why make me come all the way here to tell me when it could have been a phone call?"

"Because I needed to look you in the eye when I said it. So you'd believe me. I didn't want you to doubt me." He angles in a little closer, forcing me to either stand my ground or shift back. I don't move. "I didn't quit because I found another job."

My heart picks up the pace, thumping hard, because I already know what he's going to say. But I still want to hear it. "Then why did you quit?"

There's no distance left between us now. He cups my jaw with both hands, forcing me to look at him. Whatever remains of my anger floods away when I meet his gaze. The look in his eye is so sincere that I don't even care that this is happening in the middle of the busy train hall. Only the two of us exist right now.

"I quit so you wouldn't ever have to worry about losing your job because of me," he murmurs. "So that you would never have to choose between me and your career." He strokes a thumb over my cheekbone, the tenderness of it threatening to reduce me to tears. "I know how much you love it. And I never want to jeopardize it. I want you to keep doing what you dreamed of." He presses his forehead against mine. "Do you see now why I didn't want to tell you this over the phone?"

"I think I get it," I whisper, pressing my hands to his chest. Beneath my palms, his heart beats strong. "You quit for me."

"Don't flatter yourself," he says, but the hint of a smile on his lips softens the words. "I quit so I could keep doing this and not get in trouble for it."

There's no hesitation when his mouth finds mine. The kiss is slow, soft, teasing. It's so quintessentially Daniel that I lose my breath in a split second. He slides one hand into my hair and the other to my waist, knowing instinctively that my knees are about to give out.

He *knows* me. This man I was once convinced didn't know shit about me now understands exactly who I am and what I need. I don't know how it happened, and I don't know if I ever will. But I don't care. I'm just glad it did, because this is worth every up and down and misstep and challenge we've faced to get to this moment.

This is everything.

Eventually, he pulls back, leaving me to catch the breath he's stolen away. "I didn't do this for you," he reminds me, but the more he says it, the less I believe it. "I did it because I'm selfish. Because I don't want to be told what to do. Because it makes *me* happy to give you anything you want, and I refuse to let anyone stop me." He pauses and licks his bottom lip. "And also because this new job pays three times more than I was making before."

"That last one is a pretty damn good reason on its own," I commend. My voice is somehow level, even though my heart is threatening to burst out of my chest.

"It was the others that convinced me." The honesty in his dark eyes nearly breaks me. "That first night we were together, after the holiday party…I told you my job was to look out for the company, not you."

A wry smile twists its way onto my face at the memory. What a night that was. "I remember."

"It was a shitty thing to say, but it was true," he admits. "Now, though, I'll never have to do that again." He takes a breath, but unlike the way all of mine shake, his is steady. "No more having to take risks. No more hiding. What do you say?"

I let the question hang between us for a moment, but I've already got my answer. "I like the way that sounds."

"Good." I feel his smile as he kisses me again. His lips linger on mine, then he whispers, "Come home with me."

I pull back. "To your apartment?" I ask, but of course that's what he means. I try to make a joke of it instead. "That's a…pretty big step, isn't it? I mean, we've only ever been on a single date."

He laughs softly, shaking his head. "I think we've already taken much bigger steps."

"You're right." I give into him easily for what might be the first time—though not completely. "I mean, you *did* quit your job for me after all."

He fights a grin. He knows what he's getting into with me. "No, I didn't."

"Mm, keep telling yourself that."

I can joke all I want. I can tease him and let him tease me back. But this is what I want. No matter how much I've tried to hide and disguise it. How much I've tried to deny it in an attempt to protect my heart.

But I can't deny it anymore. I love him. I want to be with him. There's no reason to shy away. He wants this as much as I do, and he's made it abundantly clear.

Now the world can know too.

"Take me home, Daniel," I tell the man I swore to hate forever. "I'm ready."

JANUARY

EPILOGUE

I still hate New York in winter. But I officially live here now, so I guess I have to suck it up and deal.

"How many more boxes of books do you have?" Daniel asks, sounding a little irritated after carrying the latest one up to his apartment. *Our* apartment now.

Since my lease was up and Carly moved in with her boyfriend, I figured there was no better time to move to the city…and move in with my own boyfriend. Pretty sure he's regretting the invite already.

I shrug, eyeing the stack that remains in the moving truck, wishing we could be inside and curled up together instead of standing on the filthy, snowy streets and freezing our asses off. "I don't know," I say truthfully. "Maybe a dozen?"

He groans. "*Dios mío*, Selene. You're supposed to use the third bedroom as an office, not a library."

I flash him a grin and put my hands up in an exaggerated shrug. "*Por qué no los dos?*"

Daniel closes his eyes and takes a deep breath, then lifts a finger to stop me. "First of all, don't you dare quote a taco commercial at me. Second, don't think speaking my first language will put you in my good graces."

I pout and frame my face with my mitten covered hands. "How

can you be mad at this face?"

"*Selene.*"

"Okay, okay," I huff, picking up a box. "See? I'm helping."

"You could have helped by hiring movers instead of putting your stuff in a U-Haul and driving it up here."

"But isn't it hot as hell that I did this all by myself?" I prompt. "I'm a strong, capable woman who can drive a big truck on major highways *and* through a city."

"And you're cheap too," he says, rolling his eyes as he turns back toward the building where the doorman is laughing at us.

"Not all of us are billionaires!" I call to Daniel's retreating back.

"I'm not a billionaire!"

"Keep lying to yourself!"

He groans, then disappears into the building, and I wander over to Mick, who's holding open the door now.

"Thanks for putting up with us," I say, still grinning. "I annoy him, but I promise he loves me."

"You two are the best entertainment I've had in ages," he admits, taking the box from me to set inside the atrium. "I'm glad you're finally moving in. My wife keeps hounding me to get your autograph, and now I won't have to worry about missing you when you come to visit."

"Well then, it's your lucky day." I pull my new keys out of my coat pocket and cut through the tape on the box I was just holding—a box full of my own books. I grab one off the top and rummage around in my purse for a pen. When I finally find one, I scrawl my name and a short note thanking her for reading, then hand it over to Mick. "May the hounding cease."

He beams at me, tucking the book under his arm like it's precious. "I owe you one."

I wave it off. "Hey, happy wife, happy life. Just trying to make things a little easier for us all."

"Everyone except for me," Daniel says, striding through the lobby.

I give him a once-over as he moves in my direction. Dark, messy hair that I love to run my fingers through. Even darker eyes that come alive when we're close. Incredibly fit body—hidden under a coat, but I'm determined to get that off him in a bit. And it's all mine.

Just like I'm all his.

"I'll make it up to you," I promise, reaching for his hand. When we're on the sidewalk, just out of Mick's sight, I lean in and press a kiss to Daniel's jaw. "I was thinking we could christen my office-slash-library tonight. What do you think?"

He snakes an arm around my waist and pulls me flush against him. "I'm thinking I can't wait to bend you over that antique oak desk I bought you."

A shiver races down my spine, and it's not because of the cold. "Maybe I should see if I can hire last-minute movers. Maybe we can speed this process up a little." Because I would like to be bent over that desk sooner rather than later, thank you very much.

When a throat clears behind us, I spin around and come face to face with three buff men watching us expectantly.

"Already ahead of you, *mi amor*," Daniel murmurs in my ear. "Let's get you moved in." *And properly fucked* goes unsaid, but I know what he means.

"Yeah. Let's do that." Before he can move away, I clutch at his jacket. "Hey. I love you. Thank you for putting up with me."

"I wouldn't put up with you if I didn't love you too," he says, and the smile he gives me says more than his words ever could.

There may be plenty of things I hate—like New York in winter, excessive anchovies on pizza, and aggressive pigeons—but Daniel Santiago will never be on that list again.

Want more Selene and Daniel? Visit leilaburnes.com and sign up for my newsletter to gain access to bonus chapters, as well as sneak peeks of future books and other exclusive content!

And keep reading for a bonus novella...

BONUS NOVELLA
A continuation from Chapter 40

CHAPTER 1

"So. This is home."

Daniel closes the door behind us as I take in the entryway of his apartment. I'm greeted by high ceilings with beautiful crown molding and original dark wood floors. He drops his keys into a colorful dish on an antique oak side table just inside the door. In the gilded mirror hanging above it, I catch his eye, taking in how good we look side by side here, like this was where we were always meant to end up.

I don't blink as he curves his arm around my waist and pulls me into his side. He angles close and brings his lips down to brush the shell of my ear, but he doesn't break our eye contact.

"This is home," he says, pressing a hand into my belly possessively. "This is where you'll stay when you come up to the city. No more hotels. I want you with me."

I tilt my head back as his lips skate from my ear to my jaw. "What if I like staying in a hotel? There's room service. And it's closer to the office. Your place is so much farther."

"I'll convince you it's better here." He kisses the pulse point in my throat and lifts his head again. "Are you hungry?"

He can probably feel my stomach rumbling under his palm. I've been too anxious to eat thanks to his dramatic departure from Naiad, and I haven't had anything since breakfast. God, it's been a long day.

"I am, actually," I admit, leaning against him, grateful he's taken on my weight. Now that I have a moment to assess how I'm feeling, I'm exhausted. But I don't want to waste a moment of the time I have with him on sleep.

Daniel presses another gentle kiss to the corner of my jaw before he pulls back. "I'll cook."

I shake my head and turn in his arms, not willing to let him go yet. I need to feel the heat of him seeping into me. I need the reassurance that this is real and not a dream I'm bound to wake up from. "It's late. Let's order delivery."

He trails his fingers down my arms and grasps my hands for a moment before dropping one and nodding for me to follow him. "Come on."

I let him guide me down the short hall to the archway at the end. On the other side is a sleek kitchen, far bigger than I expected, with a marble island and expansive dark cabinets. He has top-of-the-line appliances, the kind I'd expect to see in the home of a professional chef, not the former acquisitions manager of a serialized story app. Every detail of the space screams wealth.

"Sit," he instructs, pulling out one of the stools at the island. "I'll get you a drink."

I settle on the cushioned seat. There's no point in protesting. He'll do all he can to make me comfortable, and I'm learning to let him; it always results in me being perfectly pleased.

He steps over to the bar cart in the corner and grabs two rocks glasses etched in gold and deep azure. The more I notice, the more I realize that this isn't the home of a man with new money. This feels old—the kind that comes with a deep history.

"Tell me about the new job," I prompt. "Is it still in publishing?"

"No." He picks up an undeniably expensive bottle of tequila from the cart as well and deposits everything on the island. Then he selects a few beautifully bright limes from the wooden bowl of citrus in front of me before pulling a knife from the block. "I went back to my investment banking roots."

I wrinkle my nose. "Ew, I'm dating an investment banker?" I tease. "Tragic. But that explains why you're getting paid so much."

A hint of a smile pulls up the corners of his mouth as he slices into a lime. "So sorry to disappoint," he says, humor tinting the words. "Will you ever find it in your heart to forgive me?"

Blowing out a dramatic sigh, I lean my elbows on the island and shrug. "I mean, I guess. If the alternative is us having to break up, I can force myself to get over it."

"You're so kind."

I don't fight the grin that comes to my face. Contentedness swirls through my chest at the way we tease and taunt each other. The spark that originally brought us together is still there, even after all the other challenges we've faced. It gives me hope that our burgeoning relationship will stand the test of time. There's no way I'm giving him up.

In minutes he slides a margarita rimmed with salt toward me, and I take a sip as he turns back toward the gleaming fridge. He gathers items and brings them over to the counter to chop and slice.

He moves with the kind of ease that tells me he does this often. On our first official date, he told me that he hates when people get in his way in the kitchen, so I'll stay on my side of the island and let him take care of everything—let him take care of me.

Once peppers and seasoned chicken are sizzling on the burner, I ask him a question I've been dying to know all day.

"When did you decide you wanted to leave Naiad?"

He sets the wooden spoon he's holding aside and turns back to me. Propping himself up against the counter, he assesses me for a moment, dragging out my curiosity. "I started thinking about leaving last year," he tells me, holding my gaze. "I was ready to move on to something different. But the morning after the holiday party, I knew for sure."

My breath catches. "Are you serious?" That was the start of everything for us.

He nods. Something in his expression softens further, like he's allowing unfiltered access to the way he feels about me—and how long he's felt that way.

I force myself to exhale a steadying breath. Once again, the earth is shifting under me. Because in this moment, I realize that we've both been in deep for a long time, even if neither of us wanted to admit it.

There's a slight waver in my voice as I joke, "I'm good in bed, but I didn't think I was good enough to make a man leave his job."

Blessedly, Daniel smiles. "Good enough to make me do anything," he replies. The honesty behind it has my eyes burning.

"I'll have to tell my pussy thank you," I say weakly, but he still throws his head back and laughs.

"You're too much sometimes," he admonishes with a grin.

He turns away and taps at his phone's screen. A moment later, a soft bolero plays from unseen speakers around the kitchen.

It has me relaxing, filling the silence that could have quickly become heavy after his confession, and I smile as he makes his way around the island to me, offering up a hand.

"You still know how to dance to this?" he asks me.

I take his hand and slide off my barstool. "I can dance to anything."

"So cocky."

"Only for you."

I let him pull me close, let his fingers curl around mine and his arm snake around my waist, let him guide me into it. We fall into the steps easily, moving together like we've had years to learn each other. When his knee slots between mine and brings our bodies flush, I debate whether I'm actually hungry enough to eat or if I'm just ready to drag him to bed.

I close my eyes and bury my face in his neck, breathing in his scent, remembering our first dance. That one dance, the one I was goaded into. How could it have led to this? Me, here. In love with a man I thought I'd hate forever and luxuriating in his love in return.

"I'm so glad you're here," he murmurs against my hair. We're barely moving in time to the music, too caught up in each other to care. It's like we've both been waiting for this moment. To simply hold each other and revel in the fact that we can.

"I'm glad to be here," I whisper back. And even though this has been the most stressful day of my life, this moment has made it all—the anxiety, the heart palpitations, the tears—worth it.

After dinner, Daniel and I stand side by side at the sink. He washes the dishes and I dry them. We work in companionable silence, damp hands brushing as he passes me plates. My chest aches at the domesticity of it. The feeling is wholly new to me and quite possibly the most satisfying experience—outside the bedroom—of my life.

When the dishes are clean and dry, Daniel gathers me in his arms, holding me against his chest. I can't read minds, but I know he's thinking exactly what I am—that we can do this with no worries now. That this is how it'll be for us going forward. No more doubts. No more looking over our shoulders. No more concerns that this isn't real.

"Thank you for dinner," I mumble against his T-shirt, my arms wrapped tight around his waist. I don't want to move even an inch away from him. I'm full and warm and happy right where I am.

"Of course. I wouldn't let my girl starve."

My heart does something funny behind my ribs as he kisses the top of my head. "Your girl?"

"That's what you are, aren't you?"

There's no hesitation in my answer. "I absolutely am."

He holds me like he never plans to let go. "Good." He inhales, just to let it out in a rush a moment later, somehow pulling me closer. There's a desperation to it. One that has me clinging to him. "Fucking good."

My throat is tight, making it impossible to express just what he means to me—he's my person too. I've finally found the one I can worship, the one who will worship me in return. I don't want to cry, because I've done enough of that already, but there's no room left in my body for the tide of emotions. They demand to be released in any way they can.

Daniel draws back a little when my breath hitches, cupping my face and looking deep into my eyes. My vision is hazy, glossed over with tears, but there's no missing the tenderness staring back at me. I appreciate that he doesn't ask if I'm okay. He just brushes away the wetness that's fallen onto my cheeks, dragging his thumbs back and forth across my skin. He understands.

"Can we go to bed now?" My voice is nothing but a hoarse whisper.

He nods and lets his hands trail down my face. They drift over my shoulders and down my arms until he's taking my hands and guiding me out of the kitchen.

We head back into the hall and step through another doorway, bringing us into his bedroom. The walls are a soothing gray, and the furniture is more dark, heavy oak, including the frame surrounding the king-size bed in front of us. After seeing other bits of the apartment, I'm not at all surprised by the quiet luxury, down to the plush bedding I can't wait to collapse into.

I'm distracted from my admiration when Daniel lifts my hand to his lips and kisses my knuckles. "I'll go get your bag," he says quietly. "Make yourself comfortable."

I nod and watch him disappear back into the hall, a little stunned that I'm actually *here* in his bedroom, a space I never could have imagined myself in. It suits him perfectly, though. It's calming and softly lit, the kind of room that has all of today's leftover tension flooding out of my body. It's a place I never want to leave.

I'm sitting on the edge of the bed when he returns with my suitcase and rolls it over to stand beside my left knee. "I have no idea what I packed," I confess with an embarrassed, breathy laugh. "I was so stressed that I wasn't even paying attention. I just wanted to get here."

He chuckles as he turns away from me again and moves to the dresser pressed to the wall. Opening the top drawer, he pulls out a faded Columbia T-shirt and a pair of boxers.

"You can wear these tonight," he says, his fingers brushing mine as I take the stack he holds out to me. "There's a toothbrush for you in the basket under the bathroom sink. We'll tackle your suitcase tomorrow, yeah?"

I don't even want to think about tomorrow. But I nod, nonetheless, and slowly rise from the edge of the bed. Daniel doesn't step back, even though we're only inches apart, like he was waiting for me to get this close again.

"Considering you've given me pajamas to put on, I guess we're not having sex tonight," I joke. Truth is, I'm so drained that the idea of doing anything more than lying beside him in this beautiful bed seems daunting.

Daniel tucks a stray lock of hair behind my ear, his fingertips lingering on the corner of my jaw. "I just want to hold you tonight. Is that okay?"

Again, my heart threatens to stage a revolt. "Yeah," I exhale. "That's all I need."

My eyes flutter shut when he dips his head and brushes his lips to mine in the softest of kisses. It's chaste and purely innocent, and yet it still has me swaying into him like he's swept me off my feet.

And I guess he has.

"Go get changed," he mumbles against my mouth. "I want to be in bed with you. I want you beside me." His hand finds the back of my neck, stroking the nape with gentle possession. "And I want to wake up with you for as many mornings as you'll let me."

"How about all of them?" I offer. He can have all of my tomorrows, as many as we're given together.

I feel his smile, the steady beat of his heart against mine, the undeniable love that flows between us.

"I'll take it."

CHAPTER 2

I wake up curled into Daniel's side. My head is on his shoulder, and I'm clutching at him like I was afraid he'd disappear into the night. But he's here with his arm around me, his chest slowly rising and falling beneath my hand. I watch it lift and lower over and over and over again, taking it all in—him, this room, us together.

This is my life now. I'm allowed to wake up next to this man whenever I want—as long as I'm in New York, I suppose. We'll have to talk about logistics at some point, but right now, I'm just so grateful for this small moment that I nearly let out a giggle of delight.

Maybe I actually do, because Daniel stirs beside me, almost like he can feel the force of my joy pressing down on him. I don't want to wake him, though, so I slip out of bed before he can open his eyes and quietly pad across the cream carpet to the en suite bathroom.

I leave the door cracked as I splash water on my face and pat it dry with the towel Daniel hung up for me last night on the hook next to his. He even put my toothbrush on my own shelf in the medicine cabinet, like that space was always meant for me. It's a silly little thing, the smallest act of domesticity, and yet it has me biting my lip to keep from grinning too widely. Daniel has made a place for me in his life in various ways already; now I get to discover them all.

I'm in the middle of brushing my teeth when the door inches open and Daniel steps in. His hair is ruffled from sleep and his boxers are low on his hips. I lift my free hand and give him a finger wave, which earns me a chuckle and a shake of his head in response. He doesn't say it, but I can hear him calling me ridiculous in my head.

He snags his own toothbrush from the medicine cabinet and joins me in the morning ritual. There isn't a second of it that feels awkward, even as we bump elbows and take turns to spit into the sink. It feels like we've been doing this for years. I'll take it as a sign that Daniel and I are meant to be.

When our toothbrushes are tucked away again, he tugs me into his arms and kisses me. His tongue tangles with mine for a quick second before he pulls back. "Good morning."

"It really is," I murmur against his lips before kissing across his jaw. "Last night wasn't a dream, was it?"

"If it was, then we must still be asleep," he answers. "Otherwise, you wouldn't be standing in my bathroom and wearing my clothes."

"Maybe I should pinch you, just to be sure."

Before I can even attempt it, he has my wrists in his grasp. But there's a spark of humor in his eyes as he shoots me a dry look. "Nice try, Satan."

I stick my tongue out at him in retribution, but I don't try to pull away. "Always spoiling my fun."

"If that keeps you from pinching my ass, then I'll do it."

"Who says I was going to pinch your ass? I could've gone for your arm."

"I know you," Daniel counters, and he's right—I *was* tempted to pinch his ass. But honestly, who wouldn't want to? The man has a great one. "And you were going to pinch my ass."

I roll my eyes, fighting a smile. But this is what he brings out in me—the playfulness, the teasing, and the taunting.

He brings out the real me.

"Yeah, yeah." I push up onto my tiptoes so I can kiss him again. There's a thrill in knowing I can steal them whenever I want. Although, considering it's nearly seven thirty, there are only so many more I can grab before we have to act like functioning adults in society. "Do you have to work today?"

He shakes his head, loosening his grip on my wrists. "I don't start until next week. Are you planning to go into the office today?"

I sink my teeth into my lower lip, worrying it back and forth. "They're not expecting me until tomorrow. I could work from here, I guess." But even as I say it, and as much as it would be nice to spend the day with Daniel, I won't get anything done if we're in the same place.

He seems to know that as well. "Just tell them you changed your train. They're always excited to see you, so they won't question it."

"Yeah, unlike you, they actually like me," I tease. But my anxiety from yesterday is sinking back in, leaving my words a little hollow. I swallow hard, linking my hands behind his neck as I meet his eyes. "Can I ask you something?"

"Of course, *mi amor*."

"When should we start telling people?" I pause to wet my lips, continuing on before he can say anything. "I already told my roommate, but what about the Naiad girls? I don't think I want to hide it from them for much longer, even though I'm kind of afraid of what their reactions will be." My next words are softer, but I need him to know how sure I am about him. "I want them to know about you. About us. I want to show you off."

He's fighting a smile, and while the sight of it after that vulnerable confession partially makes me want to curl in on myself—old habits die hard—I know he isn't mocking me. He's trying not to push me too hard, too fast with his own reaction. He's thrilled.

"I want the same." His words are measured, but the way he looks at me says far more. I'm his whole fucking world. "Now, can I ask you something?"

I nod.

"Am I allowed to call you my girlfriend?"

Unlike him, I don't hold back my grin. "Ooh, a label. Very fancy." I lean a little farther into him. "Yes, you can call me your girlfriend."

"Good." He tilts his head down, bringing us eye to eye again. "In that case, you should tell the girls tonight."

That wipes the grin off my face. "Are you sure?"

"Like you, I don't want to keep this a secret. Especially from the people we're closest with."

Worry twists through my stomach, not because I'm scared to share our relationship, but because of how long it's taken me to reveal it. "What if they hate me for lying to them for so long?"

It's not the judgment I fear anymore. People can and will judge all they want. But I don't know if I could handle it if my friends turned against me for keeping secrets.

He cups my face, holding me steady. "If they do, then they weren't your friends in the first place."

He's right. Carly's reaction is a reminder that not everyone will be upset. Plus, if Carly, an outsider to the whole situation, could understand why I kept this all a secret, then the Naiad girls absolutely will. They know all about our no-fraternization policy, plus we all bonded over our shared hatred of Daniel. They probably wouldn't have believed me if I said I was involved with him any sooner than now.

"It's going to be okay," he reassures, thumb stroking across my cheekbone. "If you decide you don't want to tell them right away, that's fine. But at least go to the office and see how you feel."

I nod. "Okay. I will." I let my head loll in his hand, basking in the support he gives me, but I still pout a little. "But that means I have to go soon. And I don't want to leave."

"It takes twenty minutes if you take the 1 train," Daniel says, dropping his attention to my mouth. The desire igniting in his eyes sends heat blooming within me. "So that gives you…an hour to get ready."

"To get ready," I repeat, bracing my palms against his chest. "Right…"

He nods, his Adam's apple bobbing as he swallows. "I should let you get to it, then."

"You should," I agree.

"I should," he says. "But I won't."

His lips crash down on mine a second later, and I respond without another thought. We kiss feverishly, the press of a timeline guiding our tempo. A sigh escapes me as his tongue brushes mine. The pressure of his hand behind my head is dominating, and his grip is meant to keep me from escaping. Not that I want to. No, I want him to take as much as he can, to make me forget anything else in this world exists except for him.

He slips his free hand under my shirt, grazing the sensitive skin of my breast with his fingers, then covering it completely with his palm. I cup him over his boxers in return, feeling the hardness underneath, hot through the thin fabric. He groans into my mouth, then turns his head, leaving my lips to fall to the column of his throat. When I lick up it, his hand squeezes me harder.

"Fuck me in the shower," I request, though it comes out as more of a plea. I'm desperate for him. "Kill two birds with one stone." Because as much as I'd like him to bend me over every piece of furniture in this place, I do still have to go to work. How disappointing.

"Let me get a condom."

"You don't need to." I kiss his neck again, scraping my teeth over his skin and gaining the shudder I'm after.

"No?" he questions, slipping his hands to my hips, dragging me closer. There's a challenge in the word and in the way he makes me grind against him, like he's daring me to take back what I've said.

I gasp as my clit pulses from the friction. "I'm on birth control," I reveal once I can find the words. "And you're the only one I've been with in…" I trail off. He knows exactly how long. I don't need to say it again. "I'm good." I want to feel him without anything between us.

"So am I," he replies. "I get tested regularly, and you know there hasn't been anyone else. You're it for me, Selene." He dips his head to find my lips again, kissing me deep and hard—thankful. It lingers for a moment before he pulls back to ask, "But are you sure?"

I can't nod hard enough. "Very."

That's all it takes. He tears away from me and wrenches open the glass shower door, flicking the handle and letting the showerhead come to life. As the bathroom fills with steam, he rids me of my clothes and steps out of his boxers, then takes my hand and leads me into the dark green tiled shower stall. It's stupidly lux and sleek like the rest of his apartment, and I make a mental note to ask him how the hell he affords all of this.

But that conversation can come later. Way later.

He positions us so our faces are out of the spray but our bodies are warmed by the water. Rivulets drip down his chest, between his pecs and over his abs, parting on either side of his thick length. The next thing I know, he's grasping me behind my thighs, just under my ass. He lifts me before I even expect it, and my back hits the wall as my legs go intuitively around his waist. The gasp that leaves me spurs him to lift me higher. A smirk tugs up the corner of his mouth at my surprise.

"I've got you, baby. Do you trust me?"

"No," I pant, already feeling the nudge of his cock at my opening.

"Liar."

The biggest.

He sinks into me with a groan, supporting me as I slide down the wall a few inches so I take all of him in one go. The searing heat of it makes me clutch at his shoulders and throw my head back, torn between wanting him to stay exactly there so I can savor the fullness and wanting him to fuck me into the tiles.

"Oh my God." I barely recognize my own voice, half-choked, half-crazed. "You're going to ruin me, Daniel."

His chuckle rumbles through his chest. We're so connected that I can't tell where he ends and I begin. "You can take it."

I whine a little when he pulls out ever so slightly and eases back in. My pussy clenches involuntarily as he tests me. I'm more than ready for him to give me more.

"I won't fuck you too hard, though," he promises, only a little breathless as he skims a hand along my waist. "You need to be able to walk."

But do I want to be able to walk if it means he's going to hold back? Even if he does, what he's doing now is still more than enough to make me cry out his name and dig my nails into his shoulders.

Each of his thrusts is deep and sharp, his hips snapping up into me in the perfect rhythm. At this angle, I swear I'm feeling things I've never felt before. Every nerve ending within me is alight and stimulated, too aware of the steady beat of water down on our bodies and the pressure of my inner walls pulsing around his cock. Between his motions and the finger he swirls around my clit, I'm not going to last long.

I buck against him, lifting my hips, but he drives me back with the force of his strokes. I grasp at anything I can get my hands on—his jaw, his shoulders, the tiles behind me—though nothing gives me the purchase I need to reciprocate. So I press back and take it, let my eyes flutter shut as the pressure builds like a simmering flame.

He nips at my ear and murmurs praise in both English and Spanish, forcing a moan to erupt from deep within me. His words—

how well I take his cock, how beautiful I look doing it, how he wants to feel me come undone around him—just add fuel to the fire. I cry out when I come, one palm slamming back against the slick tiles as the other presses against his chest.

I'm burning, but he keeps going, rougher than before, already breaking his promise of gentleness. But I don't care. I want to feel his mark on me all day. I want to keep him as my favorite secret for a little while longer. There's no more hiding after this.

I let my forehead fall against his as I try to catch my breath. When I tip back to rest my head against the tiles again, our eyes lock for a split second, but it feels like an eternity. Though neither of us has said the words in their entirety just yet, we both know what this look means.

I love you. I've been in love with you. You're everything to me.

The moment breaks when he claims my mouth again, stealing my breath away. It's hard and frenzied, the kind of desperation that comes from realizing just how emotionally intertwined we are. We knew it, there's no way we didn't, but now it's overwhelming and unignorable.

I pull back enough to drag in a ragged breath, heart beating wildly because I still haven't recovered from the intensity of my orgasm.

Daniel's strokes start to shallow out, signaling that he won't be far behind me.

"I'm close," he warns a moment later, giving me the option if I want him to pull out.

I squeeze my thighs tighter around him in answer, keeping him there, refusing to let him move away. I want this mark too, impermanent as it is. I want every bit of him.

He spills inside me, still moving in short thrusts, letting the water wash away what drips down my thighs. Eventually, he stills, breathing hard and dropping his face to the crook of my neck. It's a miracle he's still holding me up, though soon he eases me down until I'm standing on my tiptoes, still holding on to our connection, not wanting him to leave me empty until the last possible second.

He strokes my hips reverently as he kisses across my cheeks. When he pulls back again to meet my eyes, my own emotions are mirrored back at me.

"You okay?" he asks, always checking in.

I nod. "Yeah," I answer, heart pounding. "Never better."

"Good." He brushes his lips over mine one more time, so sweet that I can't help but smile. "Then let's get you ready for work."

CHAPTER 3

I only wince a little when I lower myself into my desk chair at the Naiad office.

I've already fielded shrieked greetings from Nikki and Ella, and now Zoe is standing behind me with her arms wrapped around my shoulders, her cheek pressed to mine.

"I'm so glad you're here," she slurs, thanks to our squished faces. "How long do we get you for this time?"

That's a good question. According to what I found in my suitcase this morning, I have enough underwear for two weeks, but unless I go shopping after work today, I'll have to wear this sweater with one of the five pairs of jeans I packed. Daniel laughed at me when I unzipped the case this morning and found the shit show. To my credit, I remembered mascara and deodorant.

"At least through Wednesday for the big all-hands meeting," I tell her. Though it'll probably be longer. It's not like I have to worry about where I'll stay or outrageous hotel bills; I have a home here now.

The thought knocks the air from my lungs. I have a home with Daniel. He's invited me to share it with him, to be beside him when I can. I can't break my lease, and I won't leave Carly alone anytime soon, but once January rolls around, I know where I'll be permanently. I'm ready. Plus, Daniel made it obvious this morning when he tugged me into another room in his apartment and told me that it would be my office. Would be, not could be, like it was already set in stone. I didn't protest.

"Do you want to get dinner tonight?" I snap out of my daze to look between the girls. "We need a catch-up session."

"I'm in," Nikki says without hesitation. "What about that tapas place around the corner? I could absolutely drink a pitcher of sangria by myself."

I have a feeling she's going to need that pitcher to cope with what I plan to share. "Sounds perfect."

I'm fucking nervous.

Thankfully, the girls haven't caught on to that detail yet. We're sitting around a table at the tapas restaurant, skimming the menu. I murmur agreements to the things they choose, and Nikki places our order with the server. When the man walks away and three sets of eyes turn to me, my stomach drops.

"You good?" Zoe asks, her head cocked to the side as she takes me in. "You look a little…sweaty."

Oh, great, my nerves have manifested themselves into a greasy glow, and one swipe across my forehead with the back of my head confirms it. "Yeah, I'm fine." I try to brush it off, but now Ella's looking at me curiously as well. Nikki is making grabby hands at the server, who's already returned with the pitcher of sangria.

"It's just a little warm in here."

It's not quite a lie, but I can't keep putting this off. It's been long enough already.

"Actually, I have something I need to tell you," I announce as Nikki pours sangria for us all. "And I…I want to apologize in advance for not saying anything sooner. I just didn't know how to tell you." I grab my glass and take a massive swig to steel my nerves.

Zoe, probably the most dramatic of the group, exclaims, "Oh my God, are you pregnant?"

Sangria nearly shoots through my nose. "*What?*" I splutter as I lower my drink. "No! Of course not."

"She's literally drinking alcohol, Zoe," Ella points out gently, but Nikki's head is lolling back in disbelief that she'd ask that. "How could that be what she wants to tell us?"

Zoe waves a hand. "I got overexcited, sorry. I just love babies."

"We know," Ella, Nikki, and I say in unison. Zoe is our resident pregnancy-trope lover.

As Zoe smiles bashfully, Ella motions for me to ignore the interruption. "What did you want to tell us?"

Here it is. The moment of truth. I take a deep breath and tamp down on the way my stomach is trying to work its way up into my throat, wondering if I should ease them into it or just toss 'em into the deep end.

"I'm dating Daniel," I blurt, so loudly that I'm sure every person in here heard.

My shouted confession is met with stunned silence. No one moves. No one blinks. Hell, I don't think they even breathe.

"I'm sorry," Nikki says what feels like an eternity later. The words are drawn out and slow. "But did you say you're dating Daniel? Daniel who?"

Her question is genuine, like she wouldn't dare to fathom that the Daniel in question is the one that we've worked with for years.

"Daniel Santiago," I clarify when I work up the courage to meet her eyes. "Our coworker who quit last week." I take a breath and finish, "Who quit so he and I could be in a relationship without getting in trouble for it."

The silence stretches on endlessly. They're all staring at me like I've grown a second, third, and fourth head. Zoe's mouth opens and closes like she's trying to form words but can't. Nikki's frozen like a beautiful marble statue.

It's Ella who clasps her hands together tightly and leans in, brow furrowed, and squeaks, "Start from the beginning. And please don't leave out a single detail."

We've just ordered our fifth pitcher of sangria, and I'm sure it's going to disappear as quickly as the last four did. I've gotten through most of my story, fielding disbelieving questions along the way, but so far, no one seems mad at me for lying. They barely even seem disgusted. Just...shocked.

"Hold on, hold on, hold on," Nikki interrupts again, her words slurring slightly and her usually light Brooklyn accent growing thicker. "You're saying that this—this *guy*, this asshole piss-baby *loser* who made our lives hell at work, isn't an asshole piss-baby loser after all? Am I hearing you right? Because that date you described"—she throws her head back and bites the side of her fist—"*girl*. I'd lose my mind and fuck him too if he bought me hundreds of dollars of books *and* the best croissants in the city."

"You know what they say," Ella cuts in with a giggle as sangria splashes over the edge of her glass. "There's a thin line between—"

"Oh my God, shut *up*," Zoe interrupts. She's practically halfway across the table, leaning in and clutching at my arm like she's trying to keep me from running away. "But Selene... Holy *shit*. Holy shit! I can't believe you kept this to yourself for so long. Why didn't you *tell us*?"

"Because she didn't want us to judge her, duh," Nikki answers for me. "I'm judging the hell out of her right now, that's for sure. I mean... *Daniel?* Out of everyone on the planet? Man's stupid hot, sure. He's also the worst coworker I've ever had. But you know what?" She levels her gaze on me and nods in approval. "Good for you. You went after what you wanted and didn't let anything stop you. That's brave."

"And I'm glad you told us the truth eventually," Ella adds to soften Nikki's backhanded compliment. "That was brave too. Thank you for trusting us."

"You guys don't hate me for lying?" I hedge, glancing around the table.

Nikki snorts and leans back in her chair. "Fuck no. I'd keep that shit locked down too. Fucking your mortal enemy? Talk about embarrassing."

"Nikki!" Ella scolds as she slaps her shoulder. "Come on! We're supposed to be supporting her."

"Well, it's not embarrassing *anymore*," she corrects, rolling her eyes. "Clearly, he's a decent guy underneath it all, because I really doubt you'd be with him if he didn't treat you well." She squints at me. "He's treating you well, right? Because if he's not, I'll gather up my brothers and—"

"He treats me amazingly," I stop her. "I promise. Yeah, we've had our ups and downs through all of this, but we're good." I allow myself a little smile. "Really good."

Her eyes flick over me, then she nods, appeased. "Then I'm happy for you."

"And I'm happy for *us*," Zoe cuts in, lifting her glass. "Because your relationship is the reason he won't be there to torture us anymore, thank God. You did us a solid by fucking him. Really took one for the team."

I laugh, a heavy weight lifted from my shoulders, and raise my glass to toast her. "I live to serve."

We clink glasses, and just as I predicted, the fifth pitcher dwindles down to nothing.

"I'd hold off on telling anyone else at the office, at least for a couple weeks," Zoe says after I've told them that Daniel was the one who suggested sharing our news with them. "No one else needs to know you two were getting it on while you still worked together."

She's right, though I doubt the powers that be would be too concerned, considering Daniel is no longer an employee. He really did quit for me and my happiness. What a dick.

As if he can sense me lovingly insulting him in my mind, my phone buzzes in my lap. Daniel's name appears on the screen, along with a text asking if everything is going okay. While Nikki, Zoe, and Ella rib me for it, I reply that everything is great—but that I might need him to come escort me home because I'm drunk…and also because I want to see him.

"Daniel's coming to pick me up," I tell them.

I get pelted with spare pieces of food in reply.

"Sorry that my boyfriend doesn't want me drunkenly wandering the streets of New York by myself!"

"Man, fuck that guy," Nikki says, but there's a warmth to it.

"No, literally," Zoe adds. "Go home and fuck him. Keep him occupied so he never comes back to Naiad."

Ella, the sweet voice of reason, hiccups and says, "It's very nice of him to make sure you're safe." She pauses before tacking on, "But yeah, please go get railed so we never have to deal with him in a professional setting again."

A grin so wide it hurts stretches across my face. "Your wish is my command."

The girls heckle me from down the block as I step into Daniel's waiting arms, but their lewd shouts and commentary do nothing to distract me from pressing a kiss to his cheek.

"So it went well?" he asks, his arm loose around my waist as he looks over my shoulder. "Nikki's giving me the finger right now, but she's smiling, so I'm taking that as a win."

"It went really well." I turn back, shooing the girls away. We've already agreed that tonight isn't the right time for them to meet with Daniel. If they did, I have no doubt it would lead to an aggressive interrogation. We'll give things a little time to settle. "They're happy for us. Shocked, but happy."

"Yeah?" His eyes drift back to mine, and a smile lifts his lips.

"Well, happy that I fucked you so good that you quit and now their lives are so much easier," I correct. "But what's the difference?"

"Mm, you certainly know how to make everyone happy."

"Just one of my many talents," I boast, sliding my arms around his neck and grinning. "But to be honest, you're the only one I care about making happy."

"That's funny," he murmurs, dropping his focus to my lips and dragging it up again. "Because all I care about is making *you* happy. So…" He tugs me closer, our bodies flush, not caring that we're tucked off to the side on a very public sidewalk. "Are you?"

I exhale at the feel of him against me, threading my fingers into the curls that brush his neck. "Am I happy?" I tilt my face up to the night sky as I purse my lips in thought. "Hmm…I think I could be happier."

His lips find my temple and brush over to my ear. "Oh? And how can I make that happen?"

"You could start by taking me home." I drop a hand to his chest and curl my fingers into the fabric of his shirt. "And then you could carry me to bed and let me taste your big, thick—"

"Stop talking," Daniel says, the words tight. And from the feel of it, his pants are getting a little tight too.

I bat my lashes. "Did I say something wrong?"

"You're dangerous," he murmurs, shaking his head and grasping me by the elbow.

"Just take me home so I can make good on my promises, Daniel."

"Whatever you want, *mi amor*. Whatever you want."

THE END

ACKNOWLEDGMENTS

This book is dedicated to them, but Flamingo House deserves another shout-out. Kate and Natalie, thank you for keeping me sane throughout some of the wildest moments of my life. Can't wait for our next spontaneous trip.

To my editor, Beth, for taking this manuscript and whipping it into shape. It's so much stronger because of you. You're a true miracle worker.

Mom D, you're never allowed to read this book, but I know you're proud of me, and I know Mom J would have been too. Thanks for being my chef and therapist.

To the people who read the first draft of this and gave me the confidence to put my work out there, thank you for being so supportive. Extra special thanks to Deidre for being this book's #1 supporter.

And to the real life version of Naiad Novels, thanks for the very cool job and for giving me the ability to write smut literally anywhere. Couldn't have done it without you. I'm also scarred for life because of you, so there's that too.

ABOUT THE AUTHOR

Leila Burnes spent years ghostwriting romance novels before taking the plunge and writing a few of her own. Under other pen names, she has written everything from political thrillers to young adult satirical comedies to romantic suspense starring murderous frat boys. She doesn't love sand but enjoys long walks on the beach, will never say no to a fancy little beverage, and would prefer to be sitting poolside in Palm Springs at any given moment. She still lives in Washington, DC even though she gave up working for the government ages ago, but she'll probably never leave. Leila believes in never taking yourself too seriously and doing whatever makes you happy, so go on.
Go do it.

Website • www.leilaburnes.com
Twitter • leilaburnes
Instagram • leilaburnesbooks
Pinterest • leilaburnesbooks

ALSO BY LEILA BURNES

The Naiad Novels Series

Work For It
Law of Attraction
Turn the Page

Printed in Poland
by Amazon Fulfillment
Poland Sp. z o.o., Wrocław

25848225R00188